MISSING, PRESUMED LOST

FIORELLA DE MARIA

Missing, Presumed Lost

A Father Gabriel Mystery

IGNATIUS PRESS   SAN FRANCISCO

Cover design and photography
by John Herreid

© 2024 by Ignatius Press, San Francisco
All rights reserved
ISBN 978-1-62164-663-1 (PB)
ISBN 978-1-64229-290-9 (eBook)
Library of Congress Control Number 2023944992
Printed in the United States of America ∞

I

It was at times like this that Gabriel understood why the Lord had not called him to be a lawyer. He was seated in the public gallery of the Crown Court, on the third day of the most painful trial Gabriel had ever witnessed. Like most self-respecting Englishmen, Gabriel judiciously avoided darkening the doors of a court of law, but this was the second time in as many months that he had found himself an unwilling observer of a murder trial. The long hours Gabriel had sat in this crowded public gallery had done nothing to stifle his sense of disquiet.

It had been a harrowing trial, and Gabriel had not expected it to be easy to witness. What had made this trial so agonising was the fact that it had been Gabriel's deductive powers that had caused this young woman to find herself in the dock in the first place, fighting for her liberty and possibly her life.

Marie Paige was on trial for the murder of Johannes Weber, a former fellow prisoner at Auschwitz death camp. Weber had been a *kapo*, enlisted by the guards to supervise other prisoners, and he had tormented Marie mercilessly. After the war, Weber had followed Marie to England, where he had continued to hound her. Nobody—least of all Marie—denied that she had killed the man, but her defence counsel had put forward a strong case that Marie Paige had acted in self-defence. For three long days, Marie had endured hours of cross-examination, in which the horrific details of life in Hitler's concentration camps had been revealed, discussed and disputed.

Courtrooms were, by necessity, cold, harsh places, where evidence could be tested and witness statements challenged, but listening to Marie's precise, dispassionate tone as she had told a story that sounded like a voyage into the depths of hell had made Gabriel's flesh crawl.

"Our heads were shaved," she had said. "The sick, the old, the children were sent directly to the gas chambers. . . . Yes, I am sure they were. . . . Yes, I did see them being led away. . . . Yes, I did see piles of dead bodies. . . . No, I am not mistaken.

"We were starved, beaten, worked until we dropped with exhaustion. . . . I saw prisoners shot at random; I saw a fourteen-year-old girl hanged. . . . Yes, I recollect it quite clearly."

Marie had expressed a desire to tell her story, but this had perhaps not been how she had envisaged it, standing in the dock of an English crown court with an invisible noose around her neck, being questioned with courteous forceful-ness by a wigged and gowned barrister, whilst her husband, friends, and the press looked on. But she had answered ev-ery question without once breaking down, something that could not be said for her husband, who had spent much of the trial flanked by Gabriel and their friend Alastair Brennan, and battling the urge to interfere. Once Dr Paige had been asked to leave the chamber, when the prosecuting barrister had asked Marie repeatedly whether she had been having an adulterous affair with the deceased and Paige had loudly

6

objected. It had been a reasonable enough line of questioning, but a distressed husband was never going to see it that way.

There had been audible gasps from the public gallery as Marie gave her answers, particularly when she corrected the prosecuting barrister's use of the word "violation". "He raped me, if that is what you mean. And I'm afraid I cannot tell you precisely how many times. One stops counting after a while."

Gabriel had been relieved that Dr Paige was still out of the room when Marie had reached that part of her evidence. It was bad enough sensing Alastair cringing in the seat next to him. "Steady!" Gabriel had whispered, since Alastair's fidgeting was making a little too much noise.

"I wish she hadn't killed the swine!" he had hissed. "I should have preferred to have had the pleasure myself!"

"Shh! For Marie's sake, don't go getting yourself thrown out too."

Alastair had closed his eyes and given a low growl.

Now that the trial was nearly concluded, Gabriel could feel a gnawing anxiety in the pit of his stomach. The jury had been deliberating for just under an hour when the news came that they had reached a verdict. Gabriel was unsure whether it was a good or a very bad sign that it had taken these twelve good men such a short time.

The public gallery was crammed to bursting by now, and Gabriel sweltered in a winter coat he had been too cramped to remove. He knew his discomfort was nothing compared with that of Dr Paige, whose hair stuck to his high forehead with sweat. The young doctor's knuckles were raw from the many times he had rammed his fist into his mouth over the preceding three days to silence his own groans. His hands were clasped so tightly together now that Gabriel could make out the white contours of his finger joints.

Gabriel acknowledged Alastair's nod as he shuffled in his seat, noting that Marie's old friend was almost as distressed as Dr Paige. Gabriel had no legal training, but it seemed to him that the prosecution had put up a poor case and that the chances of Marie being convicted and condemned to the hangman for murder were slight. But Gabriel suspected that every man imagined an argument to be indisputable if it concurred with his own opinion. What terrified him was the thought that men had been hanged on lighter evidence than the prosecution had presented, and even a conviction for the lesser charge of manslaughter would see Marie condemned to years of hard labour.

"You must trust to the mercy of the court," Gabriel whispered to Dr Paige as the clerk called for silence. "Justice will prevail."

"Tell that to Thomas More," Dr Paige retorted, but there was no time for further discussion. Marie was being led back to the dock, flanked by two female police constables. The twelve men of the jury were reassembling, seating themselves in their places to await the question they had been deliberating in secret.

"Has the jury reached a verdict," asked the judge.

Gabriel felt an invisible hand strangling his throat. He struggled to draw breath, but the effort only made him shudder. He saw the foreman of the jury, a short, bald, inoffensive-looking man, rising obediently to his feet. "Yes, my lord."

Gabriel's eyes moved to the diminutive figure of Marie,

who stood, calmly and silently, awaiting her fate. Dressed in black, Marie looked paler and more waiflike than ever, but her hands did not so much as tremble as she held the rail in front of her.

"Is the defendant guilty or not guilty of murder?"

"Not guilty, my lord."

"Is the defendant guilty or not guilty of manslaughter?"

"Not guilty, my lord."

A murmur of excitement—or was it relief?—rippled through the court. Dr Paige made the softest murmur before raising his head to make eye contact with his wife. Marie and the judge appeared to be the only persons in the court who did not react at all. The defendant and the elderly judge regarded one another across the courtroom like two chess players at the end of a lengthy and exhausting match. The judge gave Marie a smile of what was almost pride. "Marie Eugenie Paige," he said, "you have been found not guilty, and you may leave this court without a stain on your name. You are a free woman."

Gabriel pulled the rosary beads out of his pocket and kissed the crucifix. He was too overwhelmed with relief to pay much attention to the judge's closing remarks, and he had plenty to say, but a few words—the comments that would be published in the papers the following day—leapt out at him as he watched Marie's inscrutable face.

I have served as a judge for nearly thirty years, and I can honestly say that yours is the most extraordinary case in which I have ever sat in judgement. It was never your claim that you played no part in Johannes Weber's death, but I am satisfied that you acted in self-defence, in the sure knowledge that your own life was in danger. You have shown yourself to be a most courageous witness to the truth, and it is my greatest hope that you may now find peace and safety in this country.

As soon as the judge had left the court, there was a mad scramble from the public gallery as reporters rushed outside, racing one another to the public telephone boxes to communicate the verdict to their papers. A few would, no doubt, race round to the steps of the court in the hope of hearing a statement from the acquitted woman or her solicitor, perhaps even an exclusive interview, though Gabriel knew that Dr Paige would never allow Marie to talk to anyone in the first exhilaration of liberty.

Gabriel noticed Marie being hustled out by her lawyers. She glanced up at the public gallery for a moment, gave her husband a relieved smile, and left. Dr Paige attempted to rise to his feet, but he appeared rooted to the spot, and it was only with help from his friends that he was able to stand at all. He turned to Gabriel and gave his arm a warm squeeze.

"Thank you, Father," he said quietly, looking at Gabriel with the glassy, red-rimmed eyes of a desperately exhausted man. "Thank you for believing in my innocence when no one else would. Thank you for believing Marie."

"Off you go, old man!" exclaimed Alastair, sensing Dr Paige's sudden reluctance to move. "Go and find your lady wife before she gets carried off for a cream tea by that ghastly little man from the *Comet*. I'll look after Friar Tuck here."

Dr Paige smiled shyly and beat a retreat, leaving Alastair grinning mischievously after him. Alastair Brennan had the roguish demeanour of an upper-class man who had grown up with a charming disdain for social conventions and niceties whilst conforming to his own social stereotype without realising it. In the style of the well-bred author of satirical novels, Alastair's dress was dapper, his hair slightly too long without being bohemian, and he smoked a pipe, perfectly completing the costume of the literary dandy. But even Alastair's nonchalant pose did not hide his own sense of relief at Marie's acquittal. Like Dr Paige, Alastair had a visage pinched and pale from the long weeks of worry, and his fixed smile looked a little as if he were about to let out a nervous laugh.

"It's over," said Gabriel, leading the way out of the public gallery and down the wooden stairs. The minutes that had elapsed whilst the three men had taken stock of the situation had allowed the courtroom to clear, and Gabriel and Alastair walked unhindered out into the pale light of a crisp, overcast spring day. The pavement outside the court was abuzz with reporters, but the two men could just make out the spectral figure of Marie Paige being led away to a waiting car.

Alastair turned to Gabriel. "I say, how about if you let me buy you lunch before I drive you back to the clink? I feel I owe you that much."

"My monastery is not a clink, I assure you," answered Gabriel, falling into step beside Alastair, whom he suspected was leading him in the direction of his favourite bistro. Gabriel suspected that Alastair had not eaten very much during the trial and would now want to make up for it by gobbling up as much food as the continuing shortages permitted. "I should be grateful of a bite to eat, though," Gabriel admitted. "I've missed lunch."

"Good," said Alastair, turning down a narrow, cobbled side street that was taking them away from the historic marketplace and into the maze of higgledy-piggledy old streets that would have left Gabriel hopelessly lost in minutes without a guide. In spite of living so close to the city of Salisbury for many years, Gabriel had visited the place only once before, and he preferred to forget about that particular jaunt. The remarkable thing about being a member of a monastic community was that, in some ways, the monastery might be built anywhere. If Gabriel had not got himself a reputation for being an unbearable nuisance in the community, he might never have ventured farther than the adjacent village.

Gabriel winced as Alastair walked up to an extremely elegant-looking Georgian building with the Union flag fluttering proudly above the doorframe. Alastair paused to allow Gabriel to catch up with him before walking up the shallow flight of steps. At the top he was immediately greeted by a doorman in livery, a rotund individual who appeared to be the only man in England who had not gone hungry over the past nine years. Gabriel was sure he noticed the man looking him up and down suspiciously before letting them in.

"Relax, Father," said Alastair airily as they stepped into a high-ceilinged room like something out of a Jane Austen novel. It was easy enough for Alastair; he was clearly in his element as the head waiter minced over to them, greeted Alastair by name, and ushered them both to a table near the window.

Gabriel glanced appreciatively about him. He was sure that they were seated in what had once been a ballroom, now populated with tables draped in damask, surrounded by antique chairs. The room had certainly been well looked after, the walls and ceiling decorated as close to the original style as was possible in time of austerity. Various artefacts decorated the sides of the room to remind patrons of the building's grandiose past: a sedan chair, a portrait of a ruddy-faced gentleman in a wig, and a rather fussy arrangement of Regency-era fans in a little alcove. Gabriel's eyes were drawn to the platform at the far end of the room where musicians would once have seated themselves to entertain revellers in empire-line gowns and tailcoats. Giovanna would have loved a place like this. He could almost imagine her standing centre stage with the old harpsichord to her right, singing an elegiac love song.

Did you not hear my lady?
Go down the garden singing.
Blackbird and thrush were silent
To hear the alleys ringing.

Gabriel became aware that Alastair had asked a question and was awaiting an answer. He gave a sheepish smile and shrugged his shoulders to indicate that he had not been listening, but Alastair knew that already. Suspecting a person of murder tends to break the ice between two men of very different temperaments, and Gabriel felt he knew Alastair Brennan well enough to avoid the social tedium of putting on an act. "Wakey-wakey, Your Holiness," said Alastair good-naturedly. "You're not at Buckingham Palace, you know."

"Awfully sorry," murmured Gabriel, picking up the menu the waiter had placed in front of him without his noticing. What the menu lacked in content it made up for in aesthetics, each item handwritten in florid script, on paper mounted on leather-bound covers. "I've not entered a place like this since before I joined the monastery. I'm not even sure it's allowed."

Alastair gave a boyish grin. "You may tell your abbot I had to chloroform you to get you inside, and by the time the waiters had revived you, you were too polite to leave."

Gabriel was spared the need to respond by the waiter arriving to take their order. To Gabriel's immense relief, Alastair did not ask his opinion on the wine and ordered food for them both, simply duplicating his own choice. There had been a time when Gabriel had been rather more knowledgeable on the subject of wine than the average Englishman, having been thoroughly educated by Giovanna, but that had been a very long time ago. He glanced back at the musicians' platform as Alastair exchanged niceties with the waiter. He did not imagine that anyone had sung here since before the war.

Saw you not my lady? I . . . love her 'til I die!

"No need to look so morose, Father," said Alastair, misreading Gabriel's look. "Marie Paige has left the court a free woman. Hopefully they can now get on with their lives."

"I hope they can," said Gabriel cautiously. "I was horrified by some of the details. I know there are a lot of atrocity stories being bandied about at the moment, but it was shocking to hear it, all the same."

"She has a marvellous natural gift for telling a story," remarked Alastair. "One almost felt as though one were there, watching it all unfolding."

"Quite. I hope she will be all right."

"Of course she will," said Alastair breezily. "She's a good

deal stronger than she looks, and with Dickie at her side, she has nothing to fear. I'll warrant you'll be baptising a baby within the year."

"Now that really would be a joy," said Gabriel. "I hope God will bless them with children." He tried in vain to imagine frail, wispy little Marie carrying a child, but stranger things had happened. And as Alastair had said, she was stronger than she looked. "And how is your creation? Thriving, if your choice of restaurant is anything to go by."

Alastair laughed. "The book has been a roaring success," he agreed eagerly. "Did you read the review in *The Times*?" Gabriel shook his head apologetically. "Of course, I forgot that you chaps don't bother with such things. It has all been frightfully exciting, but I am rather feeling the strain. If one has a success, there is an expectation that every book that follows will outstrip the last. Readers expect so much."

Gabriel suppressed a smile. "I'm sure you will not let them down," he said. "Have you adjusted to life in Bloomsbury? Not tempted to return to the village?"

Alastair shook his head emphatically. "I miss the tranquillity of the mornings, and of course I miss Marie and Dickie, but I'm hoping they will come to London to visit once the dust has settled. I want to introduce Marie to my publisher. If I can't persuade her to write her memoirs, I'm sure he will."

Gabriel blinked in surprise. "You want Marie to write a book? I suppose it might help her to put it all down on paper, but I'd rather thought . . . well, I thought that was the whole point of her giving evidence in court. She has told the story now."

15

"But everyone should know what happened in the camps. If she wrote a book, the story could be read by millions of people."

"Are all books read by millions of people?" asked Gabriel, and immediately regretted it. The tone of the question was all wrong. "I mean, is there really a market for a book like that? I was under the impression that everyone was busy trying to forget all about it."

"That's what they say," said Alastair, "but I've just been reading a book by this doctor called Viktor Frankl: *Trotzdem Ja zum Leben sagen: Ein Psychologe erlebt das Konzentrationslager*." Gabriel looked nervously at the neighbouring tables, but none of the other patrons appeared to have heard Alastair's ostentatious German. "Sorry if it offends, Father, but the book is available only in German at the moment. It's Dr Frankl's story of his time in Auschwitz. Now, Marie refuses to read anything in German even though she is perfectly fluent, but I have told her about it. It's a splendid book, quite a tour de force. But it set me thinking that Marie should write her story. I could help her if need be. It would be good for her."

It wouldn't do you any harm either, thought Gabriel, then rebuked himself for his cynicism. Alastair's quiet adoration of Marie had been evident to Gabriel from the start, and it was probably for the best that they no longer lived in close proximity to one another. But a book might bind them together despite the geographical distance.

As one gloved waiter poured the wine, pausing for Alastair to sample the bouquet, another, younger waiter placed two plates of fragrant pork cutlets before them. Gabriel blenched, looking at Alastair across the table. He glanced back at Gabriel in momentary confusion before his body began to shake with laughter. "I say, Father, shall we be damned for this?"

In all the excitement, they had both forgotten that it was a Friday.

2

Alastair Brennan had bought himself a marvellous Humber with his newfound wealth and took a childlike pleasure in cruising along the empty country roads with Gabriel sitting stiffly in the passenger seat, desperately trying to relax. The pleasant diversion of food and wine having passed, Gabriel's mind wandered back to the courtroom and the long days in which the squalid details of the murder had been dissected and mulled over, and Marie's serene, clear voice had described acts of depravity part of him still did not wish to believe and could not get out of his mind.

I saw him hang a fourteen-year-old girl. He tightened the noose around her neck and pushed her off the stool she was standing on. She was struggling to breathe for over five minutes. He just stood and watched her . . .

Outside the window, he saw two sheep dogs rounding up a vast flock of merino sheep, following the whistles and calls of an elderly man who looked like Old Father Time. There was a gentle authority about the shepherd as he watched the dogs at work, then ambled slowly over to the pen to close the gate, as he must surely have done thousands of times before. Gabriel was tempted to imagine that the war had passed the old shepherd by without his having noticed the carnage taking place outside the shelter of the valley, but Gabriel checked himself. How could he be sure of that? For all Gabriel knew, the shepherd might have lost sons to the conflict; he might be out there in the fields because there was no younger man to do the work for him.

"Penny for your thoughts?" asked Alastair, noting Gabriel's brooding silence. "Or has the wine addled your brain?"

Gabriel chuckled. "It would take a lot to addle my brain. You should try a swig of Brother Thomas' cider."

"There are some advantages to the monastic life then?"

"Many," Gabriel assured him. "I'm not sure I appreciated quite how many until I had to go away. Thank God, I have been called home."

"I thought you might miss the freedom of parish life."

"I shall miss dear Father Foley's company, but I was not suited to parish life, it seems."

This was the understatement of the decade even by Gabriel's standards, and he was a master of the much-practised British art of making a molehill out of a mountain. His mind wandered back to an even darker day in the public gallery of the Crown Court, with a condemned woman's impossibly young face looking at him in calm resignation, shortly before her distraught family rounded on him. If he had stayed at Saint Patrick's much longer, Father Foley would probably have found him hanging from the church rafters, lynched by the condemned prisoner's enraged supporters. It was a perilous task, seeking the truth.

"I can't pretend I did not feel a little pang of regret as I left the presbytery for the last time," Gabriel admitted. "It was a cosy place to spend the winter. A little like living in a family home again. But . . . but well, it is a joy to be with my community. They are my family now."

An uneasy silence descended between them. Gabriel knew

that Alastair had learnt about his past, though Gabriel had no idea how, but it meant that he had no need to explain himself. Living in a cosy presbytery had been a mixed blessing, offering more creature comforts than Gabriel had come to expect in the monastery, and a good deal more freedom in terms of routine, but it had also too many reminders of the life he had left behind: listening to the gramophone and hurried mornings, gobbling down breakfast in a chilly kitchen with the clock ticking and the call of the postman as letters fluttered onto the doormat. Not that there had been a small child to feed and dress and keep out of mischief in Father Foley's presbytery, but the abbey was mercifully free of even a hint of worldly life.

When Alastair brought the car to a halt outside the abbey gates, Gabriel thanked him again for lunch and the ride before taking his leave. "Are you staying with the Paiges tonight?" asked Gabriel. "It's a long way back to London."

"No, no, they need some time to themselves," said Alastair sensibly. "I shall stay the night in Guildford with my mother. It will break the journey nicely, and I haven't seen her for quite a while."

Gabriel thought, as he waved Alastair good-bye, that he had not even realised the man still had a mother. Alastair was the sort of man, dropped off at boarding school at the age of six, who gave the impression of being a happy orphan. Gabriel walked up to the gate and rang the bell, thinking that he ought to write to his in-laws before the end of the week; he owed Giovanna's parents a letter, and for once he had something of interest to tell them. The top of the Judas gate was thrown open, and Brother Gerard's cheerful face grinned at him. As soon as Gerard registered Gabriel's figure standing in the doorway, his smile faded, and a rare look of concern spread across his features.

"Well?" Gerard demanded, letting Gabriel in. "Noose or loose?"

"Loose," Gabriel responded. "God help us all if it had been different."

"Thank God for that," said Gerard, his old smile returning. "I've been praying for that lassie all day. We all have."

As they stood in the empty corridor, a bell echoed insistently, calling them to prayer. They walked together towards the chapel, making no further conversation. Justice had prevailed and Gabriel was home, safely sheltered from whatever murder and mayhem might occur in the outside world.

Two days later, during the work hour, Gabriel was informed he had visitors. Gabriel was busy tending the monastic beehives when the message arrived. Gerard—who was petrified of the tiny, buzzing killing machines—stood some distance away, calling, "Your friends the doctor and his wife are here to see you!"

Gabriel finished his task as quickly as he could and walked over to Gerard. "Splendid!" he said, removing his hat and veil. "Are they in the parlour?"

"Yeah, I left them having a cup of tea while I came to fetch you." Gerard reached out a hand to take Gabriel's bee-keeping gear. "Give it to me and go and meet them," he said. "Mrs Paige is such a fidget, I doubt she'll be able to sit still very long once she's finished her cuppa."

Poor Mrs Paige *was* a bit of a fidget, as Gerard so eloquently put it, though Gabriel knew it was not in her temperament to be excitable. As was the case with so many of Hitler's victims, a small part of her would never leave the concentration camp. Now she had to live with the added horror of having had to fight for her survival a second time, at the cost of another man's life. Little wonder that Marie Paige found it difficult to sit primly, drinking tea and making polite conversation.

As soon as Gabriel entered the parlour, Dr Paige rose to his feet and extended a hand, which Gabriel shook warmly. He immediately turned his attention to Marie, who was smiling at him from a vast cushioned armchair that looked big enough to swallow her in one gulp. "How lovely to see you again," said Gabriel, taking Marie's bony hand in his. It was impossible to avoid noticing that, whereas Dr Paige was already very much back to his old robust self, Marie looked as frail as ever. Marie had taken some trouble over her appearance, and her carefully applied lipstick and rouge gave her face an unnatural glow of colour, but the chunky blue cardigan she wore did nothing to hide her spindly arms.

"May I pour you a little more tea?" asked Gabriel, sitting opposite them around the low table. "I hope you're not cold?"

A fire was burning brightly in the grate, warming the room nicely, but Marie still managed to look freezing, sitting somewhat stiffly, the sleeves of her cardigan pulled down over her wrists. It was Eastertide but proving to be a cold spring. Gabriel noted a warm woollen coat hanging over the back of Marie's chair. "I'm not cold at all," promised Marie, cheerfully. She did not speak with an accent, but there was something about the very deliberate way she formed her words that hinted at her Belgian background. "But I was wondering whether we might take a little walk in the garden. It's all so beautiful at this time of year with the spring flowers in bloom."

Gabriel agreed, relieved. It was always easier to have a conversation when there were plenty of distractions all around. He waited whilst Dr Paige helped Marie on with her coat before leading them out into the abbey grounds. They walked slowly, moving at Marie's pace, as she still became out of breath if she moved too quickly. Dr Paige was attuned to Marie's limitations: the moment she began to sound a little wheezy, he would slow down, placing a hand around her waist in case she fell.

The gardens were as beautiful as any visitor could have hoped, and before Marie had been so horribly attacked, she was frequently to be seen wandering through the apple orchard like a tormented soul, struggling to find the right way through Dante's dark wood. The vast vegetable patches were not much to look at, at present. The seedlings had only recently been planted out to avoid the prospect of a late frost, but the flower beds were a riot of spring colours—golden daffodils worthy of a Wordsworth poem, purple crocuses, delicate white snowdrops—and beyond the lawns the apple orchard would soon erupt into blossom, promising a bumper harvest and cider aplenty to see them through the winter.

"I shall miss the apple orchard," said Marie. "There's something so reassuring about the cover of trees."

Gabriel looked quizzically at her, but Dr Paige interjected quickly. "It's what we've come to tell you, Father," he said, stopping as if to admire the view. "Well, first and foremost, we wanted to thank you for your help. Heaven knows what would have happened if you hadn't worked everything out."

"It was no trouble at all," said Gabriel warmly. This was hardly true, as Gabriel's obsession with clearing Dr Paige's name had caused his banishment from the abbey, but Gabriel knew that Dr Paige was the sort of Englishman who struggled to express gratitude. "I am only relieved that all has worked out for the best." He hesitated before asking the obvious question. "Are you leaving the village because of what happened?"

"Not entirely," Marie put in. "Dickie has a new position."

"Congratulations! I hope you are not going far?"

Dr Paige shook his head. "Not far at all. We shall be in your old parish, as it happens. Dr Whitehead is retiring at the end of the month, and I'm taking on his surgery. It comes with a house, and there will be rather more for me to do there than here."

Gabriel started walking again as though to prevent them all from getting cold, but he could not risk Dr Paige seeing the expression on his face. "Yes, I think he'd mentioned retiring about now."

"It's probably a little sooner than he had anticipated," said Dr Paige, "but the poor chap's not at all well, and he is keen to settle his family in pastures new before he goes."

Gabriel clenched his fists behind his back, but there was no need for him to respond. Dr Paige was in full medical mode, busily explaining the minutiae of Dr Whitehead's unfortunate illness. Cancer of the lungs . . . very poor prognosis . . . won't hear of receiving any treatment . . . typical doctor, won't submit to the mercies of modern medicine . . .

probably won't last until the summer. "I shall have a hard act to follow," Dr Paige said, his voice snapping back into focus again. "He's a pillar of the community; all his patients think the world of him. I shall have to tread very carefully for the first few months, I suspect."

"It's a friendly town," said Gabriel, ignoring the fact that he had practically had to flee for his life. Dr Paige was unlikely to find himself in a similar position. Gabriel thought of the times he had sat in Mrs Whitehead's kitchen, eating her homemade fruitcake. Gabriel knew—as Dr Paige could not possibly have known—why the kindly old doctor whose place Dr Paige was taking was choosing to hasten his own death by refusing treatment. "I'm sure you'll make a beautiful house into a happy home," said Gabriel, giving Marie a smile which she happily returned. "I seem to remember the house has a very large garden."

"Yes," said Marie. "I have all sorts of plans for it. We're going to keep chickens."

"It will be better for Marie to be in a bigger place," said Dr Paige. "There will still be plenty of peace and quiet, but lots more to do. She could even take the train to Bath or Salisbury if she wanted."

More to do and more space in every sense of the word, thought Gabriel. The difficulty with small-village life was that it was impossible to live anonymously or even with a modicum of privacy. If they remained in the village, Marie would always be associated with the murder of a mysterious foreigner. Sympathetic villagers—of which there were many—would see her as a tragic victim, a war hero forced to fight for her own survival in what should have been a place of safety. The unkind villagers would only ever view her with suspicion, the troubled outsider who brought murder to their sleepy little village. Gabriel was sorry they were leaving the village, but he knew that they were doing the right thing.

"I don't suppose you know where Dr Whitehead is planning to go?" asked Gabriel, as casually as he could manage.

"I gather they are moving down to the coast," said Dr Paige. "One of their children is settled by the sea down in Dorset. I think Dr Whitehead would like his wife and the rest of the family to be close to them when he goes. Understandable, I suppose."

"Indeed."

Gabriel could not help musing, in the last moments before he drifted off to sleep that night, how much the character of the village and even the nearby town was changing. He was a Londoner by background and probably retained a romanticised idea of country life, but it seemed to him that there had been a time when villages were dominated by the same families for generations and there was very little in the way of movement. Had the war really changed all that? Or had it been a sad feature of rural life since the Industrial Revolution—the magnetic pull of the cities, especially for the young, who were always in search of work and a better life for their children? It was hardly surprising that a murder should have blasted a hole in the centre of the village, causing the main players of that drama to run for cover. Even in the nearby town with its bigger population, no one associated with that mysterious disappearance could be left in peace. The victim's children had both left the town, Douglas to get himself a smart bachelor pad in Salisbury—

hardly the metropolis but a rather livelier setting than that drab little cottage on the edge of marshland—and Agnes to India, setting sail for a newly independent country from which Gabriel doubted she would ever return. But hadn't he moved far away from the scene of his own tragedy years before? It was a natural enough impulse. New people would come to the village, and it would return to the quiet, steady rhythms of hundreds of years.

The village looked as though a small local war had broken out when Gabriel walked to Reggie McClusker's shop to stock up on some monastic provisions early the following morning. Gabriel usually enjoyed his walks into the village. He was often met by some member of the public in need of counsel or simply a friendly word, and it was a beautiful walk at this time of year with the earth teeming with life all around him. The lambing season was well under way, and the valley echoed with the bleating of dozens of tiny lambs finding their voices in a bewildering world.

That was before Gabriel arrived at the normally sleepy high street. He heard the commotion shortly before the cause of it came into view. At the far end of the street, Gabriel could make out a gaggle of men huddled near the entrance to a building. Two of them were stretching out a bedsheet or a banner between them—possibly a banner written on an old bedsheet—but Gabriel could not see the details from such a distance. A couple of other men appeared to be attempting to engage with the public, not that many were passing that way. Those who were out and about had the good sense to avoid a noisy group—and they were certainly noisy. Gabriel may not have been able to see very much, but he could hear the sound of raised male voices chanting in unison. The only word he could make out was 'No!', which appeared to form the first word of every sentence they were shouting.

Gabriel was immediately tempted to go over and find out more, but he looked down at the large—and empty—wicker basket he held in one hand and reminded himself that he was in the village on an errand. After all, he had promised Abbot Ambrose repeatedly since his return to the abbey that he would not allow his mind to be drawn to worldly matters as it had done so disastrously before. The most painful lesson Gabriel had learnt during his short exile was that he truly loved monastic life, and he could not bear the thought of being cut loose again. With a determined tread, Gabriel stepped towards the village shop and pushed open the door.

"Morning, Father G," called Reggie, as cheerfully as ever, when Gabriel appeared in the doorway. "You're a bit late this morning."

Gabriel sighed, noticing that the newspaper stands were almost empty. He tried not to feel disappointed, but he could never resist taking a peek at the headlines to see what was going on in the world beyond Sutton Westford. His few months of parish life had rekindled his interest in world events due to the omnipresence of the wireless set and Father Foley's insistence on having a copy of *The Times* delivered to the presbytery every morning. "Well, I suppose I've missed the rush. And probably most of the food," said Gabriel, handing Reggie his shopping list. He placed the basket on the counter.

Reggie chuckled, giving the list a quick glance over. "It's getting better. Not quite like the old days yet, but I can give you the monastic sweetie ration if you like." Gabriel could not hide his relief, which only made Reggie's low chuckle turn into a braying laugh. "You're all a bunch of big kids, aren't you?"

"Apart from Brother Gerard snaffling the aniseed balls, the rest of the sweets will be gobbled up by my catechism class, I assure you. It's the only reason they come." Gabriel watched as Reggie took jars partially full of sweets and began pouring them onto his weighing scales, transferring them into little paper bags with the deftness of long experience. It had been years since Gabriel had seen a full jar of sweets, but if Reggie's supply was not plentiful it was certainly varied, and all the usual delights were there—stripy mint humbugs, aniseed balls, Pontefract cakes, liquorice wheels, mint imperials, pear drops, toffees . . . Gabriel was distracted by the question of whether it would be acceptable to claim just one pear drop as his own on the way back to the abbey. No one would miss one, and the sugar would do him good as he made the journey back carrying a heavy basket . . . "Reggie, what's going on at the end of the road?" Gabriel asked the fount of all village gossip.

"Eh?" Reggie had reached the end of the jar of pear drops and was carefully siphoning off the dregs of the sugar into a separate container. "What's that?"

"There are men at the end of the road making a lot of noise. What's happened?"

Reggie groaned and made an elaborate show of rolling his eyes. "Bunch of Luddites if you ask me—or commies. It's difficult to know the difference these days." He reached under the counter and brought out a flimsy flyer, which he slapped onto the counter before Gabriel. "There's some developer come down from London. Local boy, grew up here. He wants to build some houses, and everyone is up in arms about it."

Gabriel examined the flyer. "I see. I suppose I can understand people not wanting the local landscape ruined. It is such a beautiful village. Where does he plan to build the houses?"

"In that godforsaken poky little corner at the edge of the village where nobody goes," answered Reggie scornfully. "It's not as though the poor sap's trying to bury the valley in concrete. He's selected a piece of land that is no good to anybody—an eyesore if I'm honest—and he wants to turn it into a nice little row of houses."

"Why are they at the end of the road? Shouldn't they be protesting where the houses are going to be built?"

"No, no, it's far too out of the way. They're ganging up where the poor bloke's staying. He's lodging at Mrs Lewis' place. Hounding him morning, noon, and night, they are. Maybe they think our boys should have come home from the war and lived in tents! All those homes blasted to kingdom come by Jerry. We can't keep people in prefabs forever."

Gabriel was of a conservative disposition, and any change, even the appearance of a few new houses, instinctively made him nervous, but he understood Reggie's argument. There were thousands of families around Britain who had lost everything in the German bombing raids of the major cities and were reduced to living either in squalid, overcrowded boarding houses or in the many prefabricated houses that had been hurriedly erected to provide temporary shelter. The prefabs were perfectly comfortable but not a permanent

31

solution. Gabriel knew that it was all very well for a man like him to resent the building of homes in his vicinity when he could retreat to the warm safety of the abbey.

Gabriel took another look at the flyer as Reggie finished gathering together his shopping. There was not much to look at. It consisted of a headline in heavy print which read:

LEAVE OUR VILLAGE IN PEACE!

Beneath the headline were a number of statements, which, like the words Gabriel had heard being shouted down the street, all began with the word "no": No new homes! No foreigners! No rich men taking our land! Gabriel was amazed that the leaflet was not illustrated with a figure of a man in gum boots and tweed jacket, brandishing a pitchfork. At the bottom of the page were the details of a protest meeting which was to take place in the church hall.

"It's a shocking waste of paper," said Gabriel, wondering how many of the offending flyers had been printed and scattered about the village. "I wonder who's supplying them?"

"You should go along to the meeting and find out, Father," suggested Reggie, beginning the laborious activity of cancelling the appropriate coupons from the ration books of every member of the Benedictine community. Gabriel was grateful that there was no one else in the shop, or he would be racked by that awful sense that he was holding up half the village. "You could be the voice of reason. You'll probably go the way of the prophets."

"There's a comforting thought," said Gabriel, "but if the martyr's crown is meant for me, I'd rather not claim it at the receiving end of an aged lynch mob with an aversion to modern housing." Gabriel went to pick up the now-heavy basket from the counter but stopped at the sound of raised voices outside that were getting closer and louder by the second. "May I leave the basket here a moment?" he asked, waiting for Reggie's nod before moving towards the door.

"Mind your back, they may not be so aged," warned Reggie as Gabriel placed his hand on the door handle and looked through the glass. "That Stevie Wilcox might be the wrong side of fifty, but he's a fair menace."

Gabriel suspected that he was looking at the menacing Stevie Wilcox from his position of relative safety behind the glass. Directly in front of the shop, there were two men engaged in an explosive argument. They were of similar height and build, but one was smartly dressed in the three-piece suit of the city while the other was a local man, dressed in faded corduroy trousers, a hand-knitted sweater patched at the elbows, and an ill-fitting cloth cap, which he wore stretched down over his ears like a helmet. In a rare show of common sense, Gabriel was tempted to stay where he was. He was safely ensconced away from the fight here, like a man standing at the entrance to an air-raid shelter, looking out at the black dots of bombs falling in the distance.

Temptation to common sense never lasted very long, and Gabriel threw open the door before he could change his mind, just in time to see Stevie Wilcox hurling his well-dressed opponent against the wall, shouting as he did so: "And where were you when your country needed you, you dirty coward! Daddy got you a nice little desk job, did he? Somewhere out of harm's way while the bloody Germans were blowing us all to pieces!"

The well-dressed man blushed deep red before throwing Stevie off. Stevie stepped back as though giving himself some space to plan his next move, but to his evident surprise, the man he had just accused of cowardice threw himself forward, landing Stevie an almighty punch on the nose. Stevie staggered back but did not have enough time to regain his balance before he was struck again, this time in the stomach.

"Enough!" shouted Gabriel, standing between the two men, but Stevie lay winded on the ground and was in no position to retaliate. The man he had insulted, however, looked more than ready to strike again. "I think you've made your point," said Gabriel more quietly, not daring to move in case the man pressed his advantage and treated Stevie to a kick in the head.

With his route to further revenge blocked, the city boy looked past Gabriel at Stevie Wilcox, who was recovering but had still not managed to get himself to his feet. "Aww, now aren't you a lucky boy, Stevie?" he jeered, giving Stevie the benefit of a malicious smirk. "Having Friar Tuck here to fight your battles for you?"

As pointless provocations went, it was one of the silliest Gabriel had ever heard, in a village where people were well versed in the art of the unnecessary quarrel. Gabriel stepped aside to make some space between himself and the city boy, who was standing a little too close to him. Gabriel opened his mouth to respond to the comment, but he did not need to. Stevie Wilcox staggered to his feet and—before it could occur to Gabriel to stop him—lashed out and struck his adversary full in the face, sending him tottering back against the wall. "Get out of the village, you tosspot!" roared Stevie. "Your kind were never welcome here. You should've got the message the last time."

With that, Stevie straightened his cap and marched away

down the road without a backward glance. Gabriel turned to the tosspot in question, who was pressing both hands to the side of his face. "You'd better come inside," said Gabriel, indicating the shop door. "You need to tidy yourself up."

Inside the shop, Reggie was looking suitably unimpressed. "Joseph Beaumont, I wouldn't have taken you for a street brawler," he said, without introduction. "Look at the state you're in."

Joseph groaned, moving his hands across his face and apparently noticing for the first time that his lips had split and his nose was bleeding copiously. "Have you any ice, Reggie?" asked Gabriel. "He'll look a perfect fright by the evening if he doesn't do something with that face."

"Thank you, I'm sure," said Joseph as Reggie lifted the counter and beckoned to him to come into the back room. Gabriel instinctively followed, though was not sure whether either man welcomed his presence. "I didn't set out to fight with anyone," added Joseph.

Gabriel noticed that Joseph was well spoken, but his voice retained a subtle Wiltshire lilt, which Gabriel suspected was more pronounced when he was letting his guard down. It was usually the way when a man has had to learn Received Pronunciation. Regional variations always crept in during moments of stress.

They were standing in a small storeroom, which was dark but in perfect order, boxes of nonperishable produce neatly stacked on spotlessly clean shelves. Reggie was nothing if not orderly. "Come through to the kitchen," said Reggie, indicating the door on the other side of the storeroom.

Joseph glanced back at Reggie with an unexpected grin before obeying the instruction. "I haven't been back here since I was a paperboy," he said wryly. "You're not going to box my ears, are you, Mr McClusker?"

"If I were going to give you a thick ear, I'd do it in the middle of the shop where half the village could see," Reggie retorted, laughing in spite of himself. "It wouldn't be the first time, you daft beggar."

Moments later, Gabriel was standing by the kitchen door whilst Reggie handed Joseph a cloth. "You know," said Joseph, cleaning himself up as best he could, "it wouldn't be the first time you'd broken up a fight between me and Stevie either."

"I don't know how many times I had to break up the pair of you," remarked Reggie. "You never did learn, picking fights with the big boys." He effected the tone of a whinging little boy. " 'It were his *fault*! He started it, Mr McClusker! Don't tell me dad, will you?' "

The two men laughed uproariously, leaving Gabriel feeling like Billy No-Mates. He was about to slip away discreetly when Reggie looked up at him and smiled. "It's this here fella who broke up the fight this time," said Reggie. "You want to thank our resident Sherlock Holmes that the two of you didn't end up in hospital."

Joseph looked searchingly in Gabriel's direction. "You must be from the abbey," he said, his already mottled cheeks turning a few shades redder. "I'm awfully sorry, that was not the most auspicious of introductions." He extended a hand to Gabriel. "Joseph Beaumont."

"Dom Gabriel Milson," answered Gabriel. "How do you do?"

"Not desperately well at the moment," Joseph replied. With the heat of his temper ebbing away, Joseph looked mortally embarrassed that a complete stranger had witnessed him caught up in a street fight. "I was hardly expecting a rapturous homecoming, but I thought I'd at least be safe."

Reggie patted Joseph on the shoulder and indicated the table and chairs near the kitchen wall. "Tell you what, Joe, why don't you lie low here for a bit? I've got to get on, but you could make yourself and Fr Gabriel here a cuppa. Tell him what's been going on."

Gabriel glanced nervously at the clock on the wall. His perpetual lateness had been one of the main reasons why Abbot Ambrose had sent him away from the abbey not so long ago, and he could not bear to get himself into trouble so soon after his arrival home. Yet, as always, a mixture of curiosity and the need to help a man in need of companionship caused him to falter. An idea came to him. "I really ought to get back to the abbey," he said apologetically, "but why don't you walk with me? If those thugs are still hanging around your boarding house, they are less likely to harass you if you have company."

Joseph hesitated, apparently pondering the proposition. Gabriel suspected that he was unwilling to venture into the hostility of the street from which he had only just escaped but was not going to admit his fear to anyone, least of all to a stranger. "Why not?" he said, with forced cheerfulness. "It would be a trip down memory lane. I used to go to the abbey for my catechism. Is Brother Cuthbert still around?"

Gabriel shook his head sadly. "Brother Cuthbert went to his eternal reward last winter."

"He must have had a good innings though," said Joseph, following Gabriel through the storeroom and into the shop, where Gabriel picked up the shopping basket and thanked

Reggie. Reggie was busy with another customer and gave them a brief wave as they left before returning to the task of taking a box of cigarettes down from the shelf behind him.

To the relief of both men, the street was empty when they stepped outside, the chief agitator having decided against returning to the scene and the protestors having sloped off to work. "You are a property developer then, I presume?" asked Gabriel, waiting for Joseph to get his bearings before moving in the direction of the abbey.

"Or the devil incarnate, if you prefer," answered Joseph wryly. "I thought there might be some concern about a new housing development, but I hardly expected an angry mob to stand outside my boarding house every morning to try to scare me off."

"It'll blow over," promised Gabriel half-heartedly, knowing all too well how deeply ingrained a grudge could become in a small community like this. "No one likes change."

"Father, I hoped I might do some good to the place. I grew up here; I would never do anything to hurt the village. I bought some land on the fringes of the village, a rundown wilderness of a place, specifically so that I would do nothing to tarnish the beauty of the area."

"Whereabouts is it?"

"Site of the old tin mine. The mine closed before I was born. The whole area's been a frightful dump ever since, dilapidated outbuildings, rusting old machinery. I'm going to clear it all out and build houses there. Good houses, all built using the local stone, each house with a small garden back and front. Who could possibly object to that?"

"Perhaps you want to move lodgings," suggested Gabriel, "just until the building work starts. I would imagine the clamour will die down once the work begins in earnest. There will be a sense of no going back."

"I'm not moving," Joseph asserted. "I know these men very well. They were bullies when we were children, and they're bullies now. In any case, even if I did find somewhere else to sleep at night, they'd still find me. It's a small village. At least one person claims he wants to kill me."

Gabriel stopped and turned abruptly to look at Joseph. "Are you being threatened? Oughtn't you to take this to the police?"

Joseph chuckled. "You're a Londoner, if I'm not much mistaken?" Gabriel nodded, wondering how on earth he knew and why it mattered. "No one goes to the police in these parts. When I were a lad, if you were Catholic, you never even spoke to the police unless they spoke to you, and even then, all you ever said was, 'I didn't do it, Constable.'"

"But a death threat—"

"Look, I should probably not have said anything. Some clever Dick sent me one of those anonymous letters. You know the type I mean, with the letters cut out from the newspaper. 'Go home or we'll send you home in a box.' Hardly subtle, was it?"

"But . . ." Gabriel thought for a moment about the terrible moment he and Gerard had stumbled upon Johannes Pedersen lying in a pool of blood. He, too, had been sheltering in what he imagined to be the safety of a sleepy English village. The situations were hardly comparable; Gabriel knew that death threats—like most threats made anonymously— were intended only to frighten, but past experience made him wary.

"Don't you fret, Father. I know who sent it. It was that

39

Stevie Wilcox. Always hated my guts. It was stag beetles down my neck when I were a kid; it's letters through my door and confrontations in the street now." He paused as though wondering whether or not to share the next piece of information with Gabriel, but he could not resist. "I'm happy to say I pull a rather better punch now than I used to. Stevie used to beat the hell out of me. Always the rough, tough farm boy."

"Is Stevie Wilcox leading the protests?" asked Gabriel. They had reached the edge of the abbey grounds, and Gabriel handed Joseph the basket so that he could clamber over the stile into the field. Joseph passed the heaving basket to Gabriel over the fence but made no attempt at following. "You're welcome to come to the abbey if you have time."

"It's kind of you, Father, but I ought to be getting along." Joseph's face broke into a mirthless smile. "Don't look so worried! I told you, they're just a bunch of bullies, full of wind, if you'll forgive the expression. Never done anything worth talking about, and never will."

With that, Joseph took his leave of Gabriel and sauntered in the direction of his building site with a confidence Gabriel could never hope to experience.

3

It was in Gabriel's nature to worry, and he proceeded to worry for much of the rest of the day. He worried as he stood in choir, chanting, "Thou shalt not fear the terrors of the night nor the arrow that flies by day." He worried as he knelt in his cell saying his night prayers. The nightly ritual of putting his thoughts and fears before God did nothing to still his inner trembling that evening. The events of recent months had made Gabriel needlessly anxious, but the only linking thread to all the violent deaths he had investigated was that in each case, the killer had committed the murder in his own heart many times before striking the fatal blow. Gabriel had long ago lost the belief that any act of killing was ever really committed on the spur of the moment. Accidental death was one thing, but who could honestly cross that most sacred of moral lines in the blink of an eye? On a whim? The deed had to have been played out—in the theatre of the mind at least—before the victim lay dead on the ground.

And if all murders were premeditated, was there not some way in which they could be predicted? If it were not possible to gaze directly into the human heart, surely there were warning signs, however subtle, that might save a life if they were noted in time? Might Victor Gladstone and Enid Jennings be alive today if someone had perceived the danger they were in? And what of Giovanna and Nicoletta? Had Giovanna received threats she had not shared with Gabriel because she had not wanted to frighten her own husband? Had she sensed that she was being watched, followed, that someone in the darkest recesses of London was plotting her death?

It was no good; Gabriel knew he would never sleep now that Giovanna had invaded his thoughts. He got up and stood by the window, looking out at the comforting darkness. Most people looked out of windows to see the view, but he was comforted by the fact that there was no view. Deep in the English countryside, there were no streetlights, no glimmers of light from the windows of other people's houses, not even a transient glow from a passing motorcar or bicycle. There was no light here at all to pollute the night, and he was glad of it. It reminded him that his London life was far, far away. His London life with Giovanna and little Nicoletta.

But his dead family were breaking into his thoughts more and more frequently since his unexpected reunion with his in-laws back in Cambridge. He wondered whether he would ever find again the peace he had once enjoyed at this abbey when he seemed to have laid the dead to rest and begun a new chapter of his life. It was foolish to think of Giovanna being hunted like that, in any case, as no killer had ever been found, and no police investigation had been able to give a motive for Giovanna's murder. It was very possible—indeed likely—that she had surprised a burglar and he had killed her simply to stop her from raising the alarm, starting the fire in an attempt to cover up what he had done. The killer might not have even known there was a child fast asleep upstairs.

There, an unintended killing. Two unintended killings. Gabriel had disproved his own theory, and it had not even been difficult. He knelt down a second time and prayed for Joseph's protection.

Joseph was being well looked after by his guardian angel since none of Gabriel's fears came to anything. Gabriel was mercifully protected from the continued arguments going on in the village about the housing development, as Abbot Ambrose had noticed Gabriel's agitation and sent Brother Gerard to the village shop in Gabriel's place for the week that followed. Gabriel guessed that Joseph must be extremely busy now that the building work was finally starting. Gabriel had heard no more from him after that initial conversation, which he took as a good sign—Gabriel might be confined to the abbey, but Joseph knew where to find him if he were in any trouble.

It helped Gabriel's peace of mind that the abbey was a sufficient distance from the building site such that he could not be distracted by the noise of machinery and workmen as they went about their labours in full view of an omnipresent gaggle of protesters. As Joseph had told Gabriel, the protesters were vocal and angry, but that was all they were. In the end, they were powerless to stop the building of houses that had official approval—or almost powerless. At his catechism class, Gabriel overheard snatches of conversation from the children about the goings-on at the building site, how progress was moving with agonising slowness because of mysterious shenanigans happening at night. According to little Susie Austin—an engaging child with the face of an angel and a tongue like Lucifer—the labourers were turning up for work to find tools missing and pits filled in, which they claimed had been dug only the day before.

"If that were true, Susie," asserted Gabriel, cutting off the child mid-conspiracy-theory, "the police would be guarding the site day and night."

"My father says the bobbies are all in the pockets of the Antichrist . . . anachronists . . ." Susie took a deep breath and tried again. "Anarchists. The country is going to hell in a handcart."

Gabriel cleared his throat. "Well, if it's all the same to you, my dear, perhaps we could carry on learning how not to go to hell in a handcart. Would anyone like to tell me which solemnity we will be celebrating this Thursday?"

A flurry of hands went up, but no one waited for Gabriel to choose one of them to answer. "Ascension!" came a chorus of voices. Seconds later, Gabriel was talking animatedly about why the Ascension was important, trying very hard to distract himself and the rest of the class from Susie's father's claims about police corruption. After all, everyone knew that Mr Austin was an embittered individual who saw conspiracies everywhere. There was such a fellow in most villages, and Sutton Westford seemed to have a surfeit of disgruntled males of a certain age. Gabriel flinched at the sight of Toby Salmon raising his hand, knowing that the poor dunderhead was about to say something silly.

"How did Jesus get to heaven?" asked Toby, removing a much-chewed pencil from his mouth. "Did he have a German rocket?"

44

"Don't be a silly boy," cut in Susie before Gabriel could respond. "Why on earth would Jesus need a rocket? He walked on water, didn't he? Or do you think he had special floats under his feet that time?"

A wave of appreciative laughter rolled across the class, and Toby's fat red face turned three or four shades redder. "I only asked!" he protested over the giggles threatening to drown him out. "Why shouldn't he have had a rocket if he wanted?"

"Yes, God's all-powerful, but he can't do anything without the Luftwaffe," sneered Susie, causing Gabriel to suppress a shudder. Susie was turning into her own waspish mother, always ready with a roll of the eyes and a sarcastic retort, especially when a boy dared open his mouth. There was more laughter, and this time Gabriel intervened quickly to save what was left of Toby Salmon's tattered dignity. It was a brave or foolish male who tried to outwit a girl, and Toby had learnt the hard way, but at least he had learnt the lesson nice and young.

The following morning, having judged Gabriel to have settled, Abbot Ambrose restored him to his duties, and Gabriel made his way to the village shop. It was a dull, overcast day, the sort of morning where there is not a patch of blue in the sky and it is impossible to believe that the sun will ever arrive. *Not enough blue sky to make our Lady a mantle . . .* It was at least dry, and Gabriel enjoyed the exhilaration of the walk across the dew covered grass. Despite his need for peace, Gabriel had missed these little journeys, and he told himself it was not just because of his insatiable need for information. He was blessed to live in one of the most

45

beautiful regions of Britain, and the walk was guaranteed to lift his spirits, whatever the weather.

Gabriel noticed that something was wrong as soon as the shop came into sight. The door was open, which Reggie would never normally allow at this time of year—it was hard enough keeping the shop warm for customers as it was. And something else was amiss. The paperboy's bike stood leaning against the wall when Jimmy ought to have finished his paper round and been sitting in the classroom by now. Gabriel picked up his pace, his heart hammering, and rushed into the shop before nerves could hold him back.

He was not sure afterwards whether he had really expected to find Reggie or the paperboy lying in a pool of blood in the middle of the shop floor, but Gabriel relaxed momentarily at the sight of Reggie and Jimmy very much alive, talking animatedly behind the counter. Jimmy was out of breath, having burst into the shop without bothering to close the door. Inconveniently for Gabriel, the two of them stopped talking as soon as they saw him enter. "What's happened?" asked Gabriel. Reggie indicated to Gabriel to close the door. Gabriel gave the offending door an impatient shove, causing the bell to jangle loudly enough to make Jimmy jump. "Jimmy, what's happened? Shouldn't you be at school?"

Jimmy opened his mouth to answer, but Reggie beat him to it. "There's a body been found at the building site."

Gabriel blenched, scarcely noticing that the basket had slipped from his hand. It was just as he had feared. Joseph had been murdered and his body had been dumped at the building site as some kind of horrific poetic justice for coming to the village with his fancy housing plans. Gabriel forced himself to focus his attention on the most unfortunate paperboy in the country, who had stumbled upon a dead body for the second time in less than a year. "Jimmy, where exactly did you find him?"

Jimmy shook his head, looking for all the world as if he was letting Gabriel down with the answer. "I didn't find it, Father. I heard Mr Wilcox talking about it to someone. He said the workmen had started early to avoid the protesters, and they dug up a skeleton, and now the houses couldn't possibly be built."

"A skeleton?" Gabriel looked up at Reggie for an explanation, but Reggie had already noticed Gabriel's confusion and gave him a reassuring smile.

"It's all right, Father, it's not our Joseph they've found, if that's what you're thinking. It'll be a death from years ago, I'll warrant. Don't you fret."

Gabriel picked his basket up off the floor, placed it on the counter, and handed Reggie the shopping list. "I should go and take a look," he said hurriedly, "just to see if I can be of any assistance."

"It's a bit late to be giving a skeleton the last rites, don't you think, Father?" asked Reggie wryly, laying out the stack of ration books on the counter.

"I mean poor Joseph is likely to be in rather a state. He shouldn't be alone at a time like this."

"The last thing the poor sod'll be is alone," said Reggie. "He shan't get a minute's peace now." His eyes narrowed. Gabriel had no sense of subtlety whatsoever, and Reggie knew exactly what he was up to. "I don't deliver groceries," he said tersely. "Are you coming back for this lot when you stop poking your nose in?"

"I can deliver it," Jimmy chimed in, "if you make it worth me while."

"What about school?" demanded Reggie. "You're late enough as it is."

"I'm not getting into no trouble for being late," said Jimmy emphatically. "If I deliver the groceries to the abbey, I can get to school in time for morning break and slip in at the back of the line. No one'll notice I've not been there. Miss Tuddock never remembers to take the register on Monday morning. She's too dopey after the weekend."

Gabriel left Reggie and Jimmy negotiating the price of Jimmy's courier service and hurried in the direction of the building site.

Gabriel had never visited the grim little corner of the village where the building site had sprung up. It was the wrong end of the village for Gabriel, as far to the east side as the abbey was to the west, and Gabriel had had no cause to travel in that direction before. In his mind, he imagined it rather as Joseph had described it: a dank, forbidding place full of rusted old machines and dangerously derelict outbuildings, the sort of monstrous industrial shambles to which adventurous children instinctively gravitate to make their own playgrounds. There had been rather more places like that growing up in London, derelict houses and dumping grounds for the detritus of failed factories and warehouses, the sort of landscapes in which children risked cutting themselves on rusted wire and wounding their limbs falling onto the jagged teeth of broken brickwork. As Gabriel had recalled, when these accidents had occurred—all too frequently—the children had been more frightened about their parents' responses than the risk of fractures or even sepsis.

It was almost amusing to think that in a village as beautiful as this with so many idyllic places in which children could play—clean rivers where they could splash about, green hills to roll down, trees to climb and turn into dens—children should still feel the need for an ugly, threatening playground.

Gabriel passed Barney Lodge to his left, a thatched, whitewashed cottage which stood out like the last beacon of rural civilisation, before making his way along the chalk path through a copse. He suspected that—prior to the arrival of the builders—the copse would have been completely silent apart from the odd mournful chirp of a bird. As it stood, Gabriel could hear the distant murmur of many people congregated close together, even though he was some way off. Almost as abruptly as they had covered him, the trees thinned to nothing, and Gabriel was out in open country again, with the site of Joseph's little empire looming before him.

At least, it should have loomed before him. As Gabriel left the happy refuge of the copse for the short path to the old mine, the first thing he should have seen was the building site. Unfortunately, the entire population of the village seemed to be blocking the view, huddled together watching the drama unfolding. Gabriel had never found it easy to push in, having been trained from a young age to wait his turn patiently, but he slipped through the crowd of people, politely but firmly nudging people aside until there were no longer any obstructions to his line of sight.

At first glance, this was a building site like any of the other sites popping up all over Britain. There were impressive-looking diggers and more homely-looking wheelbarrows, cement mixers and piles of bricks to one side, but the building development was in its earliest stages. The workmen were still in the process of preparing the ground; large squares were being etched into the earth, surrounded by deep trenches where the foundations of the houses would be laid. Paved paths had been set up between the squares to allow labourers to transport wheelbarrow loads of bricks and cement about. But there was no such activity this morning. A large area had been cordoned off by police, and a group of young labourers stood idly by, watching with a mixture of curiosity and anxiety whilst two professional-looking men removed something from the ground with extreme diligence.

Without thinking, Gabriel broke free from the crowd and moved forward to get a closer look. Suddenly a hand grasped his arm and pulled him back. He wheeled round to see who was restraining him; it was Joseph, white, shaking, but determined to retain control of the situation. "I wouldn't go any farther if I were you," he said in an apologetic tone. "This is a crime scene now. Stay back here with me."

"I heard they'd found a body," said Gabriel. "For a ghastly moment, I thought it was yours."

"It's worse than that, Father," answered Joseph bleakly. "It looks as though it's a child."

Gabriel watched as the two men he had observed before lifted a skull out of the ground. It was quite easy to see now that they were removing the small, underdeveloped bones of a child's skeleton from the soil. This was indeed a crime scene. Gabriel could hear gasps and whispers from the pack of villagers, who were now watching with unapologetic voyeurism. It was possible that most people had expected an archaeological find, the body of an ancient hunter perhaps, as there were many Stone Age burial grounds in the region. The body of a child was a different matter, even if it had lain in the earth for many years.

The bones would have to be carefully labelled and packaged. There would be attempts to identify the remains, and an investigation would begin that would reach deep into the past to discover what had happened to the child to whom those bones belonged. After a long and exhaustive process, these pathetic human remains might be granted a Christian burial.

"Who found him?" asked Gabriel, not taking his eyes off the two men and their work. One of them was holding up a silver necklace with what looked like a small silver medallion hanging from the chain. "Was it you?"

"No, thank God," said Joseph. "I'm not sure I would have recovered. One of the lads noticed something when he started work this morning. I've been setting to work early to shake off the protesters. They're a lazy lot and usually don't arrive until they have had a good lie-in and a hearty breakfast. My men have a couple of hours' work under their belts by then."

"Where is he now?"

"Who?"

"The chap who found the skeleton?"

"I sent him home. Poor man fainted when he realised what he'd found. He said he thought it was a dead animal to begin with. He got on his hands and knees to clear away some of the muck and felt tiny fingers poking through the soil. Would have been enough to give anyone a turn."

Gabriel became aware of a man's voice shouting authoritatively, and the sudden ripples of movement as groups of onlookers began to scatter at the man's bidding. Gabriel knew that voice very well and turned quickly to Joseph. "I think it might be better if I made myself scarce," he said as calmly as he could. "The inspector's arrived to survey the scene, and I've a feeling he'd rather not see me."

"Don't run away!" commanded Joseph, blocking Gabriel's attempt at a swift exit. "I'll say you've come to hear my confession."

"On a building site? Joseph, he's not stupid!"

"You can hear it for real if you like, but it's a bit public." Gabriel gave Joseph a warning glance. "Sorry, I didn't mean to be flippant. Look, the inspector chappie will be far too busy doing his job to notice who's watching, mark my words."

Gabriel had to acknowledge that Inspector Applegate was not a man to beat about the bush. Without any introduction, he went directly over to the shallow grave, where the last parts of the skeleton were being removed. Gabriel could see the men talking through what they had found, showing Applegate the silver necklace they had discovered with the bones. "Unless my presence is useful to you," said Gabriel finally, "I have to return to the abbey. I shouldn't really have come, but I was worried about you."

"If you can bring yourself to stay, I'd appreciate it," said Joseph. Gabriel suspected that Joseph was the sort of man who found it extremely difficult to ask for help, and this was not a nightmare Joseph wished to face alone. "I daresay the inspector will need to talk to me, and I've no idea what's going to happen now. I hadn't really thought beyond the discovery of the body. I'm not sure I know what to do."

Gabriel looked about him. The villagers had taken the hint from Inspector Applegate and dispersed, but he knew that most of them would return after a discreet interval to see what other bits of juicy gossip they could glean. The workmen would not be permitted to leave until the police had taken statements from them, but they did not seem overly troubled by the indefinite cessation of activity. "You should probably go over there and introduce yourself to the inspector," said Gabriel, considering the matter. "A body has been found on your land, and you need to make it clear that you wish to cooperate with the police in their investigation."

Joseph nodded, braced himself for the task, and moved forward, but he had waited a moment too long. As he stepped towards the imposing figure of the inspector, Applegate turned round to face him, immediately noting Gabriel standing guiltily in the background. "Well, well, well, I should have expected to find you loitering with intent," said Inspector Applegate, marching swiftly in his direction, but to Gabriel's infinite relief, his stern, thin face broke into a grin and he extended a hand to Gabriel like an old friend. "So, they've called you home, have they?"

Gabriel nodded. "As long as I behave myself," he said, wincing at the thought that it had not taken very long for him to wander off the beaten path. He could justify this excursion on pastoral grounds, since Joseph was in a distressing situation, but he was still not supposed to be here. "Is it true what they're saying, that it's a child's skeleton they've found?"

"I'm afraid so," said Applegate grimly. "Quite a young child by the look of things, and I have a nasty feeling I know which child she is. I'll need to be sure before I name names, though." Applegate turned sharply towards Joseph, who had made the mistake of relaxing slightly as the two

53

men talked. "And who might you be?" asked Applegate, giving the stranger a terse handshake.

"This is my land," said Joseph. "My men were at work when they found the bones."

"Which one of them made the discovery?" asked Applegate, glancing back at the group of labourers, who had begun whispering amongst themselves when the inspector had arrived. "Would you point him out to me?"

"He's not there, Inspector," Joseph explained. "I'm afraid he fainted when he realised he'd found human remains. Always been one of the more delicate types. I can supply you with his name and address."

Applegate nodded. "I'd be obliged if you'd do that, sir. You will need to give a statement to one of my constables before you leave, as will any other man who was at the site when the discovery was made. Beyond that, there's not much else I need from you since this appears to be a very old case. Building work will have to cease temporarily until this matter is cleared up, of course."

"Of course," Joseph agreed, a little too readily. Whether or not Joseph was willing to acknowledge it, Gabriel knew that dragging out the building work indefinitely could prove extremely costly to a businessman like Joseph. It might even put paid to the whole scheme.

Inspector Applegate turned back to Gabriel. "There's something I'd like you to look at."

Gabriel raised an eyebrow. It was one thing Applegate warming to him a little, but it was a novelty to be asked for help. There had to be a catch somewhere. "Of course."

Applegate gestured for Gabriel to follow him and walked back to the grave, causing the two excavators to stop their work and look up. "Gentlemen, this is Father Gabriel. He's a Roman priest, so he should be able to help you with that thing you discovered in among the bones."

On closer view, Gabriel could see that the two men were of different generations, a senior and a junior man. The young man was a serious, bespectacled specimen, very much in the mould of a person who has elected to spend his life picking over bones and bloody fingerprints. The older man had the affable air of a bartender, which wrong-footed Gabriel immediately. "How do you do, Father?" he said cheerfully, refraining from shaking hands, only—Gabriel assumed—because his gloved hands were filthy. He handed Gabriel the silver necklace, waiting as Gabriel examined the worn, dirt-encrusted medallion. The markings were almost illegible, but he could just make out a figure holding the baby Jesus. For a moment he thought it was a Madonna, but the figure was slightly too masculine, and there was no sign of the telltale mantle. He knew that pose very well. "It's a medal of Saint Anthony of Padua," said Gabriel, suppressing a shiver. If that medal belonged to a child, it might have been a First Communion gift or even a baptismal token. It spoke of precious moments in a child's life that should have been followed one day by confirmation and maybe marriage. So many moments never experienced by a life cut short.

"Am I to take it that our victim was a Roman Catholic then?" asked Applegate.

"Probably, though some high Anglicans have similar devotions, I gather. Of course, it might have been a present from a Catholic relative. But I suspect the child was Catholic." Gabriel hesitated. "You said victim. Might the child have met with an accident? I've been told that this was quite a popular place for children to play in once, and it would certainly have been very dangerous. Might the child have suffered a fall? If he had been playing alone, no one could have helped him."

Applegate shook his head, handing the necklace back to a subordinate. "I'll leave you to carry on here," he said to the man before walking with Gabriel towards his car. "Tell you what, Father," he said, a little more loudly than was strictly necessary. "Let me give you a lift home. It's not far out of my way, and we can't have your abbot throwing you out on your ear when you've only just come back, can we now?"

Gabriel looked surreptitiously round him, wondering with whom Inspector Applegate was really communicating, but he saw no one of note apart from Applegate's own team, Joseph, and the workmen. Not a bad list, Gabriel conceded, and he shared a policeman's unease about being overheard. "That would be most kind of you, Inspector," he said, turning to take his leave of Joseph. "Come and see us at the abbey, Joseph," he said. "You would be most welcome."

Gabriel felt a huge sense of relief as he got into the back of the car with Applegate, greeting Police Constable Richardson warmly as he did so. If he returned to the abbey in a police car, it would lend credence to his story that he had remained away from the abbey only out of necessity. Not to mention the thought that Gabriel's appearance outside the abbey gates in the company of a detective inspector would cause enough of a distraction to stop anyone asking too many questions, including possibly Abbot Ambrose. "Glad to be back in your monastery, Father?" asked Richardson as he turned the key in the ignition and the engine growled to life.

"Rather," answered Gabriel. He looked sideways at Applegate, wondering when he was going to start talking, but Applegate waited until they were some distance from the crime scene before speaking.

"I didn't think it wise to begin a lengthy conversation in the open," Applegate explained, taking his cigarette case out of his pocket. "These villages are cauldrons of gossip. If just one of them heard the word 'murder' whispered from my mouth, it would be all over Sutton Westford before you could say 'post mortem'."

"You think you're looking at a murder?" demanded Gabriel, feeling a knot tightening in his chest. He remembered Douglas Jennings talking about the day his sister had gone missing, and the terror that had consumed them as the hours passed and they had scoured the surrounding countryside in mounting panic, fearing the worst. Gabriel could not bear to think of the other child. Child murders were so horrific, such an abomination that the very subject inevitably brought out a man's protective instincts. Everyone had a child in his life for whom he would shed blood to protect. Gabriel exhaled slowly, counting silently to five before resuming the conversation. "How can you be sure with just bones to look at? Surely you can't even identify the remains now?"

"Cause of death may be difficult to ascertain, certainly," Applegate agreed, "unless someone is overcome with remorse and confesses, but I'm not holding out for a miracle."

"Has anyone ever voluntarily confessed to murder to you, Inspector?" asked Gabriel, curious. He was pretty used to people confessing their sins to him—though, contrary to popular belief, rarely anything very serious. Gabriel wondered whether the general public viewed the police the same way as they saw priests.

"Never in my entire career has a guilty person admitted he's done wrong. I've had convicted murderers whom I practically caught with blood dripping from their hands, going all the way to the gallows pleading their innocence." Applegate busied himself tamping and lighting a cigarette, a well-worn ritual guaranteed to steady his hands and his thoughts at the same time. "As to your other question, it will not be so difficult to identify the child. Children don't disappear from tiny communities like this very often. I can think of only one case in this village in the past thirty years. I can't tell you the name yet, of course—I'll have to reopen the case file—but I'm pretty sure already who the victim was."

"But murder? I don't know, I always try to give humanity the benefit of the doubt. If he died in an accident . . ."

A cynical chuckle erupted behind a small cloud of smoke. "I stopped giving humanity the benefit of the doubt years ago, Father. Let's face it, the body was buried. The ground is not marshy or boggy; there's no way the earth reclaimed her by itself. Someone buried her; someone had something to hide—a crime."

"Her?"

Applegate fidgeted in his seat. "Slip of the tongue, of sorts. The missing child was a girl. As I said, I can't confirm anything until I've reopened the file, but I'd wager you anything it's her."

Gabriel glanced out the window at the neat row of houses

that made up the more respectable side of the village. These houses had traditionally belonged to artisans rather than farm labourers and as a result were larger, more solidly built, with bay windows at the front to let in plenty of light, and trim little gardens with rose beds, not vegetable patches. He noticed a girl aged perhaps six or seven sitting on the wall outside her house, dressed in a warm woollen frock and chunky red cardigan. He wondered for a moment why the child was not at school, then remembered who she was. Lilian Williams had stopped attending the village school after an attack of the measles had left her virtually blind. Her mother had told Gabriel that there had been snow on the ground when Lilian had taken sick, and she had closed the curtains in the girl's room and forbidden her to get up because the light would hurt her eyes. Like all children, Lilian had been desperate to go out and play in the snow. When her mother was occupied in the kitchen and her brothers and sisters had gone off to school, Lilian had crept out of the house and into the sparkling white wonderland of the garden, far too young to realise that the sunlight reflecting off the snow was destroying her eyes forever. It had been a harsh punishment for a moment of childish disobedience, and all the villagers indulged her a little.

"I hope you don't mind my asking this, Inspector," said Gabriel, with all the hesitance of a man who knows perfectly well the inspector will mind a great deal. "I know you have not exactly appreciated my involvement in your cases in the past."

"Interference, you mean," clarified the inspector. "No, I haven't. Not that it seems to have stopped you."

"I suppose all I mean . . . ," Gabriel continued bravely,

trying hard not to be unnerved by the interruption. "Well, it's just . . . it seems to me that it would be easier if we worked together. If you think about it, sometimes people are happier talking to a priest than a policeman. It might be easier for me to investigate because nobody notices me quite so much. I don't want to be a nuisance, you understand, and my abbot won't want me making trouble either."

Applegate laughed softly to himself. "Father, you *are* a nuisance. You have always been a nuisance, and I suspect you always will be. But I owe you one for helping me collar Gladstone's killer. I'm prepared to admit I couldn't see the wood for the trees in that case. I would have seen the wrong man hang." Applegate looked up at the impressive exterior of the abbey, into which he would soon deposit Gabriel. If he had been inclined to do so, Applegate could have gone in with Gabriel now, demanded to see the abbot, and begged him to keep Gabriel confined within the walls of the abbey for the duration of the case. He knew that Gabriel was in a vulnerable position and would be obliged to do as he was told, but Applegate had not spoken lightly when he had thanked Gabriel for his help with the Gladstone case. For the first time, an investigation had brought the two men together, and Applegate could see the benefits of two minds at work on a cold case which would most likely prove extremely difficult to solve.

"I hope I haven't spoken out of turn," said Gabriel finally. It had not taken long for him to give up hope of a positive response from Applegate. "I suppose I was just hoping that—"

"No," said Applegate emphatically. "I meant it when I said I owed you one. The fact is, cold cases are always hard to crack. Years have passed; the killer will have had a long time to cover his tracks, assuming he's even still alive. If we have found the missing girl I'm thinking of, she disappeared during the first war. There were such movements of people and so many deaths, it's difficult to say what we will find. So yes, I'll share any information I have, and you can feel free to dig around. Tactfully."

"Thank you." Gabriel grinned and made to get out of the car, only to feel Applegate taking him forcefully by the arm and pulling him back into the car, which made Gabriel feel like a naughty schoolboy being dragged indoors by the scruff of the neck.

"On one condition, Father," said Applegate tersely. "If I tell you to stop, you stop. Understand? If your abbot tells you to stop, you stop. You don't get in my way, you don't get under my feet, and you don't annoy absolutely every-body you talk to."

"That sounds like more than one condition to me," Gabriel retorted, his spirits sinking.

"Do I make myself clear?" continued Applegate relent-lessly.

"I understand your terms perfectly," answered Gabriel, getting out of the car without hindrance this time. He hes-itated before closing the car door, wondering whether his next request would be a step too far. "I don't suppose you could explain this to my abbot, could you? Otherwise, he might think I'm going off on some flight of fancy again."

4

"I cannot begin to describe to you, Dom Gabriel," said Abbot Ambrose from behind his mahogany desk, "quite how far my heart sank when Jimmy arrived at the abbey with the provisions I had sent you to purchase."

Gabriel shifted his weight from one foot to the other. He knew Abbot Ambrose found the habit maddening, but—as usual—Gabriel had not been invited to sit down, and the effect of standing before a seated judge always made him uneasy. "I'm awfully sorry, Father Abbot," he began. "As I've explained, my first thought when I heard that a body had been discovered was that the young businessman had been killed. He had warned me that he'd received death threats, but he was not willing to go to the police. Even when I was told that it was someone else, I thought he might still be in some sort of trouble."

"There is no need to go over all that again," Ambrose replied, finally motioning for Gabriel to sit down, if for no other reason than to stop his moving constantly. "I have no doubt that you acted out of a sense of pastoral duty, not mere nosiness or anything as base as that." Gabriel looked down at his hands. "Since the inspector has specifically requested your assistance, Gabriel, I am inclined to allow you to pursue this case. If a child has indeed been murdered, then we surely owe it to her family and to her own memory to see her killer brought to justice."

"Thank you, Father Abbot, I swear I shall—"

"There is just one small concern I feel I should share with you," continued Ambrose, looking steadily across the desk at Gabriel, who quickly looked away again. It was becoming a habit, but Abbot Ambrose was a difficult man with whom to make eye contact. He had the gift of spiritual night vision, capable of seeing through every layer of obscurity until the truth leapt out at him. "When you first entered this abbey, you did so because you were seeking peace after suffering a terrible tragedy. Perhaps the worst tragedy any man may suffer."

"Father Abbot—"

"I'm afraid I have to ask you this: Are you seeking justice for this child because your own child received none? If so, I should warn you that going after another child's killer is unlikely to bring you any peace."

There was a long silence, which Gabriel took as a sign of weakness on his own part but which Ambrose found encouraging. Gabriel was thinking, not dismissing the idea out of hand as he might so easily have done. And he really was thinking. Gabriel saw Nicoletta sitting on the stairs the last time he had ever seen her, singing a nursery rhyme perfectly in tune, with the breathless determination of a small child to get the words out as quickly as possible.

Up above the world so high
Like a diamond in the sky!

Gabriel blinked and forced himself to look at Abbot Ambrose. "I cannot lie to you and pretend that my wife and child are ever far from my thoughts," he said quietly, "and it does grieve me that there can be no justice for them. But this child had parents too, and they are living with the daily agony of knowing that their child's killer is still living free in this world. Can it be wrong for me to want to spare them that?"

Ambrose smiled sadly. "And what of your pain, Gabriel? How will you feel, working on a case that might turn out to be quite like your own?"

"My pain is my own," said Gabriel simply. "I know now that nothing I do will ever make it go away. I can't have my child back; I can't give this family back their child either. She's dead. I saw her bones being removed from the ground. But someone knows what happened, and someone knows who killed her."

Ambrose nodded, apparently satisfied. "What is it that Inspector Applegate wants you to do?"

Gabriel felt himself breathing more easily. They were moving on to practical details now; he commended Nicoletta to God, as he always did when she came into his thoughts, and did his best to focus his mind on the here and now. "He's sending the car for me tomorrow morning after I've said my Mass. I shall endeavour to be away from the abbey as little as possible, but it's difficult to know how things will pan out. Inspector Applegate said that he is going to read through the notes on the missing persons file today, and we can talk further tomorrow. He hopes that much of the excavation work will have been completed by then too. They'd only removed the skeleton when we left this morning, and I daresay they have to look for other clues." He remembered the Saint Anthony medallion. "I think the child was

Catholic," he said. "They found a Saint Anthony medallion with the remains."

Ambrose started violently. "When did this child go missing?" he asked, making no effort to hide his agitation.

"I'm not sure," answered Gabriel. "I think Inspector Applegate said that there was a child who had gone missing some time in the past thirty years. It was the only unresolved case of a missing child they had had in all that time, which is why he thinks it's the same one."

"Primrose Harding."

"What?"

"Little Primmie Harding," said Ambrose, visibly moved. "She was eight years old when she vanished. I was only a novice at the time. I'd prepared her for her First Holy Communion."

"You knew her!"

Ambrose put up a hand to stop Gabriel's thought processes going down a rabbit hole as usual. "If it's her, of course. And I suspect it is." Ambrose sat back in his chair, distracted in a manner Gabriel had never noticed before. "The inspector will tell you tomorrow if it was, I suppose. But as he said, there aren't so many missing child cases in a place like this." Ambrose shook his head dejectedly. "I suppose it should not be a surprise, really. It's just that I have always half-hoped that she might be alive somewhere. One always hopes."

"How the devil did you know her name?" demanded Applegate, looking askance at Gabriel across his insubstantially sized office. "Have you started snooping about already?"

"Not at all, I promise," said Gabriel, sitting himself down

in the only comfortable-looking chair in the room. He had startled Applegate as usual by barging past the constable at the front desk and bursting into the inspector's office and saying Primrose Harding's name before either of them could get so far as a "Good morning." Now Applegate was staring at him, and Gabriel was in the predictable position of trying to explain himself. "Abbot Ambrose knew her. I suppose everyone in the village over a certain age must have. He said her name as soon as I mentioned that the dead child might have been a Catholic. He said he prepared her for her First Holy Communion. As there's no Catholic parish here, the few Catholic families in the village come to the abbey for the sacraments and catechism."

"I see," conceded Applegate. He could hardly call it snooping on Gabriel's part when all he had done was to have an innocent conversation with his own superior. "Well, if he taught the girl, he might be able to help us."

"Yes, I think he knew it was her as soon as I said that a child's body had been found. He kept saying 'she'. But he didn't want to talk about it anymore until I was sure about the child's identity."

Applegate pushed a thick cardboard file towards Gabriel. Gabriel had not quite got over the novelty of Applegate volunteering information, and he stared at the folder as though afraid to touch it. "Primrose Harding, eight years old," declared Applegate, as though addressing a meeting. "I suspected as much yesterday but had to be sure before I started bandying her name about. Hers was not the only missing child case; children do go missing, but they are usually recovered quite quickly. It's the only missing child case in this village in which the child was never recovered. It was my predecessor's last case, and it broke him. The whole village was after him, demanding answers, demanding that he find her, but the little thing had disappeared into thin air. The only item discovered was a metal button, but it was so generic, it might have come off the coats of half the men in the county."

"Where was it found?"

"In the old mine, in the area where she was known to play. It was suggestive of foul play but not conclusive."

"It seems extraordinary that a child could vanish like that in a small village where everybody knows everyone and everybody's always minding one another's business. One can't walk down the street without curtains twitching and neighbours whispering."

"Yes, but as you remember from Agnes Jennings' case, we are surrounded by miles of countryside. Plenty of places to lure an unsuspecting child away. Plenty of places to hide a body. According to the file, there were policemen and volunteers combing the countryside for weeks trying to find her, but they never found a single trace."

Gabriel picked up the folder gingerly. "May I have a moment to look through this?" he asked Applegate. "I'll be more useful to you if I have all the information there is."

"Be my guest. I meant you to read it," said Applegate, "not that you'll find very much information of any use. The poor lass went missing three decades ago. I get the nasty feeling, reading the file, that old Inspector Gardiner suspected the mother. It usually is the mother or father, but he couldn't find any evidence to pin it on her, especially without a body."

"Or a murder weapon," said Gabriel. He moved his chair

away from the desk so as not to distract Applegate, settling himself near the window, where there was plenty of light. Information was indeed scanty despite the thickness of the folder. The girl had been reported missing by her mother at ten o'clock on the night of April 1, 1918. The mother claimed that the girl had left the house before the rest of the household had awoken that morning and had never returned. The mother was not concerned as the child often wandered off alone, liking her own company, and she had become concerned only when evening came and the girl did not return for her supper.

Gabriel could not help thinking immediately that there was something odd about the observation that an eight-year-old girl would like her own company. He had not been the most sociable of children himself, but most children—male and female—gravitated towards the company of other children. A love of solitude was usually associated with adult life, the desire for peace and quiet, the need to put one's thoughts in order. Gabriel knew he might be being a little judgemental of young children, but the image of a lonely child troubled him. He was even more troubled when he saw the faded monochrome photograph of the girl. The photograph of Primrose Harding had been taken by a professional in a studio. The girl was dressed in a long floral-print frock with many layers of frills and a large, uncomfortable-looking lace collar. Her long curls were impeccably coiffured into bunches tied with extravagant ribbons. Her face could have been called beautiful, except that her expression did not belong to a little girl at all. Her face had none of the puppy plumpness one might expect from a child that age; if anything, the cheeks were sunken, making her eyes look almost a little too large, and she stared into the camera with a look of suspicion and mild reproof.

"Was she ill?" asked Gabriel, looking up from the folder.

"It doesn't say she was," answered Applegate absently.

"Poor then?"

"Not at all. The Hardings were pretty well-to-do as far as I could make out."

Applegate went back to his paperwork, and Gabriel looked back at the photograph. There was something else wrong with her, but he was almost embarrassed to admit to himself that he had noticed. Her clothes were all wrong, even allowing for the fact that this was a professional photograph taken many years before, when children typically dressed more formally. Her frock looked overly elaborate and old-fashioned—ludicrously so. She was dressed in the sort of expensive, cumbersome gown that a minor royal or a child with high-society parents might have worn in the days of the old queen. It was hardly unfair to say that she barely looked like a child at all: she looked more like a porcelain doll or a model posing for a portrait painter who was trying to capture the essence of a lost age.

"Inspector, is Mrs Harding still alive?" asked Gabriel, rising to his feet.

"Yes."

"And Mr Harding?"

"Died long before Primrose disappeared."

"I should like to speak to Mrs Harding. Has she been informed that her daughter has been found?"

"I sent two of my men to see her yesterday evening, simply to warn her that we may have found her daughter's remains," Applegate explained. "I wouldn't normally speak to the relatives until we had confirmation, but I didn't want her hearing about it from some talkative villager. It was better for her to hear it from us, even if the body had turned out to belong to somebody else."

"And now you are quite sure the skeleton is that of Primrose Harding?"

Applegate nodded. "Frankly, we all knew as soon as those bones were unearthed, but mistakes have been made before, and it always pays to be cautious. We've been able to confirm that it is Primrose Harding, as far as you ever can."

"How? There was nothing left! No hair, no clothes. Only the Saint Anthony medallion, and thousands of Catholics have possessions like that."

"Except that there aren't thousands of Catholics in Sutton Westford, for a start, and it's amazing what you can tell from bones and teeth. It said in the notes that she had broken her arm the year before she went missing, which was why her mother claimed she didn't like her to play with other children. Too boisterous, you see. Our man was able to see a faint line on the right humerus, indicating a healed fracture. The mother said that Primrose's front teeth were missing as her adult teeth had not yet come through."

Gabriel shuddered, handing Applegate the folder. "It's a bit sobering to consider that when we die, all that will be left to identify who we were will be missing teeth and the fractures we gave ourselves as children."

"Don't you people have pictures of skeletons all over the place? Skulls on your desks to remind you of death?" asked Applegate, getting up to put on his jacket and hat. Gabriel picked up his soup-plate hat and followed Applegate out of the office.

"I can assure you, there are no skulls in my possession," Gabriel retorted, falling into step next to Applegate as they walked down the corridor. "Though it's humbling to consider what a leveller death is. We'll all return to dust one day."

"Talking to you makes me lose the will to live," snapped Applegate. "You're worse than a pathologist."

Outside the police station, Gabriel found himself hesitating to get back in the car. "Wouldn't it be easier to walk to the Harding residence? It's not very far, surely?"

"Quicker to drive," answered Applegate tersely, ushering Gabriel into the back of the car. "I'm a busy man."

You don't want to be seen walking around in the company of a Catholic priest, thought Gabriel wryly, but he let it pass. He did not get the impression that Applegate was particularly allergic to papists, but he would no doubt balk at the idea of advertising that he had elicited the help of the village's very own mad monk. "Did Mrs Harding accept that her daughter was dead, all those years ago?" asked Gabriel. "It would help to know how she is likely to respond."

"The presumption was always that the child had died, and she was declared dead seven years later, but whether the Harding family accepted this is difficult to know. There's something horrible about a permanently missing person, especially a child. One knows that the child is almost certainly dead, of course, but hope always remains in the absence of answers. If she'd been my girl, I know part of me would have kept wondering whether she was alive out there somewhere, if she might just knock on my door one day as if nothing had happened."

Gabriel shuddered. He could not bring himself to tell

Applegate or anyone that—even with definitive evidence of death—it was possible to think like that. Perhaps those charred bones were the remains of someone else's child; perhaps my wife and daughter had gone out for the evening, and two vagrants had broken into the house for shelter and been caught up in the subsequent fire . . . It was easy enough for a grieving mind to believe all manner of impossible things when the alternative was too horrible to contemplate. "Mrs Harding must be a grand old age by now," Gabriel observed. "Primrose would be nearly forty if she had lived."

"Yes, Mrs Harding is well into her seventies. I suppose I can console myself that she lived long enough to get some answers. Perhaps. Inspector Gardner said that he always liked to be able to tell families what had happened, even if it was something unbearable. However terrible the circumstances, if there is a body, there can be a funeral. There can be grief and remembrance; the family can begin to face what had happened."

Gabriel was almost relieved when the car pulled over and he could busy himself with the mundane act of opening the door and letting himself out onto the pavement. He could hear Abbot Ambrose's words of warning in his ears and wondered how often he would have to hide his troubled feelings in the days and weeks to come. It certainly gave him an incentive to help Applegate clear the matter up as quickly as possible.

They were standing outside one of the grander residences of the village, a red brick villa separated from the road by a hedge clipped into a perfect green cuboid, and a large expanse of garden that turned out to be a croquet lawn. Gabriel wondered, as they walked along the path to the front door, whether there had ever been an actual game of croquet played on that lawn. The house and surrounding acreage was so deathly quiet, it was impossible to imagine guests in frocks and straw hats, laughing and chatting as they whiled away a lazy summer afternoon. It was not that the gardens were overgrown and unloved as the residences of some elderly widows inevitably were. The place was almost unnaturally neat and tidy—a loveless tidiness.

"Didn't the notes say that Mrs Harding had other children?" asked Gabriel, slowing down to give himself more time before they reached the door.

"A son killed during the first war, and a spinster daughter," Applegate filled in, moving ahead of Gabriel to climb the three steps to an imposing front door framed by mock Roman pillars. "Let me do the talking." Applegate seized the lion-shaped door knocker—which Gabriel half expected to turn into the face of Jacob Marley—and gave it an authoritative rap. "I'll break the news, then I'll say I brought you along because they are Roman Catholics and I thought they might need your ministrations."

The door opened slowly on its well-oiled hinges, and Gabriel and Applegate found themselves facing the spinster daughter herself. Swathed in an Edwardian-style dress that fell about her tall, spindly figure in heavy black pleats, a woman stood before them who could have been any age from fifty to seventy. Her hair was an unappealing grey-white, and she had tied it back in a straggly bun. She even wore a pearl choker to complete the style of a nineteenth-century dowager. *Never mind Jacob Marley,* thought Gabriel, swallowing a wave of nerves. *I might be in the presence of Miss Havisham.*

74

"Good morning," said Applegate, cutting through Gabriel's thinly disguised astonishment. "My name is Inspector Applegate. Would I be addressing Miss Harding?"

A bitter smile crept across the woman's pale face, and she gave a pert nod. "You would be addressing Miss Harding, Inspector. I assume that you have come to inform me of what I already know?"

Applegate cleared his throat. "Miss Harding, we suspected that the skeleton discovered yesterday was that of your sister. I can now confirm that there was no mistake. It was important to be sure——"

"I was born in this village, Inspector," interrupted Miss Harding, as though she were cutting off an impudent servant. "I have lived here all my life. Indeed, I have barely ever left it. Children do not vanish into thin air as a rule. My mother and I knew perfectly well that the body you found yesterday was Primrose." The woman gave Gabriel a piercing look as though assessing whether he was worthy to cross the threshold of her house. "I presume you have a tongue in your mouth, sir?"

"This is Father Gabriel Milson from the abbey," Applegate explained, aware of the faux pas. "I gather that you are Roman Catholics, and I thought you might want——"

"Thank you for your concern about my spiritual welfare, Inspector," replied Miss Harding in that peculiarly upper-class English manner that is both impeccably polite and appallingly rude at the same time. "Is there anything else you may tell me about my sister's death, or are you here simply to tell me that she died? As you may imagine, I have some questions."

Both men bristled at the cold, acerbic tone. There was

something unnatural about the way the woman was talking, even if one made allowances for shock and grief, both of which might cause a person to appear harsher than he really was. "At present I can only assure you, Miss Harding, of my deepest sympathies and my determination to discover as much as possible about what happened to your sister. Obviously, when many years have passed, it can be difficult—"

"Yes, yes," Miss Harding cut in, deliberately looking away from him. "I'm sure you have your excuses very well prepared. The police did nothing to save my sister at the time; I can hardly expect that you would deign to catch her killer now—if, indeed, she was killed." She turned to Gabriel, surprising him by giving him an unexpectedly warm smile. "Your community was very kind to us when Primmie went missing. No one else was, and I suppose I should be grateful for that. Would you like to come in? I daresay Mother would like to meet you, Father."

Applegate glanced sidelong at Gabriel, clicking his heels together and walking towards the car before he could be formally dismissed. Gabriel would never admit it to Applegate, but he would have given anything not to enter that well-polished mausoleum alone, and he had to force himself to return Miss Harding's smile as she led him indoors.

"I don't want to impose on your grief, Miss Harding," ventured Gabriel as his eyes adjusted to the poor interior light. He was standing in a spacious hall. There was a wide wooden staircase to his left, Persian rugs of considerable vintage on the floor and a grandfather clock looking sternly at them from the wall, which Gabriel was not surprised to discover had stopped.

"You may call me Florence, Father," she said, indicating a

heavy wooden door on the right-hand side. "Father Gabriel, isn't it? I'm afraid Mother is very frail these days, and she's been much distressed by the news, but I'm sure she would like to see you."

Gabriel nodded, remembered his manners, and pushed open the door to allow Florence to pass through in front of him into the sitting room. "Thank you, Florence," he said, but any further social nicety Gabriel might or might not have thought to deliver was strangled in his throat as he entered the room. An impossibly old matriarch sat before him, giving off all the warmth of a spider curled up in wait for a hapless insect. "Good morning, Mrs Harding," he said unsteadily. "My name is—"

"I know precisely who you are," came the dismissive retort. "I may be old, but it does not follow that I'm deaf. I overheard your little conversation with my daughter."

"I see."

"If you have come to console me, Father, I'm afraid you are a little too late," Mrs Harding continued. "You chaps were kind enough at the time, God knows, but I have been living with my daughter's death for many more years than she ever lived. You can have nothing further to say to me."

Gabriel swallowed hard. In his experience, it tended to be the relatives who protested most forcefully that they were in no need of counsel, who turned out to be hurting the most. All the same, it was hard to know how to speak to this woman without appearing to patronise her. She looked precisely as he knew Florence would look when she reached that age—their features were strikingly similar—and he shuddered at the thought of what sort of a life Florence would have to endure in her old age, without even the company of a daughter to break the loneliness of the long days. As Gabriel might have expected, the older woman was dressed and seated in a style more reminiscent of the 1840s than the 1940s. Like Florence, she was dressed head to toe in black, though her dress had puffed sleeves and lace trim around the wrists and hem. She wore no jewellery except for a brooch at her throat which held up her pie-crust collar, whilst she wore her hair in short grey curls, scraped away from her face by invisible pins. She was seated in one of those Georgian wooden chairs with engraved armrests and feet, perched on a surfeit of elaborate cushioning, which gave her the look of a marchioness seated on a throne.

"Would you like me to offer Mass for your daughter?" he asked when the silence became troubling. "If you wish, I could . . ."

"My daughter was an angel, Father," Mrs Harding pronounced, surprising Gabriel with the sentimental choice of words. "She was an innocent, sheltered from the world and all its evils. That she was so pure is the only comfort I ever had." She looked to her side; to his acute embarrassment, Gabriel became aware of a woman in nurse's uniform standing silently in the shadows. "If you'll excuse me, Father, I'm extremely distressed and I need to rest. Hillard, if you would be so good as to assist me to my room."

Gabriel watched as the nurse—a young woman Gabriel imagined must have trained in her profession during the war—helped Mrs Harding to her feet and assisted her in walking out of the room. For such a frail-looking woman, Mrs Harding walked with her back straight and an unexpectedly firm tread, barely needing the nurse's support.

"I'm sorry if my mother seems a little distant," said Florence once the two women had left and the door had closed firmly behind them. "I'm afraid she's never entirely recovered from Primmie's death. Within a week of her disappearance, we all knew that Primrose must be dead; she would never have gone off like that without a word. And someone would have seen her. It's not as though she could have got very far if she had run away . . ." Florence trailed off. "Forgive me, how rude of me. Please sit down, Father."

Gabriel noticed two wooden chairs and a small table near a desultory fire and sat down gratefully. The arrangement was for the benefit of visitors, no doubt, but like the empty croquet lawn, Gabriel had the sense that the Hardings rarely received visitors into their home. "Would you care for some tea?" asked Florence, making for the door.

"Thank you, yes," answered Gabriel, then wondered— as Florence slipped noiselessly out of the room—whether he had made a mistake. The family was clearly not as grand as it once was, if Florence had no maid to make the tea for her; with the increasing cost of labour, the Hardings might have had to choose between a nurse for the elderly mother and a housekeeper.

Gabriel noticed a photograph in a silver frame over the fireplace and got up to inspect it. He had learnt that photographs and paintings were a particularly useful source of information about a family's history. This photograph was a sad reflection of what he already knew. A young man in a subaltern's uniform stood flanked by a girl Gabriel judged to be just a couple of years younger than himself and a little child, elaborately dressed. Primrose. Gabriel judged that the

79

photograph must have been taken while Florence's brother had been home on leave. He had the proud, dutiful expression of an officer who had already lost the youthful excitement he had felt before answering the call to serve king and country. Like so many young men who had experienced the carnage of trench warfare at first hand, Dennis Harding would never have admitted to any sense of horror at his imminent return to the Front, but Gabriel thought he could see the exhaustion in the prematurely aged face. Florence and Primrose were dressed in the same conspicuously old-fashioned manner Gabriel remembered from the photograph of Primrose in the police folder. Primrose held a doll in her arms as though it were her most treasured possession, and both girls bore the same guarded, wary look as they posed for the camera.

Gabriel studied Primrose's neck for any sign of the Saint Anthony medal, but she wore no jewellery at all and neither did Florence—no necklace, no bracelet, no earrings. The young man, however, like many men of his class, wore a signet ring. Gabriel had always found the practice of wearing a signet ring a little pretentious, but then, he found most ostentatious signs of social status pretentious.

There was the light clink of cups rattling as the door opened, and Florence emerged into the room bearing a tray. Gabriel attempted to help her, but she put down the tray skilfully enough and invited him to sit again. "I'm very fond of that photograph," said Florence, glancing at the picture before focusing her attention on pouring the tea. "Sugar?"

"No, thank you."

"It was the last time we three were photographed together, a picture taken to celebrate Dennis returning safely home on leave. Primrose was terribly excited because he'd brought her that dolly all the way from France. Two days later Primrose went missing, and they made Dennis return to his regiment in spite of everything. He was dreadfully cut up about leaving us in that state." Florence handed Gabriel his tea and picked up her own cup and saucer. "It was a terrible time for us. Dennis was killed in action just eight weeks after arriving back at the Front. Caught up in a German raid. I gather he was frightfully brave, but I daresay they tell all families things like that. They would hardly have told us he was a coward, would they?"

Gabriel heard the strain in Florence's voice and sighed inaudibly for the millions of families around the country who had received the sort of letter Florence described, a desperate attempt by an officer at the Front to give some sense of purpose to the loss the family was facing. The telegram always came first. Gabriel remembered the agony of delivering those miserable little envelopes all too well—the terse, officious message that a man was dead. By the time a kindly letter arrived, the family was already reeling from the body blow delivered by that message, and no insistence on the man's bravery and the significance of his death could offer them any consolation. "I'm sorry for your loss, Florence," said Gabriel, hating the formulaic nature of the words. "You and your mother have truly suffered."

"You cannot begin to know how much," answered Florence, a cold tone returning to mask whatever torrent of emotion she was feeling.

Gabriel wondered whether this might be the moment to tell her he knew exactly how it felt to suffer the loss of two loved ones without warning, but as on so many previous occasions, he kept it to himself. He doubted it made any difference to a person to be told that a stranger understands; who really believes that in his darker moments? In any case, it would provoke too many questions, and he wanted Florence to remain focused on her own family. "I trust it's not too impertinent to ask, Florence, but did you lose a sweetheart to the war as well? Many women your age—"

Florence interrupted him with a bitter laugh. "My mother would never have allowed me to walk out with the village boys! After the war there was rather a dearth of eligible young men, even in the fashionable towns. I preferred to remain unmarried than to force myself into an undesirable union, simply to avoid becoming an old maid."

"That's very sensible," said Gabriel, but he was finding Florence's quiet resentment exhausting to bear. Polite resentment always troubled him more than displays of temper, partly because he had seen such feelings corrupt a person beyond recognition before. The slow nursing of grievances over a period of years really could destroy a man's soul, and he wondered how far Florence had journeyed along that path following the loss of her two siblings. "You . . . you have always lived with your mother?"

"I was a governess to Lord Pilburton's family for eight years after the first war. They were generous to me, and my father had left us well provided for. After my little charge went away to school, I returned home to manage my mother's affairs. It felt wrong to leave her alone when I was all she had left."

You do not have much to show for your life, thought Gabriel glumly, watching the prematurely aged woman before him as she sipped delicately at her tea. She had enjoyed a few short years of independence, though it was hardly independence to be ensconced in a grand house in the middle of nowhere, living the life of a better class of servant. Then she had returned to this loveless family home, the sole survivor of her generation, condemned to be her mother's attendant for the best years of her life. Florence's mother might die in her sleep at any time, her body worn out by the long years of unresolved grief, and what would happen to Florence Harding? Would she continue to live alone in this place, surrounded by the memories of lives unlived—her own life unlived—until she died without anybody noticing?

"Florence, how much do you remember of the day Primrose went missing?"

Florence leant her head to one side as though she was thinking hard. Gabriel had noticed that the people he spoke to tended to do that, even when he asked about a day they must have replayed in their minds thousands of times. "It was an awfully long time ago, Father," she said tonelessly, "though it does not always seem that way. I was sixteen at the time. It was a Saturday, and I'm afraid I had been naughty and slept late. Mother did not usually allow slovenly behaviour, but she had been a little under the weather herself, and I knew she was unlikely to notice if I left my room late. By the time I had come down to breakfast, Primrose had left the house."

Gabriel cleared his throat. He could already see the glaring discrepancy between what he had read in the notes and the picture that was forming of life in this house. If Florence's mother had had strong views on the time at which her children should be up and about, Gabriel doubted very much that she would have taken kindly to a child of hers leaving

83

the house without permission. "Was it usual for Primrose to wander off on her own?" he asked. "Had she perhaps gone to play with a friend?"

Florence gave the low, unpleasant laugh that Gabriel was already beginning to associate with her. "Little Primrose had no friends, Father. We were never permitted friends. None of the village children were good enough for us, you see."

"So, you knew she had gone out alone. Your mother's statements suggested that it was quite usual for her to go out and play for hours, that she was not concerned until late that evening when she had not returned."

Florence was staring fixedly down at the floor as though scrutinising every detail of the rug beneath her feet. "I should not wish to give the wrong impression, Father," she said, in little more than a whisper. Gabriel moved his chair closer to hers to avoid having to ask her to repeat herself. The woman was positively mumbling. "My mother has always been an honest woman. She would never normally lie; neither of us would. We were all in such a state when Primrose went missing. I suppose none of us really knew what was coming out of our mouths. It's easy enough to become confused at such a time."

"Of course, I quite understand."

"I suppose she said those things because it would normally be quite reasonable for a child to go off to play on a Saturday morning, especially in a village like this where children tend to run wild. It's just that Mother never allowed it. Primrose had broken her arm the year before, and Mother blamed the village children. She said they were too boisterous, too rough. She did not think it seemly for a nicely brought-up girl to be seen playing with ragamuffins. After that, Primrose was never allowed out to play. She played alone in the garden. Sometimes I took her on outings."

"Your mother must have been extremely worried all day then, if Primrose had acted out of character."

Florence shook her head, and for a moment it looked as though she were going to break down; but Florence was not a woman who shed tears easily, and she stood up, turning towards the fire as though to warm her hands. "Mother did not worry; she raged. She was in a filthy temper all day, convinced that Primrose had slipped out to play with the nasty village children. I don't think it occurred to her once that some disaster might have befallen the child. She was convinced that Primrose had acted out of spite, walked away to challenge Mother's authority. She fully expected Primrose to come crawling back to the house later on when she was hungry and cold, but of course she never did."

"What time was it when your mother alerted the police?"

"She didn't. I did. Unbeknownst to Mother, I spent much of that day going round the village trying to find Primrose. I knew something must have happened to her. She was a timid little thing, brought up to believe that the world was against her. If she had decided to run off out of sheer frustration, she would not have lasted long outside. She would have come running home, contrite and frightened."

"Had anyone seen Primrose?"

Florence shook her head, resting her hands against the wooden mantel of the fireplace. "No one had seen her. Not one person had caught so much as a glimpse of her, and if she had been out and about in the village, someone would have noticed her. She was always so conspicuous. Someone would have remembered."

Gabriel sat back in his chair, attempting a pose of nonchalance. "Conspicuous? How so?"

Florence turned to look at Gabriel, her lips pursed into a smirk that made him want to look away. "Mother has always had many strong opinions about the way things ought to be done. She is not a bad woman; you must understand that. It's simply that the world has changed, and she never cared to. In her mind it has always been the 1880s. We were forced to dress in ludicrously old-fashioned clothes, and it provoked a great deal of comment in the village. That is what I mean when I say that she was conspicuous."

Gabriel waited for Florence to sit down again before daring to ask his next question. "Is it possible that Primrose was lured away from the house? If it was out of character for her to wander off, is it possible that someone she trusted may have convinced her to meet him somewhere?"

Florence shook her head. "I have thought about this so many times. I knew it was not in her character to wander off like that, so yes, I have wondered whether someone coaxed her away. It occurred to me that someone might even have stolen her from the house. It's a big house; it would not have been impossible for a kidnapper to climb into her room and take her, but the police said there was no sign of an intruder." She shook her head, raising her hands to her face out of sheer exhaustion. "I'm sorry, Father, but after all these years I still cannot make any sense of what happened to her. Part of me still thinks it's a bad dream and that she'll come skipping into the room at any moment, just as she was then. An eight-year-old girl in a frothy pink dress, with her hair in plaits."

Gabriel stood up and placed a hand momentarily on

Florence's shoulder, causing her to look up at him. "I'm sorry to have brought this up with you again," he said. "I know how hard this must be for you, but if there is any chance that Primrose's killer may still be found . . ."

"I know," she said softly. "Finding the body has almost been a relief, but it's also the end of hope. She really did die that day; she hasn't had that secret life away from us that I've sometimes imagined she might have had. She's been dead all this time."

Florence made to rise, but Gabriel gestured for her to stay where she was. "It's all right, I'll see myself out," said Gabriel, moving towards the door, but a sudden thought struck him. "Please excuse my asking, Florence, but did Primrose own a Saint Anthony medal?"

Florence flinched but quickly recovered. "No, she didn't. I did, but I mislaid it. Why?"

"Because a medal of Saint Anthony was found with her body."

Florence brushed away a demeaning tear from her eye before it could shame her by falling. "I always wondered what had happened to that. The naughty little minx must have gone off with it; she was always doing that. But yes, it was mine."

Gabriel nodded and left the room.

5

It had been Gabriel's intention to find Inspector Applegate immediately and discuss the case with him. Gabriel had the sense that the easiest way to remain in Applegate's good books would be to be as cooperative with him as possible, even if he retained the instinctive desire to stay well out of the man's vicinity. As Gabriel walked back towards the village high street, however, he became aware of a commotion outside Joseph's boardinghouse and picked up his pace to see what was going on.

As Gabriel drew closer, he could see a young man up a ladder, impatiently doing the bidding of a woman in housecoat and curlers, who was holding the ladder whilst shouting instructions to him. It was the landlady and her long-suffering son, who was deftly boarding over a broken window without the need of any assistance or instructions. The landlady turned round in time to see Gabriel walking towards her. "Take a look at this!" she called, loud enough for the whole street to hear. "Is this decent? Is this fair?"

Gabriel looked up at the broken window. "What happened?"

"Some thug's hurled a brick through the window! What's it look like?"

"Who?"

"How am I supposed to know?" shrieked the landlady,

giving the ladder a dangerous nudge. Her son bellowed at her to desist. "He weren't so daft as to run down the street in the middle of the day! I were in the kitchen cooking the breakfast when I heard it. At that hour, only the milkman or the paperboy might have seen him. And they didn't."

Gabriel felt his chest tightening. The room could not be very large. If Joseph was in bed at the moment the brick flew through the window . . . "Was anyone hurt? Was your lodger in the room at the time?"

The landlady shook her head impatiently, as though it would have been infinitely better if her lodger had been brained by the flying brick. At least a blameless brick and an equally blameless window would not have been damaged for nothing. "No, always leaves early. And anyhow—"

"Is he here now?"

"Oh, he's here now, for a minute anyhow. I know it ain't the poor lad's fault—I'm sure he didn't do nothing—but I can't have no more trouble. I run a respectable boarding-house!"

Gabriel sighed. "So you're sending him packing then?"

"I got no choice!" the landlady protested, her voice rising by several decibels. "I'm only a poor widow trying to earn an honest living. I can't have people throwing bricks through windows—how would you like it?"

"I understand," said Gabriel. "I'll have a word with him." He ducked under the ladder and went inside, ignoring the woman's protests that he ought not to be bursting into her house without her permission. Gabriel closed the door behind him and paused in the dark, dingy hall to get his bearings. The house smelled of boiled cabbage, ersatz coffee, and the stale smoke residue that spoke of generations of bored men smoking cheap cigarettes. Joseph must have been desperate for lodgings to have settled for a room in a place like this when he could afford so much better. The trouble was that there were very few places for a stranger to lodge in a small village. The pub had a few rooms on offer but would probably have slammed the door in Joseph's face on account of the landlord being friends with the Wilcoxes, and even the hotel in the nearest town might well have refused Joseph a room in protest at his building houses in the area. This landlady might not have decorated her house in decades; she might think it perfectly acceptable to keep her paying guests within four walls stained with nicotine and grease; she might have filled the rooms with furnishings that looked as though they had been salvaged from a shipwreck fifty years before—but she had at least had the decency to welcome Joseph. Temporarily at least.

Gabriel made his way up the creaking wooden stairs, following the sounds of heavy footsteps moving about a room on the opposite side of the landing. Without pausing to collect his thoughts, Gabriel knocked on the battered door and awaited an answer.

"Please leave me in peace, Mrs Lewis!" wailed an exasperated male voice from within. "Five minutes and I'll be gone."

Gabriel knocked again. "Joseph, it's me," he said. "Would you like—"

Gabriel never had the chance to finish asking the question. The door flew open with an angry *whoosh*, and a haggard

Joseph stood before him. "Who the hell is—" began the man, but he spluttered to a stop, registering Gabriel's presence. "Oh, sorry, Father, I didn't realise it was you. Come in."

Gabriel followed Joseph into a room that could not have been particularly welcoming even before its occupant had started hurling his worldly possessions into a suitcase. It was a good-sized room for a single man, and with a little care, Joseph could have been quite cosy, but there was no getting around the fact that the monks' cells at the abbey were in considerably better shape than this place. Joseph's suitcase lay open on a metal-framed bed, its weight causing the horsehair mattress to sag dangerously. Besides the bed, the only furnishings were a monstrously oversized wardrobe that leant to one side as though it were perpetually inebriated, and a tattered armchair—currently containing a pile of folded shirts—next to an empty grate.

"You missed the brick then?" said Gabriel, desperate to break the silence.

"Fortunately," answered Joseph, picking up the shirts and dropping them unceremoniously into the suitcase. "The idiot who threw it got the wrong window. The poor soul in the room next door got his window broken. Well, he's out at work. Nice surprise he's going to get when he gets home later."

Gabriel backed up against the door; he could never shake off the feeling of being in the way. "I suppose it's possible that the brick was not intended for you," he said, but even he was not convinced.

"It was very definitely meant for me, Father," Joseph

replied matter-of-factly. "It hardly needed to have my name written all over it."

"Where do you plan to go?"

"At the moment, I'm not entirely sure. My first task is to get out of here. The police don't want me to scarper, and I can't anyway. There's the small matter of a building site to deal with. Unfortunately, this was the only place I could find a room." He closed the suitcase with considerable difficulty and proceeded to stuff several bundles of papers into a satchel. "I suppose I could ask the police to place me in protective custody," he quipped joylessly. "A few nights in the Sutton Westford lockup might be an improvement on Maison Lewis here."

"Come to the abbey," said Gabriel on impulse. "We always have room for a stranger."

Joseph looked up from his work in surprise. "Is that allowed? Would I have to pretend I wanted to be a monk or something?"

Gabriel laughed, which broke the tension between them. Joseph blushed in embarrassment. "Don't worry, we shan't make you take any vows or anything. You need somewhere safe to stay, and we have room. Do you have a car?"

"Yes. If you give me a minute to finish off here, we can drive to the abbey together."

Gabriel sat in the now-empty armchair and watched as Joseph finished packing up the room. He worked methodically if not very tidily, showing none of the military precision Gabriel often saw in men Joseph's age. "Joseph, were you called up?"

Joseph continued buckling his satchel shut without

93

looking up. "I was too young during the first war and too asthmatic for the next one," he answered tersely. "Yet another point against me, as far as certain people are concerned. No one likes to be called a coward in time of war."

"Or any time, I suppose," Gabriel agreed. "There must be many men who were treated like that during the war, through no fault of their own."

"It's the curse of the hidden condition, Father," said Joseph, slinging the strap of his satchel over his shoulder and picking up his suitcase. He declined Gabriel's wordless offer to take the suitcase for him. "Not that it felt very hidden when I was gasping for breath. If I'd walked with a limp or had a crippled hand, I might have been entitled to some sympathy." He took a quick, final glance around the room. "Well, I shan't miss this place, if I'm honest. I shan't miss having to walk past screaming protesters to get about my business in the morning."

The next few minutes were taken up with going downstairs and Gabriel waiting back in the unlovely hall whilst Joseph settled up with Mrs Lewis. There were some arguments about various extras she had added to his bill, especially her attempts to make him pay for the broken window, on the grounds that it never would have happened if he had not been resident in the house. Gabriel could see Mrs Lewis' predicament. The shabbiness of the interior of the house was not entirely due to laziness or parsimony on her part. He suspected that her few paying guests only just kept the wolf from the door, and it was unlikely that the man who had broken the window would ever be compelled to pay up. Calling in a glazier to replace the broken pane was an expense Mrs Lewis could do without, but a boarding-house with a boarded up window looked disreputable, and she could not afford to leave it alone either.

Eventually, with the argument resolved, the two men stepped outside. "Where have you left your car?" asked Gabriel, looking up and down the street in puzzlement. Apart from a bicycle propped up against a lamppost, Gabriel could see no wheels anywhere, and his first thought was that the car might have been stolen.

"I left it around the corner," Joseph explained, leading Gabriel in the direction of a nearby side street. "I thought it might be a bit of a target if I parked it outside my residence. I thought, 'Park it somewhere else, and who's to know it belongs to me?'"

It was not often that Gabriel could call another person naive, but it was the only word he could think of as he followed Joseph in the direction of the hidden vehicle. Few people owned motorcars in the village, and most people would have seen Joseph driving about in it. If anything, parking the car some distance away might have made it more vulnerable to attack.

Sure enough, when the car came into view, the first thing both men noticed was Stevie Wilcox standing on the other side of the car, stooped forward with his face partially concealed by the bodywork. He stopped abruptly as soon as he realised that he was being watched, and looked guiltily at the two men. Gabriel noticed the door key in Stevie's hand and realised that he had been scoring a jagged line along the paintwork of the car. Joseph darted over to where Stevie was standing, gave him a shove, and looked at his enemy's handiwork. It was a good deal worse than Gabriel had suspected. Stevie had not been scoring a line; he had etched the word MURDERER in large capital letters.

"How desperately subtle of you," said Joseph in a brave attempt at a devil-may-care attitude which did not suit him; Gabriel noted the slight trembling of Joseph's hands behind his back. Joseph was enraged or shaken, but Stevie was never going to know it. "Have you quite finished?"

Stevie put the key back in his pocket and effected a nonchalant pose. "I know what you are. Not all folks do," Stevie answered by way of explanation. "Now you can have the pleasure of letting the whole village know what you are."

"I don't know what you're talking about," said Joseph, meeting Stevie's cold, hard gaze with a glare of his own. Now that the confrontation had started, Joseph was getting into his stride. "That body has been there for years. I had nothing to do with it."

"Yeah, it's been there for years. You meant it to stay there forever, didn't you? You knew it were there."

Joseph flushed red, but he did not look away. "Nonsense! If I'd known there was a body hidden on that land, I would hardly have started digging it up, would I?"

Stevie returned Joseph's look of unmitigated contempt. Gabriel discreetly moved forward in case he had to separate the two men once again. "You never meant to dig her up. You meant to build lots of posh houses over her so no one could never find her."

Almost on cue, Joseph dropped his suitcase and launched himself at Stevie, but Gabriel missed the cue, and Joseph had Stevie pinned to the bonnet of the car before Gabriel could attempt a rescue. "Stop!" he shouted, grabbing Joseph's arm. "Have you gone mad?"

Joseph, who looked very much like a man who had lost his mind, spat directly into Stevie's face, placing his hands around Stevie's throat. "Give me one good reason not to wring your scrawny little neck!" he hissed. "That's the thing about kicking the little 'uns—we grow up and kick back."

To Gabriel's relief, there was the sound of a policeman's whistle, a shrill-enough warning to pierce even Joseph's rage, and he stepped away from Stevie shortly before the blue-uniformed bobby arrived to restrain him. "What's all this about, lads?" he asked, offering Stevie a hand, which he resolutely ignored. "Aren't you a bit old to be brawling in the street like a pair of urchins?"

"He attacked me," said Stevie, and Gabriel noticed his attempt to walk away from the car so that the policeman might not see the graffiti. "Ask the padre. He saw him!"

"He's defaced my car," answered Joseph, slipping effortlessly back into the role of city businessman. If both the constable and Gabriel had not seen the altercation, it would have been impossible to believe that a gentleman as apparently poised as Joseph could have rammed a man against his car and threatened to strangle him. "I caught him in the act, as did Father Gabriel here."

The constable moved deftly to the left of the car and took in the word MURDERER etched incriminatingly into the side. Stevie had committed an impressive act of vandalism; the letters were huge. The constable turned to Gabriel. "Did you see anything?"

Gabriel nodded uncomfortably. "I'm afraid I did. He used a door key. It was still in his hand when we arrived."

"I see," answered the constable, in that noncommittal tone country bobbies use just before making an arrest. "And did you see the car owner attacking this gentleman?"

"He was rather provoked," Gabriel began, sensing that talking to the policeman was an act of disloyalty towards Joseph.

"Did he or did he not attack Mr Wilcox?" the constable persisted, in the same measured tone.

"You don't have to get the thumbscrews out, Constable," Joseph chimed in. "I'm not afraid of accounting for my actions. I did have the pleasure of giving the little pipsqueak here a scare. I'll come quietly."

The constable looked at the three men in turn before addressing Stevie. "Do you wish to press charges against this man for common assault?"

Stevie took his time answering, but if the pregnant pause had been intended to unsettle Joseph, it did not appear to have worked. "I wouldn't stoop so low," he answered with a smirk. "I can fight me own battles, if it's all the same to you."

It was Joseph's turn to be addressed. "Would you like to press charges against this man for vandalising your car, sir?"

Gabriel was genuinely unsure as to how Joseph would respond and felt a flutter of disappointment at the answer when it came. "I would, thank you. I'm a great believer in the rule of law."

Gabriel turned away as the constable read Stevie his rights before marching him away to the village lockup. It was hardly as though the man were going to swing for an offence like that, but he might well face being arraigned before the magistrate and the imposition of a fine he could ill afford. He waited until the sounds of two heavy sets of footsteps had vanished into the distance before turning back to face Joseph. "Was that necessary?" he asked. Joseph had opened his suitcase across the boot of the car and was rummaging around in it. "What are you doing?"

"Be prepared, as our scoutmaster used to say," said Joseph, taking out a small round tin and a shoe brush. "I can hardly drive to the abbey with that thing scrawled all over my paintwork, can I?"

"That's very resourceful of you," said Gabriel, watching as Joseph opened up the tin of black boot polish and began smearing it adeptly over the incriminating letters. Gabriel doubted it would withstand the wind roaring past the metalwork as they drove along or, God forbid, a downpour of rain, but he supposed the boot polish must be quite resilient if it did not wash or flake off boots at the first contact with a puddle. It was not a subject to which Gabriel had given very much thought. "You're good at covering things up," said Gabriel admiringly, as the letters slowly vanished. The compliment had come out completely wrong. "Sorry, that wasn't quite what I meant. I mean—"

"I didn't do it, Father," said Joseph bluntly, taking his time closing and snapping the tin shut. He walked round to the boot of the car, dropped the brush and tin into the bag and took an immaculate white handkerchief out of his pocket to wipe his hands. "But Stevie's going to go around telling everyone I'm a killer. That's the story now: I bought a plot of land because I knew there was a body there, and I thought I'd build houses on top of it to make sure that the body could never be found. It's nonsense, of course, and a good defence counsel could pick that story apart in minutes. Anyone who works in this field knows that one has to dig quite deep to lay the foundations for a house. If anything, I could argue that my opponents were the ones with something to hide."

Gabriel felt distinctly unsettled as he got into the passenger seat of the car. "Are you saying you think someone opposed to the building development killed Primrose Harding?"

Joseph waited until he had manoeuvred the car away from the kerb before answering. "Well, someone in this village knows who killed that little girl. I'd venture a few people do. That being the case, someone had a lot to lose when I turned up to start digging the land. Whoever it was knew what I would find."

"The question is who," said Gabriel, thinking of the many people in the village who must have opposed the building development. So many people, all with different reasons: Luddism, genuine fear for the future of the village, xenophobia—and in the case of this village, that meant an ingrained hostility to anyone who was not born and bred here. The Benedictine community had been granted some kind of unofficial dispensation in that department; Catholics were usually regarded as suspicious foreigners, wherever they came from. The death had occurred so long ago that everyone under a certain age could be discounted immediately, but this was a small advantage in a murder investigation in which every possible trail had long grown cold.

"The question is always who," said Joseph, giving Gabriel

a sidelong glance. "I said it was more your department than mine, Father."

"You know, Joseph, I'm not sure you should have pressed charges against Stevie Wilcox," Gabriel began, knowing he would not be easy in his mind until he had said it. "It was a vicious thing for him to do, but the Wilcoxes are a poor farming family. If he can't pay the fine, he may go to prison. It will hardly help heal the feud between you."

Joseph chuckled. "I very much doubt anything will heal the feud between us, Father. Our families have been at each other's throats for generations. No doubt our descendants will be exactly the same."

There was an awkward silence, both men regretting the unfortunate choice of words. Neither Joseph nor Stevie had children. "Is that the way you want it?" asked Gabriel.

"I didn't say it was the way I wanted it, just that it is the way it is." Joseph looked across at Gabriel, noting his pensive expression. "I'm not sure you've ever really hated anyone, have you?"

Gabriel felt himself becoming hot. He saw again the interior of that police inspector's office, the grim expression on the otherwise kindly face of a white-haired old copper who had described the findings of the pathologist after the death of Gabriel's wife.

"I'm sorry to have to break this to you, Mr Milson," the policeman had said, "but your wife was murdered. There is no sign that the child was injured before the fire, but your wife's body showed signs of trauma."

"How on earth can you tell? There was nothing left of either of them."

"Sir, the skeletal remains showed signs of numerous fractures, including several to the skull. I'm afraid it looks very much like . . . before the fire was deliberately started to cover up the tracks. The killer may not have known about the child."

"My wife was battered to death? But why? Everyone loved her her . . . everyone. We all loved her. Why?"

Returning to the present and Joseph's question, Gabriel said dully, "We all are capable of hatred . . . I am not exempt."

"I say, are you all right, Father? You're awfully white."

Gabriel could not answer without lying and instead focused his attention on the facade of the abbey as they drove along the path. No man was incapable of hatred, but not all men had the refuge Gabriel had sought and found. "It's all right, Joseph. You'll be quite safe here."

Joseph brought the car to a gentle halt near the abbey gate and switched off the engine. "Don't get cut up about Stevie Wilcox, Father. If he does get fined, I won't let his family go hungry on my account. I'll waive it if the money is granted to me, or I'll pay the court myself. That will be better revenge than I could hope for."

"When mercy is used as a weapon, it ceases to be mercy," said Gabriel, letting himself out of the car.

"When justice is ignored, it ceases to be justice," Joseph retorted, heaving out the suitcase. "Vandalism is a crime."

"So is assault."

"I was provoked; he acted in cold blood. No comparison."

Gabriel sighed, unwilling to begin Joseph's stay at the monastery with a prolonged argument. "Well, let's just hope

you can have some peace and quiet here," said Gabriel, ringing the bell. He listened for the reassuring skip of Brother
Gerard's feet as he scampered along the corridor, then the
slow groan of the door being swung open on its hinges. All
was well. They were home.

6

Despite all his years in the monastery, Gabriel had never completely lost his sense of being summoned to the headmaster's study upon entering Abbot Ambrose's room. Fortunately, Ambrose anticipated Gabriel's possible uneasiness and greeted him with a warm smile as he crossed the threshold and closed the door behind him. "I gather from Brother Gerard that you have picked up a stray," said Ambrose, motioning for Gabriel to sit down.

"I hope you don't mind my bringing the man here unannounced," said Gabriel, perching himself on the edge of the chair. He was out of breath from a combination of having climbed the stairs a little too quickly and residual nerves. "You see, I think Joseph Beaumont may be in some danger. He has half the village up in arms against him."

"There is always room for a stranger among us," Ambrose reassured Gabriel. "We were all strangers to this house once. Perhaps you could explain why the gentleman in question has to claim sanctuary with us; then you had better ensure that he is settled at the cottage."

Gabriel looked up in alarm. "Father Abbot, surely he cannot stay there? I thought he would stay within the abbey walls?"

Ambrose's smile did not flicker. "Not superstitious, are we, Dom Gabriel?"

"It's not that," promised Gabriel, shaking his head fervently. "I'm more concerned about living monsters than the man who died there. The fact is, Joseph's work has made him extremely unpopular among some of the more . . . well, malevolent forces within the village. Wealthy men who build houses are never popular, but since the discovery of that body, things have escalated. One of Joseph's enemies is putting it about that he is the culprit, that he bought a plot of land with the intention of covering it with houses to hide the body buried there."

"What nonsense!" Ambrose interrupted, leaning forward so that his arms rested on the desk before him. "But far more nonsensical stories than that gain credence in a place like this. If the man was unpopular to begin with, he hardly stands a chance now."

"My thoughts exactly," said Gabriel. "It's not that I imagine a mob with pitchforks is going to come after him or anything like that, but he's already been forced out of one boardinghouse. Someone threw a brick through the window. Other places wouldn't take him to begin with. I couldn't leave him without a safe place to lay his head at night. The cottage is perfectly comfortable, but—"

"Yes, yes, yes, I quite see your point," Ambrose cut in, standing up to indicate that the meeting was over. "You had better let the guest master know that the cottage will not be needed after all. He can sleep in Cuthbert's old cell for the present."

"I can make up the bed and make it comfortable for him," said Gabriel, getting to his feet. "I need to speak to Joseph and find out what childhood memories he has about the dead girl. It might be easier to talk if we're busy doing something practical."

Ambrose nodded, his face suddenly grave. "They have confirmed the identity of the child then?"

"Yes," answered Gabriel softly. "It is Primrose Harding, the girl who went missing many years ago. I met her mother and sister this morning."

Ambrose put up a hand to signal that he did not wish Gabriel to leave. "Gabriel, God has given you the gift of deduction. You have a talent for getting to the truth, which is why I have allowed you to work with the inspector on this case. But are you sure about continuing with the investigation? If it involves a child . . ." The sentence hung unfinished between them, and they let the uneasy silence wash over them.

"The murder of any child is an outrage," said Gabriel in a whisper. "This little one was killed and dumped like a piece of rubbish. She had a right to a Christian burial. Her family have a right to justice."

Ambrose put a hand on Gabriel's shoulder. "Do what you have to do, with my blessing. But if I suspect that this case is doing you any harm, I will order you to stop, and you will listen to me. Do you understand?"

Gabriel nodded, but he could not look at Ambrose. He bowed and fled the room, waiting until he reached the stairs before impatiently wiping the tears from his eyes.

"I do feel a bit of an imposter," admitted Joseph. "I feel as though I ought to be wearing a habit or something."

Joseph was sitting on the wooden chair in the corner of

the cell, watching as Gabriel tucked a sheet expertly round the mattress. Gabriel, who had not entered the cell since Cuthbert had gone to his eternal reward, was surprised by how anonymous it felt. Brother Cuthbert had spent most of the final months of his long life in the abbey infirmary, and shortly after his passing, the cell had been stripped of whatever meagre possessions Cuthbert had left behind. The process would have taken minutes at most, to gather up the spare habit, a rosary, a breviary, and a Bible, emptying out this little space for the next occupant. Cuthbert had left few traces of a life that had spanned nearly a century, yet seldom did a day go by when Gabriel did not find himself imagining Cuthbert looking up at him from his sickbed to reassure him or to warn him that he was going about things the wrong way.

"You're most welcome, Joseph," Gabriel promised him, trying not to wonder why Joseph did not offer to help. Gabriel suspected that it had been a very long time since a man like Joseph had had to make his own bed. A short spell at the abbey might be quite good for him. "Of course, should you wish to join us for prayers you are most welcome, but I suspect you have a good many matters of the world to attend to. I'll ask Gerard to take a look at your car. He's quite an expert with machines."

"Thank you, I'd be most obliged," said Joseph. "I can hardly drive about the village with the car in the state it's in, and I'll need to be getting about."

"Will it be all right for you to go about alone?"

Joseph gave an unmistakably nervous laugh. "It's not quite that bad, Father. I shan't be needing a bodyguard, though that Brother Gerard of yours wouldn't be bad in a tight spot.

Wilcox and his ilk aren't about to do me in; they just want to make my life a misery. If he manages to persuade other people that I'm the killer, though, it might be a different matter."

"Have you any idea who might have killed Primrose? You lived in the village when it happened."

Joseph gave no sign that he was startled by Gabriel's direct question, other than to hesitate a little longer than was strictly necessary to consider his answer. "I was only a boy, Father. Grownups were too boring to bother about, and I hardly knew Primrose. Lads my age barely noticed little girls, and her family always kept to themselves."

"Her sister Florence was a little closer to your age, wasn't she?"

"She was worse than Primrose; she was older than I. I kept well out of her way!" The attempt at levity fell flat, but Gabriel made no attempt to rescue the situation. He watched as Joseph swivelled in his chair so that he faced the wall rather than meet Gabriel's enquiring glance, which Gabriel took as a good sign. "Father, it's a beastly thing to say, but the Hardings were insufferable snobs. They didn't mix with the hoi polloi of the village. They were far too genteel for all that."

"They must have mixed with someone."

"Apart from the village doctor, I would imagine that all their friends—such as they were—were from the town. But I honestly wouldn't know. No one cares about people who turn their noses up. I'm sure poor little Primmie was a perfectly sweet girl, but she never stood a chance. Always dressed like the Ghost of Christmas Past. Everyone laughed at her."

Gabriel went back to the task of tucking in the bedclothes, aware that an invisible door was being slowly unlocked. Joseph was not the sort of man who failed to notice anyone, especially an unusual child. "The Ghost of Christmas Past? People do seem awfully put out by the way that family dressed. How important is it in the grand scheme of things?"

"Father, there is old-fashioned and there is self-deception," Joseph declared. "Plenty of people are a little old-fashioned, particularly in the country. They get set in their ways, and they're suspicious of change, but the Harding family took it to an extreme. I remember Primrose walking to school or catechism class looking like a walking wedding cake—layers and layers of lace and frills, hair tucked up in a little lace cap. She looked beautiful, but I don't think any child had dressed like that for fifty years. She had to walk the long way to school, across the fields, away from the main road to avoid anyone seeing her."

"Did the other children make fun of her to her face?"

"I never saw anything, but they must have been merciless. You know what children are like. It was wicked making her stand out like that, giving other children reason to bully and torment her. My first thought when I heard that she was missing was that she must have suffered some accident wandering alone, or even tried to run away. I think I would have run away if I were that lonely." Joseph stood up abruptly. "It's awfully close in here. I need some air."

Gabriel smiled, pointing to the door. "Off you go then. Why don't you have a turn around the garden while I finish off here? Then we can talk some more."

Gabriel watched Joseph slip away, feeling fairly certain that Joseph would really rather not talk to him again given half a chance, but Gabriel had too many questions to let him go that easily. A picture was forming in his mind of the sad little life that had ended in a desolate, abandoned mine all those many years before. If Joseph—who claimed to have barely noticed Primrose Harding's existence—had known that she was in the habit of wandering off the beaten track to avoid her tormentors, then many others must have known about it. And someone had acted on the knowledge. A little child in an isolated place could not have been more vulnerable. She could not have defended herself or even been heard if she had had the presence of mind to call for help. If Joseph was right, Primrose need not have been lured away to an isolated spot; she had willingly taken herself away from the presence of people who represented unkindness to her.

But who would do that? Who would follow a little girl into the back of beyond with the intention of hurting her? This was where Abbot Ambrose was mistaken in his fear for Gabriel. Gabriel's own child crept into his thoughts with agonising frequency, often when he least expected it, but he had the smallest, tiniest shred of comfort that Nicoletta may not have been deliberately killed. Whoever had started that fire might not have known that there was a child sleeping upstairs, and Gabriel clung to that hope, as only a desperate man can. But whoever was responsible for the death of Primrose Harding had known exactly what he was doing. That was the true horror of the case. There was no room anywhere to give humanity the benefit of the doubt.

Gabriel was aware that he had taken a little too long going to find Joseph, but his mind had a tendency to go skittering off down blind alleys, and he arrived downstairs to find Joseph and Gerard deep in conversation. "Ah, there you are!" called Gerard the moment he noticed Gabriel approaching. "You took your time!"

"I've been thinking," Gabriel explained, bracing himself for the inevitable jocular response, but Gerard merely grinned. Gabriel turned to Joseph. "Has Brother Gerard been giving you a tour of the place?"

"I'm afraid there hasn't been time," said Joseph, almost apologetically. "I'd forgotten how quickly news travels in this part of the world. The inspector's put a call through for me. Apparently, he tried to phone my landlady, and she told him I'd gone off with you."

"Well, I suppose he'll need to speak with you. It will only be a formality. You'll need to ask him a few questions too, find out what's going to happen to your land now."

Joseph shook his head almost sulkily. "I have already made a statement to the police about yesterday morning's discovery. I went so far as to say that I thought the remains were Primrose Harding's, and I certainly wasn't obliged to volunteer that information. He wants me to present myself at the station as soon as possible."

Gabriel looked searchingly at Joseph, who turned toward Gerard and said, "It was kind of you to offer to paint my car. Perhaps we can get hold of some paint. It can't be very difficult to find some for sale if one asks nicely." Joseph looked at Gabriel in a way that made him feel as though he were being accused of something. "Not that asking nicely is likely to do me very much good at the moment. Reggie might have something I could buy."

Gabriel ignored the bitter tone. "Why don't we walk back into the village together? You can speak to the inspector, and I can go in search of paint. Reggie sounds like a good man to start with."

The mortified look on Joseph's face distracted Gabriel happily from the question of whether the abbey's new guest was guilty of deceit. Gabriel had every intention of returning with some paint in hand, but he would never have left the seclusion of the abbey on so frivolous a task. "We're walking all the way back into the village?" asked Joseph incredulously.

"Well, I don't imagine you'd fancy driving around with 'Murderer' all over your car," answered Gabriel. "It's really not far. You've become too used to city living, my friend."

Joseph's shoulders drooped comically as he admitted defeat.

"There's nothing wrong with city life," said Joseph a little testily as they made their way out of the gate and across the fields. Joseph's dapper little shoes were not at all suitable for long grass and mud—Gabriel should have tried to find him a pair of galoshes—but it was a little late to think about that now. The brown leather shoes, the colour being the only nod to country living, were already wet and plastered with bits of snapped grass. "There are plenty of admirable things to be found in the city: big red buses, restaurants, shops selling everything money can buy—assuming one has the correct coupons—picture houses, theatres . . ." Joseph looked down at his feet. The ends of his trousers were splattered with tiny globules of mud. "Pavements. Did I mention the pavements? Splendid invention, pavements."

Gabriel laughed. "You forget I was a Londoner once.

And yes, one does not appreciate a good pavement until one is walking along a dirt track."

"You must miss a lot more than that, Father," Joseph protested. "The hustle and bustle. The mere existence of other people. Interesting people."

"Joseph, you forget that I turned my back on the world. I chose to leave London behind, and I shan't be going back." They had reached the fence, and Gabriel climbed over the stile, landing softly on the chalky path on the other side. Joseph grimaced as he stepped up onto the slippery, precarious wooden step, swinging over his leg so violently that Gabriel hoped the man would not split his elegant trousers in the process. That really would ruin the day. First a hasty eviction from his lodging, then his car vandalised, then mud on shoes and a split trouser seam . . . "All right there, Joseph?" asked Gabriel solicitously. "Sutton Westford is your home, you know. If you find it so offensive, why did you come back? There must be plenty of sites in London that need redeveloping. All those bomb sites."

Joseph stood next to Gabriel, holding onto the fence for support as he caught his breath. There was no disguising the fact that he was hopelessly out of shape, but Gabriel was sure that there had been a time when Joseph could have run that distance and not cared two hoots about the state of his shoes. "You mustn't imagine that I'm trying to impose the city upon the village, Father. I have precious little reason to feel affection for this place, but as you've said, this was my home once, and I want to do some good. People are so set in their ways. They don't seem to realise that the village is dying. Very few people like you, city folk, ever settle in the villages, but hundreds—thousands—of young men are

114

leaving the countryside to find work in the cities every day, and they won't come back."

"But the farms are always short of labour," said Gabriel, "with the loss of so many young men. We can't rely on prisoners of war to grow our food for us now that the war is over."

Joseph stood up straight and began walking again. Now that they were back on a path, albeit a rough, partially overgrown path, Joseph appeared to have regained confidence. "Industry was mechanised a hundred years ago; it was what made Britain great. Farming is already being mechanised. With more machines replacing human labour, there will be no call for anyone to live in a village within a generation. Building more homes means building a community; it means giving people a reason to settle in this part of the world and bring their money and their enterprise with them. I don't want to see the village die."

Perhaps he means it, mused Gabriel to himself, *even if he stands to gain a great deal more than the village will benefit from this enterprise of his.* "Does it change anything that that plot of land is now a grave?"

Joseph shrugged, apparently confused by the question. "Hardly a grave, Father. They've already moved the bones. I daresay her family will want you to give her a Christian burial on consecrated ground."

"A murder scene then."

The unintended barb struck Joseph so forcefully that he stopped dead in his tracks, struggling to find an answer. Gabriel waited patiently as Joseph swallowed, opened his mouth to answer, closed it again, then finally whispered, "Father, all any of us know at present is that the skeleton of a child has been found on my land. No one knows how it got there, and no one knows what happened."

With that, he turned on his heel and marched towards the police station, not stopping to see whether Gabriel had followed. Gabriel noted that Joseph was so unsettled, he did not even hesitate at the police station entrance when he saw old Archie Wilcox standing outside the blue door smoking a Woodbine. Gabriel hung back from the entrance, knowing that it would be better for Joseph if they were not seen entering together. In Gabriel's company, Joseph might be presumed to be a suspect, and he had been tainted badly enough by the discovery as it was. What Joseph did not seem to realise was that unless the truth emerged about Primrose Harding's fate—and quickly too—Joseph and his houses would be perpetually marked by an unsolved murder. The smartest houses in the world would never be occupied if the ghost of a murdered child were haunting village folklore for years to come. Worse, Joseph's name would be associated with the death, even if his only crime had been to purchase a plot of land containing little Primrose Harding's remains.

"Penny for your thoughts, Padre?" came a gravelly baritone voice that still managed to contain a faint sneer. Archie Wilcox was stubbing out the pathetic remains of the Woodbine and flicking it onto the ground. "You ought to be more careful who you be consorting with."

Gabriel fixed Archie with a steady gaze. He did not know the Wilcoxes well, but Archie was so unmistakably Stevie's Father that it was almost eerie. He had Stevie's watery blue eyes and thickset features, distorted by age and the ravages of more alcohol and nicotine than was good for a man. He was the Stevie of the future, a grimier, fatter, greyer version of the middle-aged man currently receiving a dressing down from a policeman inside the building. "Good day, Mr Wilcox," said Gabriel, ignoring Archie's grimace. "Are you waiting for your son?"

Archie shrugged, taking another Woodbine from his pocket. He tapped it against the box before placing it in his mouth and rummaging for his matches. "I might be. Damned fool's gone and taken the law into his own hands as usual. I told him not to cross a toff."

"Joseph Beaumont is hardly a toff," protested Gabriel. "He's a local lad like you."

"Makes no difference now, as he's got money. Thinks he can do what he likes. Thinks he can lord it over the rest of us."

Resentment. It was at the heart of most rivalries, especially in a community such as this. Gabriel might not be entirely sure about the purity of Joseph's motives, but he was right about one thing. The village was poor, and its future existence fragile. Families like the Wilcoxes might be a dying breed, eking out a meagre living on a small farm that had been passed from father to son for generations but perhaps not for much longer. Then there was Joseph Beaumont, who had left the village when he was little more than a boy and had returned a wealthy man with his smart clothes and expensive motorcar. Of course he appeared to be lording it over the others, whether or not that was his intention.

"Whatever you think of Mr Beaumont, Stevie had no business vandalising his car," said Gabriel, suppressing the urge to cough. Archie really was smoking sailors' socks. "Murder is a strong word, especially when it's written without evidence."

117

"You don't have to lecture me," Archie retorted. "The lad's been a damned fool. He's given our Joseph a way to hurt him now."

"He may have hurt Joseph," suggested Gabriel. "Do you really think he killed that child?"

Archie lowered his eyes abruptly but not before Gabriel noted his darkening expression. "I know perfectly well he didn't do it," mumbled Archie. "He were only a lad himself at the time. Why would he have hurt a little kiddie like that? I've never had no time for the Beaumonts, but that there Joseph's no killer."

Gabriel glanced quickly in the direction of the station door in case there was any sign of Joseph or Applegate emerging, but all was quiet. "You must remember those days very well, Mr Wilcox. Do you have any idea who might have wanted to hurt Primrose Harding?"

Archie looked at Gabriel as though it took the greatest effort in the world to make eye contact with him. "I can't say nothing without proof. It's like you said, murder's a nasty word. But I can tell you who might have wanted to do it." He looked over his shoulder in a needlessly dramatic gesture. The need to avoid the local lockup was almost a superstition in this village, and no one went near it voluntarily. The two men were very much alone. "They say, when a child dies a violent death it's always the family what done it. That narrows it down a bit for you, because little Primmie, she didn't have much family. Just that horrible mother and a toffee-nosed sister who thought she were the queen of Sheba. But there were only one person in this village who really hated that poor child, and that were Miss Baines."

Gabriel blinked. "The old schoolmistress? I've heard she was a little harsh, but surely you can't imagine she'd—"

"She weren't always so harsh and bitter," Archie cut in. "Phyllis Baines were a lovely lass in her day, but life passed her by. No husband, no children, not even a home of her own. Stuck in that miserable little schoolroom with the village brats to educate. Then little Primmie Harding walked through her door."

"Mr Wilcox, I'm really not sure . . ." Gabriel hardly knew how to finish the sentence.

"Primmie never belonged. Her ma made sure enough of that, and children who don't fit in are always trouble, even if they don't mean to be. I had a daughter not far off Primmie's age, and I used to hear what they all said about her. That Miss Baines had it in for her, but it were easier for the others that way. Even a schoolmistress like Miss Baines needed only one kid to torment. Said the Hardings needed taking down a peg or two."

"Mr Wilcox, if every teacher who had ever picked on a child went on to murder him, they'd be hanging schoolmasters every day of the week!"

Gabriel was almost relieved at the sound of the door creaking open, compelling the two of them to step aside for whoever was trying to leave. Stevie stood in the doorway, looking fit to commit a murder himself, no more so than when he noticed Gabriel in conversation with his father. Archie gave Stevie no time to speak with Gabriel, grabbing him by the arm and dragging him out onto the pavement. It was a gesture of paternal indignation Archie must have employed many times, but it looked almost slapstick between an elderly man and his middle-aged son.

"Well, what's the damage then?" demanded Archie, looking Stevie up and down as if he half expected to find his son in shackles. "What's the charge?"

"No charge," snapped Stevie, turning his back on Gabriel. "His Holiness Joseph Beaumont has withdrawn the charge of criminal damage on condition that I repair his car. There now, wasn't that decent of him?"

"Sounds perfectly decent to me, you daft beggar," answered Archie relentlessly. "Scratching cars, getting into brawls in the street at your age! You ought to be ashamed of yourself. Now come on home." Archie gave Stevie an undignified shove, which would once have sent him sprawling on the ground. Instead, Stevie got the message and stormed off in the direction of the family home, showing no interest in whether his father deigned to follow. Archie turned back to Gabriel. "Tell Joseph I'll paint his car for him. I can't face talking to him meself."

"Thank you, Mr Wilcox, he is staying at the abbey. His car is there."

Archie nodded. "I hope I've not spoken out of turn mentioning Miss Baines. If she did it, I doubt she meant to. She were seen losing her temper before. It happens. There were a man killed his wife here years ago when I were only a boy. He said he never meant it either."

"One must keep an open mind, I suppose," said Gabriel warily. "I've seen some very unlikely murderers before, it has to be said."

Archie's expression softened for the first time. "Father, all anyone here will tell you is what were wrong with the Hardings, what were wrong with Primmie. But her family weren't her fault. It's not as though she could choose who bore her. She were a sweet little thing; she didn't deserve such a death."

It was only then that Gabriel remembered Archie's reference to his daughter, made in the past tense. The two men had little in common, but they shared a loss without a name. There were names for men and women who had lost a spouse, and children who had lost parents, but there was no word to describe men who had lost their children.

"No child deserves to die a violent death, Mr Wilcox," said Gabriel quietly, "but I will find out who did this. I swear."

7

The next five days left Gabriel with very little time to investigate. Since the Hardings were nominally Catholic, Mrs Harding had requested a Catholic funeral for Primrose, and Abbot Ambrose had agreed to take care of all the arrangements. It was the first time a Requiem Mass had been offered for a child at the abbey. There had been mercifully few infant deaths in the village in recent years, and what few Catholic families there were tended to want their loved ones buried in the Catholic cemetery in the nearby town, but no one was going to refuse little Primrose Harding a Requiem.

"Is it usual for police inspectors to come to a victim's funeral?" asked Gabriel incredulously when Inspector Applegate signalled his intentions the day before.

"Just paying my respects on behalf of my predecessor," Applegate explained, "and doing my job. Absolutely everyone comes to a funeral, especially if there's free food afterwards."

"Even killers?"

"Always. Every murderer I've ever arrested has had a touch of the voyeur about him. And I can't have you going round that crowd of fake mourners, gathering clues without my assistance, can I now?"

They had had this brief conversation in the abbey grounds.

Applegate had done Gabriel the honour of coming to visit him for a change, though Gabriel was fairly certain that Applegate was using it as a pretext to talk further with Joseph. Gabriel had been in the process of attending to the monastic bee colony—a task that was taking up more and more of his time—when Applegate had arrived. Gabriel had tried hard not to enjoy Applegate's discomfort at being forced to watch him—swathed in white like a mediaeval penitent—moving around the hives pumping smoke into them. He knew Applegate was concentrating too hard on appearing relaxed to be able to defend himself from an unwelcome question. "I swear I shan't ask again, but are we definitely looking at murder? If there is any possibility—"

"We're looking at murder," answered Applegate testily. The man had quickly given up trying to appear nonchalant and simply sounded annoyed now. "It's confirmed. They found signs of a fractured skull and broken knuckles. Will you for goodness' sake come away from those bees!"

The confirmation of murder had thrown Gabriel, even though he had known his hopes of an accidental death were without any foundation. Gabriel peered at Applegate's exasperated face through the mesh of his face protection. It was no good; he had to come away from the safety of the bee-hives where all pain was innocently inflicted. "Where were the fractures?" he asked numbly, removing his headgear.

Applegate tapped his own forehead, then squeezed his hands into fists. "The broken knuckles rather suggest that she tried to fight off her assailant, not that she would have stood much of a chance."

"So, whoever assaulted her would have had to look her directly in the face as he struck her."

Applegate nodded. "It's a devilish business. There are very few people in this world capable of such a deed."

"Do you really think it was Joseph? Is that why you wanted to talk to him the other day? He was so young at the time . . ."

"No, I wanted to know what the assault conviction on his record was all about. Turns out he got into a fight with Archie Wilcox years ago and beat him unconscious."

Gabriel could sense Applegate's continued discomfort and walked with him, well away from the hives. "Archie, not Stevie?"

"Yes. I was a bit taken aback too. He doesn't look the type to pick fights with older men."

"My thoughts exactly. What on earth were they fighting about?"

"That's what I wanted to find out. I doubted it was going to be important, and it wasn't. I gather they'd both had a skinful, then Archie started insulting Joseph's old man. Next thing, the fight's being broken up, Archie's in hospital, and young Joseph is left in cells cooling his heels."

Gabriel floundered for the right response. "I don't know, Inspector. It strikes me that Joseph is just the sort to fight back—recent events make that clear enough—but I can't quite imagine him socking an older man. It would be like striking one's own father in these parts."

"Family loyalties run very deep in these parts too," said Applegate, "and neither of us really know him. How do you know if you'd have been capable of attacking an older man years ago? Were any of us the same person when we were young?"

It was a fair-enough point, but it left Gabriel thinking hard about the implications as he took his leave of Applegate and went back to work. Or tried to. Gabriel's thoughts were in disarray at the image of a little girl raising her fists to her face to try to fend off an assailant twice her size. Primrose Harding's death had been even worse than he had imagined— the killer had looked that terrified girl in the eye as he had killed her; he had acted in full knowledge of the terror and pain he was inflicting on a child in a completely helpless situation. Even Nicoletta had not had to . . .

Lord Jesus Christ, have mercy on me, a poor sinner. Some wise mentor from years ago had taught Gabriel to recite the Jesus prayer if he became hopelessly entangled in his own dark thoughts, and it worked every time. Gabriel turned his attention back to the state of his beehives and indulged in a little mild fretting about various completely soluble problems. Bees did not need him to worry about them and solve their domestic crises. He was sure there were no mysterious murders among the bee population, they just got on with things. Gabriel pumped smoke into the hive he was working on and listened to the reassuring sound of the bees reacting to the threat in the way they always did.

Gabriel had never quite lost his qualms about pinching large quantities of honey and substituting it with sugar water whilst his unsuspecting bees dozed contentedly, the smoke having tricked them into gorging themselves on honey and sending themselves to sleep. They gobbled up the sugar water happily enough, but it was hardly as though they were in a position to form a union and complain about their poor working conditions and theft of earnings, all to provide the abbey with pots of honey and pretty candles to sell on market day.

Concentrate! Gabriel commanded himself, snapping his mind back to the question the inspector had asked. That was what made a sleeping murder so much more complicated. It was not just that there had been plenty of time for evidence to be destroyed or simply to disappear; it was that the people themselves among whom the murder had been committed had moved on, died, or changed beyond recognition. Joseph in his three-piece suit and with his apparently altruistic plans for the village had once turned on a man old enough to be his father and beaten the living daylights out of him. If he had been capable of doing a man quite so much harm in a fit of temper, had the Joseph of yesterday been capable of murder?

It is not the same thing! Taking on some lout of a man in a fistfight is not the same as luring a child to her death! And he was only a . . . But that was the other brick wall Gabriel found himself facing. With the body deteriorated to the bare bones, how was it possible to know anything of the motive behind Primrose Harding's murder? If she had been raped, it would be impossible to know now unless the culprit confessed— and what man would admit to such a detestable crime if he had concealed it successfully for decades? Was it—as Archie had implied—that an adult had attacked the child in temper and pushed her too far? Did anyone really do that outside the boundaries of the home? Murders of that nature were almost always committed by family members behind closed doors.

Gabriel concentrated on finishing his work, ignoring the occasional sharp sting from an alert bee that had found its way through Gabriel's protective clothing. He was virtually immune to bee stings now and would remove the stingers from his skin after he had finished. Gabriel realised that he needed to build up a picture of the kind of child Primrose Harding had been, not just the superficial references people made to her bizarre dress and her life in that decaying Victorian pile. Children who are the routine targets of bullies, particularly in a small community where there are few hiding places or alternative circles of friends, react very differently depending upon their temperaments. Where one child might respond by becoming hostile and aggressive to anyone who approaches him, another might become supercilious and self-important, determined to rise above the level of the thugs who persecute him. Yet others might become withdrawn and nervy, easily intimidated, easily manipulated.

That was another problem. He could go to see Mrs Harding and ask to see Primrose's old room, but even if she did not throw him out for his impertinence, even if—as some families did—she had left Primrose's bedroom perfectly preserved, he would have no way of knowing whether any incriminating evidence had been destroyed over the years. Tomorrow, the child would finally be granted a Requiem Mass and a burial, a proper burial this time in consecrated ground with her final resting place marked out by a stone cross. For years to come, for as long as she would be remembered, someone would attend her grave and leave flowers there every so often. But none of the people who attended the Mass would give Gabriel an accurate view of the child they were mourning. After so many years, she was a memory, an eight-year-old girl in an antiquated frock, frozen in time whilst others aged. But a flesh-and-blood child had been killed—not a memory, not a doll, not a pretty face in a faded, monochrome photograph. Somehow or other he had to find her. He had to find Primrose Harding and let her lead him to her killer.

As Gabriel had anticipated, the chapel was full for the Requiem Mass, with even the most ardent Protestants and even more ardent disciples of John Stuart Mill scrambling for a seat at the back. He liked to think that the beauty of the liturgy might touch a sceptical heart or two, but he was bewildered by the palpable lack of emotion in the church, even as the villagers fell into their familiar patterns of exclusion. Florence Harding and her mother sat alone at the front of the chapel. The only free space in the entire place was to be found on the pew directly behind them. Even at this most distressing of moments, no one seemed willing to get too close to them, and some chose to stand at the back rather than sit with the Harding women.

Seated in choir, Gabriel noticed a number of familiar faces. The inspector was there as promised, looking very solemn indeed in his black tie. Gabriel could see Stevie and Archie Wilcox standing together, Joseph having seated himself as far away from them as possible. There were other characters from the village whom Gabriel suspected had come out of a general sense of respect, such as Reggie McClusker; or for the free food, like Gordon Merriott, the village's very own handyman, malicious gossip, and sponge. Gabriel tried to make out Phyllis Baines in the congregation and finally found her near the front, partially concealed by a pillar. She certainly looked the part of a retired schoolmistress, dressed in a black gown and a hat, which looked as though it had lain on top of a wardrobe for years, gathering a stubborn layer of dust the wearer had not quite removed.

Gabriel tried to calculate the ages of the different members of the congregation, mentally dividing them between those who were old enough to remember Primrose Harding and those who were clearly too young. As the Kyrie rang out around him, Gabriel tried to subdivide the older group into those who were children at the time of Primrose's disappearance and those old enough to be suspects or at least mines of information.

Only a handful of members of the congregation went up for Communion when the time came, and Gabriel noted that neither Florence nor her mother moved from their seats. They were both stubbornly dry-eyed, unnaturally so. He had learnt not to judge a person's response to loss; in many cases, an individual who was reeling from the knowledge that a loved one was gone would be too shocked to react at all. The tears would come later, in the privacy of the home, behind a locked door, whilst gossips spoke disparagingly about how heartless they were.

They might not feel able to cry in public, thought Gabriel, watching the women staring directly ahead, with the coldness of two strangers standing on a railway platform waiting for a train. *But surely they must feel the need to comfort one another?* They were not even touching. At no point during the entire Mass did they so much as look at one another, let alone pause to see how the other was bearing up. It was all wrong. Even within the bounds of the formal behaviour expected in church, Gabriel would expect the two of them to acknowledge the presence of the other in this most distressing of situations. And what more distressing event was there in a woman's life than the funeral of a beloved child?

Beloved child. Another assumption Gabriel had no right to make. He had no way of knowing whether Primrose had been loved by anyone. The horrific thought haunted Gabriel as Abbot Ambrose gave a short homily. *What if no one loved that child? No one at all?* The thought continued to echo in Gabriel's head as the small white coffin was carried out at the front of the procession of mourners.

The cold air hit Gabriel like a slap in the face as they stepped outside and walked the short distance to the burial ground, where a grave lay open and waiting to receive Primrose Harding's bones. A drizzle of rain added to the misery of the scene, and Gabriel felt a certain relief that nature was weeping for this lost innocent even if no one else was.

Gabriel looked round the small crowd assembling at the graveside and glanced discreetly from face to face. Surely no child was completely unloved? There was always someone, even just one person who had been close to a child, close enough to be heartbroken when she came to grief. They were all very dour, certainly—every single person gathered had the decency to look sad—but where was the raw grief for this murdered child? Gabriel remembered the funerals of his wife and child, and his realisation, as he had stood trembling and weeping at the graveside, that everyone in his vicinity was in tears. Not one of those present failed to be moved by the ungodly horror of an innocent woman and child being laid to rest together after suffering horrible deaths.

There she was. A grieving woman. Gabriel's eyes rested on the spectral figure of Miss Phyllis Baines. Her large hat cast her face into shadow, but Gabriel could see tears sliding down her cheeks, which she was making no effort to wipe away. He knew that a woman like Phyllis Baines would not cry easily, especially not in front of a large group of people, but there she was all the same, silently weeping for a child it was claimed she had despised in life.

"Thoughts?" asked Applegate, with his usual lack of preliminaries. Following the burial, the mourners—those who chose to remain—had been shepherded into the abbey refectory, where the monks were handing out cups of tea and cucumber sandwiches that were already curling at the edges. The quality of the food hardly mattered, as few seemed in the mood to eat, except Gordon Merriott, who was tucking in with graceless alacrity.

"I've never known such a cold congregation at a Requiem," answered Gabriel in a stage whisper. "She was eight years old, for heaven's sake! I wanted to weep, and I didn't even know her."

"After all this time, I'm not sure anyone really knows how to react," ventured Applegate, taking the uncharacteristic role of diplomat for a change. It did not suit him one bit. "Even to those who knew her, the child must be a distant memory by now."

"But her sister? Her mother? The only person in tears was her old schoolmistress."

Applegate helped himself to a sandwich. "I don't know about you, but I'm going to take a stroll around the room. What they don't tell me directly I may just overhear. I suggest you do the same."

Gabriel had no intention of taking an aimless stroll around

the room. There was one particular person to whom he wished to speak, and she was standing conveniently alone, sipping at a cup of tea without enthusiasm. "Miss Baines?" he asked, approaching the black-clad figure with caution.

The woman looked sharply in Gabriel's direction. *Once a schoolmistress, always a schoolmistress,* thought Gabriel anxiously. To his surprise, however, Miss Baines gave him a friendly smile, removed one black glove from her spindly right hand and extended it to him. "I know who I am, young man," she said, shaking Gabriel's hand firmly. "Who might you be?"

"Dom Gabriel Mil—Father Gabriel," Gabriel corrected himself. The Benedictine title tended to cause confusion among the uninitiated. "Thank you for coming to pay your respects. I'm sure the family appreciates it."

"I very much doubt they do, I'm afraid," Miss Baines answered ruefully. "I was only Primmie's teacher, and it was a very, very long time ago. But I could not let the poor girl go without"—she paused as though she found the expression inappropriate—"paying my respects, as you say. We all knew she was dead, of course. Everyone knew it was the only way things could have turned out, but at least the family needn't torment themselves with false hope now."

"Indeed," agreed Gabriel. "There's something very hard about the word 'missing'."

"Don't I know it!" Miss Baines muttered, looking up into the far corner of the room. "My nephew flew off in his Spitfire five years ago and never returned. Missing, presumed lost. As with little Primmie, I knew as soon as I read the telegram that he was surely dead; but somehow one would like confirmation. It took me a long time to stop imagining all the ways in which he might have parachuted to safety in France or the Netherlands and perhaps lost his memory . . ." Miss Baines smiled again, suddenly embarrassed by the revelation. "Well, one imagines such irrational things when one is desperate."

"I'm sorry for your loss, Miss Baines."

"There cannot be a family in the country who has not lost someone, but dear Rupert was the only member of that generation our family had. I have no children of my own, and Rupert was good to his old maiden aunt, far more attentive than most young men. And at least he did not die in vain, unlike poor Primrose." Miss Baines looked up at Gabriel, and he noticed that there were tears in her eyes again. "That is surely the greatest horror when a child dies. It's all so pointless. She was killed for *nothing*."

Gabriel looked round briefly and realised that a number of heads had turned momentarily in their direction before people began resuming their own conversations. "It's a little warm in here," he said. "Would you like to take a turn about the gardens?"

Miss Baines nodded gratefully. "Thank you. I'm afraid I don't get out very much these days, and I find social gatherings very trying. A little fresh air will do me good."

Gabriel accompanied Miss Baines out the side door and into the gardens, secretly wishing that it were a little warmer. A chill northern wind swept over them as they walked the perimeter of the lawns, and Gabriel used the excuse of the grass being wet to keep Miss Baines on the more secluded path. He knew that they had been witnessed leaving, and he would not put it past the likes of Gordon Merriott to start shadowing them, seeking some juicy piece of gossip to spread.

The sharp light of outdoors gave Gabriel a better look at Miss Baines' face. He noticed that, though advanced in years, she was a woman who had kept herself fit and healthy. She walked with her back straight as her governess had no doubt taught her, her stride firm and regular, without the slightest hint of unsteadiness or fatigue. "I couldn't help noticing how distressed you were during the Mass, Miss Baines," said Gabriel, searching for a discreet way to begin the conversation, finding none, and going directly to the subject at hand. "Did you know the child well?"

The corners of Miss Baines' mouth flickered, but she did not smile this time. "A schoolmistress gets to know her pupils very well indeed, especially in a small place like this. I have always taken the trouble to get to know each and every one of my pupils—their characters, their weaknesses and foibles. I find it makes the art of teaching a good deal easier if one knows one's audience."

"You were very diligent."

"I was very harsh," answered Miss Baines, discarding the compliment like an unwanted gift. "I know that's all they will have remembered."

"They were harsher times."

"They certainly were." Miss Baines made a show of looking around herself intently, as though genuinely curious about her surroundings, before looking back at Gabriel. "Primrose stood out from the others for all the wrong reasons, and when that happens, one is tempted to single the child out. I am quite sure Primmie thought I was the devil incarnate."

Gabriel sensed that this was as close to a confession of cruelty that he was likely to get from this woman, and he kept walking slowly in the hope that she would remain distracted enough to continue talking. Only when Miss Baines went quiet did he try to prompt her. "Many children feel that way. I had some fairly dark thoughts about some of my schoolmasters when I was a child. One forgives and forgets over time."

"But she never had the chance," said Miss Baines, stopping in her tracks for a moment. "She never had the chance to do anything, and I could never tell her that I missed her presence in my classroom. I don't mind telling you that I never allowed another child to sit at Primrose Harding's desk after she disappeared. *I* am not a superstitious person," Miss Baines added hurriedly, placing the emphasis to indicate that Gabriel obviously was. "It just seemed wrong to allow another child to take her place."

"I understand." Gabriel swallowed hard, imagining a sad little desk and chair in the middle of a bustling classroom, the strongest possible reminder of what a lost child really means to a community—that absence, that constant sense of a hole in the world that can never be filled.

"This village has seen a great deal of death," continued Miss Baines, "young men leaving the fields to die in the trenches, then the next generation sent to die all over the world—at sea, blasted out of the skies. There are a few of my past pupils lying dead in those ghastly war graves. But Primrose was the only little child who went home one day and never returned to school."

"Have you considered what might have happened?" asked Gabriel, bracing himself for an unfriendly response.

Miss Baines glanced sidelong at him, her eyes narrowing as though she thought him a blithering idiot. "None of us in this village considered any other subject for many, many weeks after Primmie's disappearance. Everyone had his own theory, usually of a needlessly ghoulish nature."

"And you?" Gabriel persisted, since she had conspicuously failed to answer the question. "What was your theory?"

"I hope this shan't shock you, young man, but when I heard that Primrose's brother had been killed in action, my only thought was that it was better than a hangman's noose. At least that way he could be remembered as a hero rather than what he really was."

Gabriel attempted to keep walking as though nothing had been said, but he stumbled, only just preventing himself from falling. "I see. A young man killing his little sister seems a little farfetched. It's hard to imagine—"

Miss Baines held up a hand as if he had interrupted her in the middle of a grammar lesson. "Dennis was no worse than your average spoiled young man. With him being the only son, you can probably imagine the sort of oaf he turned into, but I daresay he might have been saved if the war had not turned his head."

"But murder? He was a soldier; he was trained to kill Germans!"

Miss Baines laughed bitterly. "You strike me as something of an innocent, Father. Surely you cannot imagine that no woman or child has ever been harmed or killed in time of war? You are perhaps too young to remember the first war—"

"No, as a matter of fact—"

"Those poor boys saw some terrible horrors, and for a man as weak and silly as Dennis, it was always going to turn his head. Even before he went to war, he used to bully his sister shamelessly. I reprimanded him for it once or twice."

"Bullied?"

"A lot of young men don't know their own strength, of course, but I noticed bruises on the child on one occasion. I tried to talk to the mother, but it was beneath her dignity to discuss the matter with me." Miss Baines paused for breath, and for the first time, she looked hunched and weary, but not with age. "I suppose that's why I feel so cut up about the whole thing. I could have saved her, but I had no idea where to turn."

Gabriel opened his mouth to answer, but Miss Baines did an about-face and stalked off in the direction of the abbey building. She was back to the haughty, strong-willed woman she had been just before her admission of weakness, but Gabriel doubted she would be rejoining the funeral party. He determined to follow her—he had so many more questions for her, and she was a valuable witness— but Gabriel became aware of the pungent odour of cheap cigarette smoke and cider close by. He turned just in time to see Gordon Merriott emerging from behind a tree.

"You should have made your presence known," said Gabriel curtly, glancing at Gordon's surly, unshaven face. Gordon had the newly lit cigarette clamped between what remained of two rows of yellowing teeth, his heavy white brows knitted into their customary frown. "Mr Merriott, it's awfully bad form to eavesdrop."

"Never done me no harm before," drawled Gordon.

"Not to you perhaps." Gabriel tried not to think of the misery Gordon Merriott's eavesdropping and gossiping had caused the village over the years. He was the embodiment of everything that had gone wrong with his generation. Called up in 1916 when conscription had been introduced, Gordon Merriott had had a disastrously short and ignominious war, taken prisoner after a bungled raid in which he had panicked and failed to obey a single instruction he had been given before venturing into no-man's-land. Rather than do his country a favour and get himself killed—or at least wounded at the Somme or Passchendaele—Gordon had returned home to the village after the cessation of hostilities, malnourished, lice-ridden, and a source of permanent embarrassment to his family.

Gordon's bitter determination to drag everyone else into the mud from which he had never entirely extricated himself had wrecked a few reputations, and Gabriel dreaded to think what he would claim he had overheard during Gabriel's brief conversation with Miss Baines. "You're wasting your time, Father," said Gordon, walking towards him with slow, insolent steps. "There's no mystery what can be solved here. Primrose Harding's killers have been gone a long time."

"Killers?" Gabriel knew he should not indulge Gordon's whisperings, but Gordon was another of those rare witnesses to the events of years ago. It could hardly hurt to ask a question or two. "You said killers, not killer. Why?"

" 'Twas Gypsies what got her," pronounced Gordon, taking a long, noisy drag on his cigarette. For the second time in the investigation, Gabriel regretted being a non-smoker, having to fight the urge to turn his head away from the toxic blue-grey tendrils. "She were always hanging about the Gypsy encampment like a stray dog. Spoilt her rotten, them tinkers did. Treated her like a little dolly."

Gabriel felt a flicker of temper troubling him and clasped

his hands together under his scapular. The Gypsy community was blamed for everything—a stolen chicken, or anything of any value that disappeared for that matter, a minor act of vandalism—but the death of a child? This was ugly territory, even for Gordon Merriott. "If they spoilt her, what reason could they possibly have had to kill her?"

Gordon's face twisted into an unsavoury smirk. "The reason little girls do end up dead," he whispered. "To keep them quiet. Forever."

Gordon's croaking insinuations made Gabriel's flesh crawl. "Mr Merriott, that's a very serious allegation to make about anyone—"

"I ain't allegating nothing," Gordon broke in. "I'm telling you straight. One of their men had his wicked way with her and killed her to hide the crime. As soon as it were done, they could be on their way, and no one would be none the wiser."

"I'll bear your theory in mind," said Gabriel, giving the man a perfunctory nod before hurrying back inside. Any encounter with Gordon Merriott left Gabriel feeling as though he had waded through an open sewer. As a Catholic in a hostile country, Gabriel knew how easy it was for a seemingly respectable community to turn on groups who failed to conform, particularly groups whose rituals and way of life were entirely alien to outsiders. Catholics and Gypsies had plenty in common, including the tendency to be used as scapegoats. There had been no mention in Primrose Harding's file of a Gypsy encampment anywhere near the village.

Gabriel stepped indoors and heard the subdued murmur of many voices talking in the refectory. No one ever dared be too enthusiastic at an occasion such as this, but people were making the most of the event and showing no sign of dispersing. Except for Phyllis Baines, who had left as Gabriel had feared she would. Phyllis Baines. A woman who knew too much.

8

"If I didn't know you better, I'd say you were being a teensy-weensy bit melodramatic," commented Applegate, turning the key in the ignition whilst Gabriel parked himself in the passenger seat and closed the door. "Why shouldn't a grown woman leave when she's ready to leave?"

"There's nothing wrong with her going home; she was upset," Gabriel explained. "But I'm sure she was holding back. Worse, you-know-who was skulking about while we were talking."

"Merriott? What was the old duffer up to this time?"

"Besides eavesdropping as always, he told me Gypsies did it."

Applegate let out a maddeningly protracted groan. "The Gypsies get the blame when they're not even here! They never arrive until early June. It's the same every year. Primrose Harding disappeared in April, long before any tinkers turned up."

"I suppose it shows how hard it is to expect people to recall what happened so long ago," said Gabriel. "Details start to blur."

"That's not a mistake; it's a flat lie," snapped Applegate. "I wouldn't trust Merriott as a witness to murder if he produced the smoking gun. In this case, the Gypsies weren't there, and Merriott would've been tucked away in the trenches."

Gabriel glanced nervously down the street, hoping against all hope to see Miss Baines walking along the pavement; but the village high street was eerily quiet, and there was no sign of that wraith-like figure anywhere. "I . . . I don't think he was in the trenches quite yet," said Gabriel, but his mind was elsewhere. "He . . . I'm sure he was a conscript. The other men mock him about it even now."

"A conscript? Hmm. Well, well, Parliament had long introduced conscription by the time Primrose Harding vanished, so he was almost certainly well out of the way by 1918. It won't be hard to find out."

Applegate had barely brought the motor to a standstill and said, "She lives at number 22" before Gabriel had hurled himself out onto the pavement and rushed for the door. He hammered the brass door knocker loud enough to rouse half the street, but Phyllis Baines must have only just arrived home, as she was still wearing her coat and hat when she threw open the door with an indignant swoosh.

"Miss Baines, are you all right?" gasped Gabriel, trying to ignore the woman's hard stare. "Are you . . . erm . . ."

"I am quite all right, my man," Miss Baines answered tartly. "Might I enquire what the matter is with you?"

Applegate was bringing up the rear, which was fortunate for Gabriel, as he could not see the look on his companion's face. "Begging your pardon, Miss Baines," began Applegate, removing his hat and gently pushing Gabriel aside in one deft movement. "My friend was concerned for your safety."

Gabriel glanced both ways down the street, a gesture that

made him look absurdly paranoid. There was no one about, and nobody appeared to be watching, though one could not be too careful. "Might we come in, Miss Baines? We probably oughtn't to be seen—"

"I don't think that will be necessary, Father," said Miss Baines, giving him a cold smile. "Good day to you."

Gabriel and Applegate stood awkwardly on the pavement as the door closed in their faces, looking like a pair of snubbed carol singers. "What would I do without your assistance?" asked Applegate, turning back to the car. "I don't suppose you might explain what you were playing at?"

"I was not playing at anything!" exclaimed Gabriel, getting back in the car. "She knows something she's not telling! If I've worked that out, the killer may also have worked it out. Can't you see?"

"So, Miss Baines is in imminent danger of being brained with a piece of lead pipe because she has a secret? Perhaps she witnessed the whole thing! Perhaps she did it!"

Gabriel looked disconsolately out the window, resisting the wave of sulkiness that swept over him. "I'm worried, Applegate."

"That much was abundantly obvious," Applegate retorted. "Don't take up poker, will you?"

"What?"

"Nothing." Applegate busied himself starting the car and pulling away. "Perhaps you'd best leave the interviews to me in future. I don't tend to annoy the witness in the first ten seconds."

"I don't suppose you found out anything useful?" asked Gabriel.

"Not really. Even those who remembered the lassie didn't

have much to say. Reggie McClusker went on about giving her sweeties when her mother wasn't looking."

"I wonder if there was anything that poor girl's mother actually approved of?"

Applegate shrugged. "You get types like that. Mrs Harding wasn't so unusual. If that child had lived to be a woman, she would either have been a hopeless wet lettuce or have turned against everything."

But she never grew up! raged Gabriel inwardly. *Someone made sure she could never grow up, and Phyllis Baines is lying about who really did it.*

"Well?" demanded Applegate. Gabriel became aware of the uncomfortable silence in the car and realised that Applegate was awaiting the answer to a question Gabriel could not remember him asking. "Father Gabriel, when you've applied for naturalisation papers to planet Earth, you will let me know, won't you?"

"Sorry," murmured Gabriel. "I'm just feeling a bit lost."

"You're not the only one," growled Applegate. "It's hard enough pursuing a murder investigation in the immediate aftermath. When the victim's been in the ground for decades, it really does get tricky. There's something else I need to tell you."

"Hmm?"

"You need to pull yourself together, because it may not be long before you're investigating this murder alone."

Gabriel looked up sharply, his head suddenly clear. "What? What's that supposed to mean?"

"I mean that the police force has limited resources, and the powers that be are not going to leave me running around indefinitely trying to solve a cold case. It won't be long

146

before someone wakes up to the fact that the killer may be dead and I may therefore be wasting my time."

"But . . . but justice!" exclaimed Gabriel. "What about that? What about Primrose? Surely we owe it to her memory to find out what happened?"

"I'm not here to tie up loose ends, Gabriel, and that's a fact. I owe it to my predecessor to try to clear this up; but I also know that I shan't be given much time. There are crimes being committed now, today, and some would argue that men like me would be better placed keeping law and order in the present rather than bringing up the past."

Gabriel could think of no answer to that. As always, there was a brutal logic to any argument surrounding police work when it came to funding and resources, but he knew that exactly the same argument had been used to close the investigation into the deaths of his own family. They had no leads; they were very sorry. They doubted they could pursue this; they were closing the case. The murder of Giovanna and Nicoletta would be yet another unsolved case in the archives of Scotland Yard.

"This isn't a cop-out," Gabriel heard Applegate explain, in the closest to an apologetic tone as he was capable of expressing. "I want to clear this up: I want to find out who killed Primrose Harding. But I need you to know that time may be short. We can't afford to be chasing false leads."

"I understand."

Gabriel desperately needed to clear his head. Early that morning, Joseph had driven off in his shiny, newly repainted car in the direction of the building site, whilst Gabriel remained in the abbey, planting potato seedlings in the monastic vegetable garden. Gabriel had lost his taste for potatoes however they were cooked—fried, boiled, mashed, sautéed—by the middle of the war. Potatoes were easy to plant and grew quickly, meaning that the humble spud had become the abbey's staple diet as soon as rationing had begun. There had been little meat, sugar, or fat; no oranges, lemons, or bananas; but there had been a tediously plentiful supply of potatoes to fill their groaning stomachs.

"Are you listening to a word I'm saying?" demanded Gerard, who had joined Gabriel in the vegetable garden and was already covered in mud. "Wakey wakey!"

Gabriel groaned, glancing wearily at Gerard. He absolutely *detested* that particular expression. "I'm not asleep," said Gabriel. "I'm not even tired. I'm trying to solve a murder before the case gets closed again."

Gerard looked up at Gabriel in surprise, the metal blade of his spade jarring against stone. "I thought Appleface was quite keen for once?"

"You won't ever call him that, will you?" asked Gabriel, unsure as to whether he should reprimand Gerard for being so disrespectful. "Applegate's very keen. It's his superiors who might not be. It was a long time ago, after all."

"Tell that to the poor lassie's family," said Gerard, stamping down on the step of the spade. There was another scrape of metal striking stone, and Gerard dropped to his knees to search for the obstruction. "A crime's a crime."

"That's my belief, but the more I think about it, the more I wonder how it will ever be possible to solve."

"Actually, I reckon it should be very easy to solve if you go about it the right way," said Gerard. Gabriel thought he would have sounded smug if he had not been clawing the ground like a stray dog. "It's a small village; there are only so many people it could have been. Process of elimination." He reached into the shallow hole he had made and prised out a lump of chalk, causing Gabriel to wince visibly. "What's up?"

Gabriel grimaced. "The way things are going at the moment, I actually thought you'd dug up a bone."

"Now that would be awkward," Gerard agreed, throwing the chalk aside and picking up the spade. "Though I suppose if you dug deep enough pretty much anywhere, you'd find some evidence of human remains. When I were a kid, I found a Civil War cannonball when I were out playing footy with me brothers. We were up half the night imagining whose head had been knocked off."

Gabriel shuddered again. He was too squeamish to be a sleuth. He began counting names off his fingers, distracting himself from the thought of buried remains and the smashed skulls of doomed Cavaliers. "Primrose Harding's brother Dennis, Reggie, Gordon Merriott, old Mrs Harding, Florence, Stevie and Archie Wilcox, Joseph, Phyllis Baines. They were all in the village at the time, and they were all connected in some way with Primrose."

"There you go; it's a start."

"Except that none of them had a motive to kill Primrose; there is no evidence that any of them did any such thing, and we can't rule out the possibility that she was snatched by a stranger."

Gerard shook his head, making him look even more like a stray dog. It would take him days to get the soil out from under his fingernails. "I don't think you believe it were a stranger. She knew all the people you've listed, and she would have trusted all of them."

"None of them had a motive," said Gabriel. He then almost whispered the next thought that came to mind. "But what motive is there to kill a child? None of them had a motive because there could be no motive. But one of them is almost certainly a killer."

The two men stopped talking at the sound of an urgent voice calling Gabriel's name. A moment later and Joseph stomped into view, somewhat the worse for wear and very much out of breath. "There you are!" he called.

Gabriel noticed that Joseph was carrying a brick in one hand and a piece of paper in the other. Gabriel sighed. "Another message then?" he asked glumly.

Joseph threw him a withering look. "I do wish this person would simply send me a telegram. It would make rather less work for the glazier that way."

"Where was it?"

"In the driver's seat of my car. It was hurled through the windscreen." He held out the note to Gabriel. The paper was moist and crumpled, but the message was clearly visible, spelt out once again in letters cut out of a newspaper. CHILD KILLER. "I can't take much more of this."

"This makes no sense," said Gabriel, but he could not understand why he found the note so baffling. "When did it happen?"

"I had been at the building site only half an hour when I heard the crash. I rushed over to the car, but it was too late. I should have left Stevie to the police when I had the chance!"

Gabriel indicated the abbey building, and the two men walked together to the privacy of indoors, leaving Gerard to face the task of planting the potatoes alone. Gabriel knew that Joseph needed a cup of tea and the chance to calm his nerves, or there would be another fistfight to break up before the end of the day. "You're very sure it was Stevie?" said Gabriel, opening the door to the parlour. "Why don't you sit down and catch your breath."

"Of course it was Stevie! First, he defaces my car, then goes one step further and smashes the windscreen. I wager it was him who threw the brick through my boardinghouse window. He always was the sort of lout whose idea of communication was smashing things up."

"I think I should have a word with Mr Wilcox," said Gabriel, stepping backwards towards the door, only to be struck in the small of the back by the door flying open. It was Gerard, determined not to be excluded from the action—or just shirking his potato-planting duties. The slapstick moment at least caused Joseph to smile, but he quickly shook his head.

"I'll not have you fighting my battles for me, Father."

"I'll not have you fighting any battle: that's the point."

Joseph jumped to his feet, choking with mortification. "I'm sorry about that ridiculous scuffle! It was beneath me; I see that now. I mean only to speak with him this time!"

Gabriel turned to Gerard. "Make sure Mr Beaumont has a nice cup of tea while I'm gone. I shan't be long."

Joseph made to follow Gabriel, but Gerard somehow or other managed to get himself between the two men, and Gabriel was in the corridor before Joseph could make his way to the door. Gabriel smiled at the sound of Joseph raging at Gerard: "You're a sneaky piece of work! Are you sure you're not a Jesuit?"

"I am very, very sneaky, but definitely not a Jesuit." There was the scrape of a chair against wood as Joseph sat down heavily again. Gerard had won.

Gabriel hurried out before Joseph could make another break for freedom, making his way in the direction of the Wilcox farm. He remembered, a little late as ever, that he was not supposed to go out on his own, but it was the least of Gabriel's sins against the Order of Saint Benedict. It was Gabriel's hope that Gerard would get the hint and do some sleuthing of his own whilst he had a suspect seated impatiently in the parlour, awaiting tea.

9

Gabriel clambered over a stile that marked the edge of the abbey grounds and dropped carefully onto the narrow path. It was not raining as Gabriel walked through the tunnel of trees towards the Wilcox farm, but he could feel that light drizzle all around him like a net of mist. The damp had the effect of releasing all the pungent, fertile odours of wild land—peat and cow parsley and moist tree bark. The neighbouring farm's chestnut gelding leant his head over the five-bar gate, anticipating food when he heard Gabriel's footsteps.

Gabriel was fond of horses and would have liked to have paused for a moment to stroke the soft brown hair and feel the gelding's warm breath on his hands. He had ridden a horse only when he had been at school. It had been almost as significant a part of the curriculum as rugby and cricket, but Gabriel had quickly been scared off after a few accidents and the constant reminder that he was never going to compete with boys who owned their own ponies and could decorate their walls with multicoloured rosettes.

The Wilcox family farm lay less than a mile away to the east of the abbey, but Gabriel had never ventured onto the Wilcox land before. The Wilcoxes were the sort of men who kept to themselves as far as they could, which made Stevie's determination to whip up the village against Joseph all the more puzzling. Joseph's building site was nowhere near the

Wilcox land; the building of those houses could not inconvenience the two men in the slightest. They would have no cause to go near the development when it was completed unless they wished to sell their produce to the new residents. Both Archie and Stevie could avoid a monument to another man's success if it troubled them so deeply.

Jealousy again. Might that be all there really was behind Stevie's determination to thwart Joseph? People had done worse when driven by that sin—the first jealous man had murdered his own brother—but envy was the deadly sin Gabriel understood the least well. He had never experienced it before, even when he had been deprived of what mattered most to him in life. It was hard to get his head around the notion that a man could be so consumed with envy that he might make it his mission in life to destroy another, not because it would benefit him in any way, but simply to spite a rival.

Gabriel hesitated at the gate that marked the rear entrance to the Wilcox farm, half expecting the Hound of the Baskervilles to come hurtling towards him—fangs bared and glowing—if he dared step on the hallowed ground of another man's territory. Gabriel said a quick *Ave Maria* and clicked open the latch, slipping through as quietly as he could. It did not help Gabriel's sense of foreboding that he was immediately alarmed by what appeared to be a human figure standing some feet away from him. It was the world's creepiest scarecrow; its head was made of a stuffed potato sack with buttons for eyes and a hideous frown that put Gabriel in mind of the sort of monstrous humanoid alien one might find in the pages of an H. G. Wells book.

"Are you to keep the crows away or to keep everyone away?" Gabriel asked the glowering scarecrow before turning back to the narrow dirt path that sliced through the field. He had not gone five paces before he became aware of a very definitely human presence gaining on him. Definitely not a scarecrow this time; Gabriel could hear the laboured breathing of a man who was exerting himself, the stamp of boots on sticky, muddy ground. He spun round to face his stalker. "Good day, Mr Wilcox. Just the man I wanted to see."

Stevie's face broke into a mischievous grin. "I wouldn't talk to the scarecrow if I were you; you'll never convert him. He's a heathen."

"I was rather hoping to talk to you," said Gabriel, hoping his acute embarrassment did not show. "Where did you pop from? The field looked empty."

"I were clearing a ditch back there. You wouldn't be able to see me behind all that undergrowth." Stevie took off his thick hemp gloves. "Now what was it you wanted? Joseph Beaumont sent you, did he?"

"Not exactly," answered Gabriel quickly; Stevie Wilcox was no fool. "But some kind person keeps sending him bricks, no doubt to help speed up his building work. I wonder if you know who that might be?"

Stevie did a good act of looking astonished. "What's happened this time? I heard about the brick through his landlady's window."

"Someone threw a brick through the windscreen of his car, with a note attached, accusing him of being a child killer." Gabriel looked intently at Stevie's face for any sign of guilt, but Stevie looked away sharply. "Stevie, if you had anything to do with this, it might be better if you told me now. The police will take a very dim view of this."

Stevie shook his head violently, still unable to meet Gabriel's eye. "I didn't do it! I know I damaged his car before, but it were a daft thing to do. Me dad gave me hell about it afterwards. But I ain't done nothing with no bricks."

"Stevie, it's not going to look very good for you when Joseph reports this latest attack to the police. You've already been caught red-handed damaging his car. The police will say that you've got it in for Joseph Beaumont because you're trying to stop him from building houses."

"Damn his houses!" shouted Stevie before putting a hand over his mouth like a naughty schoolboy. "Begging your pardon, Father, but I done nothing! I don't think he's a child killer any more than the next man. None of us really believe that. I just don't want his ugly houses in our village."

"The houses aren't being built anywhere near your farm. They may not be ugly. They certainly won't be uglier than the land they're being built on."

Stevie looked up at Gabriel. For the first time, Gabriel noticed how vulnerable he looked. Slightly hunched as he was, his whole figure wore a look of unaccepted defeat, the way an old soldier might appear when he has been stood down from a battle he believes in but no longer has the strength to fight. "Father, everything is changing," said Stevie. "The world is changing; nothing's certain no more. Apart from my days as a soldier, I've never left this village. It's all I've ever known. I won't let change come here! I won't let those city nancies come and wreck a village that's been left alone for hundreds of years. I won't let it happen!"

"Stevie, who do you think threw those bricks if it was not you?"

"I don't know," answered Stevie quickly. "Let's face it, he's plenty of enemies."

No thanks to you, thought Gabriel grimly, but he said nothing.

"Do you really think Joseph killed Primrose Harding?"

Stevie shook his head wearily. "No," he all but whispered. "I'm sure a kid could kill another kid, but I've never really believed that."

"Then who did?"

Stevie did not hesitate this time. "Someone from out of the village. Must have been. No one would have killed her what knew her, and we all knew her. She may have been a mad little madam, but she were one of us."

"Mad?"

"No one likes people what won't fit in. There's something unnatural about a child who wanders off on her own, won't join in with the others."

"I understand that her mother forbade her to wander freely," said Gabriel, recalling his conversation with Florence. "She was confined to the house or the garden."

Stevie gave a laugh that was almost a snigger. "Her mama loved laying down the law, but she were too wrapped up in herself to notice where that child was half the time. Too busy moping over her dead husband."

Gabriel cleared his throat, suppressing the urge to take that line of questioning any further. "I see," he said.

"I'm not saying it were her ma's fault," Stevie put in hastily, as though suddenly aware of his own accusatory tone. "Children should be able to run free somewhere like this. Who would kill a kiddie?"

This was the brick wall Gabriel was going to keep hitting. No one ever wants to believe that their own friends or neighbours—even family—could be killers. "Stevie, I know it was a long time ago, but could you cast your mind back to the day Primrose disappeared?"

Stevie smiled. "It's no good, Father. If I seen anything important, I'd have remembered it by now. She were missing for hours before her mother took the trouble to raise the alarm. No one with any sense went to that bit of the village anyway. Horrible mouldering outbuildings, rusting machinery."

"It sounds like the perfect children's playground."

"Primrose didn't play," Stevie retorted. "My sister were at school same time as Primmie, and she said she always sat alone, even in the playground."

Gabriel recalled his conversation with Archie. "You had a sister?"

"She were carried off in the flu epidemic."

"I'm sorry. There's been so much loss."

"It were a long time ago, Father," said Stevie, in the tone of a man who considers the subject well and truly off-limits. Only one child's death was open for discussion, and it was not his sister's. "Bessie were a mite younger than Primmie, but all the village children knew each other."

"Did she ever talk about what happened?" Gabriel was not even sure whether it was decent to pursue the subject, but he wanted to see whether Stevie's and Archie's recollections matched. "Children sometimes notice things."

Stevie shook his head. "The little kiddies got it into their heads that Miss Baines done it. They were all scared to death of the old trout—not that she were so very old at the time—and their imaginations filled in the rest. You know the way it is."

Gabriel smiled, thinking of the insane rumours that had floated about the schoolroom when he was a child: the headmaster had hurled a boy out the window and told his parents it was an accident; the chemistry master poisoned his laziest pupils . . . "What do *you* think?" he asked.

"Who knows? Miss Baines were clever enough and cold enough, but would she have?" Stevie's shoulders sagged as though carrying an unbearable burden. "Look, Father, I dunno who killed that little one, but sure as eggs are eggs, Joe Beaumont had nothing to do with it."

"You know what you have to do then," said Gabriel. "Telling lies to destroy a man's good name is a filthy business. And whipping up the village against Joseph Beaumont was never going to help your cause. Those houses may never be built now, anyhow."

Stevie nodded. "I know that now. I hadn't thought of it, but I daresay the poor sod will be well out of pocket with everything stopped." He looked at Gabriel with the sheepishness of a man who has seldom had to admit to being in the wrong. "It were never anything personal, you know . . ." He trailed off with what Gabriel hoped was an unwillingness to tell another lie. "Tell you what, Father, why don't you tell him to come over for tea tomorrow?"

"Tea? Oh, well . . . well, yes. I'll tell him, of course," Gabriel virtually stammered, failing miserably to hide his alarm.

Stevie threw back his head and guffawed, which was the

best reaction Gabriel could have hoped for. He had seen what Stevie looked like when he was offended. "He'll be safe enough in my home, Father; I'm not that daft! We'll never be friends, but it's pointless feuding at our age."

"Indeed."

Stevie smiled, looking a good deal more self-assured than he had a few minutes ago. "Life's too short for all this. You can have so much to say, and suddenly it's too late."

Rumours were not to be taken seriously, especially rumours started by bored—and probably resentful—schoolchildren, but Gabriel had to reach Phyllis Baines. Children made up stories all the time, but they were also masters at noticing subtle hostility. If Miss Baines had been overly severe with Primrose, if she had given the impression of a personal animus against the child, the other children would have picked it up very quickly.

Gabriel knew he ought, by rights, to be more concerned for Joseph's safety. He liked to see the good in people, but even Gabriel could not avoid the thought that Stevie's offer of tea after years of feuding had come remarkably easily. Gabriel told himself that there would be time to warn Joseph that he might be walking into a trap; it might already be too late to warn a woman who knew too much. A good psychiatrist would probably have said that Gabriel had become preoccupied with the belief that Miss Baines was going to meet the traditional end meted out to all reluctant murder witnesses in the pages of Mrs Christie's books.

There were all manner of rational explanations, no doubt, but as Gabriel walked back in the direction of the abbey, the flutter of fear quickly became something akin to panic. He broke into an undignified run. If he could find Gerard, he might persuade him to drive them both to Phyllis Baines' house. If he walked all the way to the far side of the village, he was certain it would be too late. The abbey gardens had never seemed so large. Gabriel felt the stabbing pain of a stitch in his side and was forced to slow down in spite of himself. He reached the door and shoved it open, tumbling virtually into the arms of Abbot Ambrose.

"Forgive me, Father Abbott," Gabriel gasped before Abbot Ambrose could make any comment; he could not possibly have anything complimentary to say. "It's an emergency! I need Brother Gerard to drive me into the village."

Abbot Ambrose put a hand on Gabriel's arm and looked—to Gabriel's relief—concerned rather than annoyed. "What is it? What's happened?"

"There's no time to explain! I have to get to the village immediately! A woman is in terrible danger!"

Abbot Ambrose nodded. "Go directly to the car. I will send Brother Gerard to you immediately."

Gabriel waited just long enough for Abbot Ambrose to give him a quick blessing, before hurrying to the front door and the abbey's clapped-out old motor. Gerard, he knew, would waste no time in joining him.

"It's a good job you didn't tell Father Abbot you had a funny feeling someone was in danger," shouted Gerard over the roar of the tired old engine as they hurtled in the direction of Phyllis Baines' house. Gerard was a hopeless driver, but he did at least drive fast, and that was all Gabriel could think of as he clung to the edge of his seat for dear life. "You got pretty short shrift last time you tried to rescue the lady."

"That was then, this is now! This time I'm right! God help me, I wish I weren't. When Stevie mentioned her name, I just knew . . ." Gabriel went silent. Talking felt pointless at moments like this, and Gabriel closed his eyes and prayed, prayed with every ounce of his strength. He prayed that Phyllis Baines was still safe at home, that she had locked the door, barred the windows, refused to allow anyone in. If she had finally come to understand the seriousness of the danger she was in, she might still save her own life.

When the car lurched onto Phyllis Baines' street, Gabriel felt a flicker of relief. The street was as quiet as always; but almost immediately, Gabriel thought that a quiet street would be an easy street on which to commit a murder. It was a vile thought, but Gabriel was starting to see danger everywhere. If a child was not safe in a village, no one was, and certainly not the sort of woman who had overheard the tittle-tattle of generations of village children, a lady who had been ignored for decades as she quietly observed everything and everyone . . .

Gerard had not quite brought the car to a halt when Gabriel threw open the door and jumped clear, jarring his ankle as he landed awkwardly. Phyllis Baines' front door was closed, and with net curtains hung at every window, it was impossible to see whether there was anyone inside. Gabriel hurried to the door and pushed it open, calling out as he did so. "Miss Baines! Miss Baines, are you there? Are you all right?"

The silence of the grave clung to him. Worse than silence, Gabriel could smell the bitter, metallic odour of blood coming from somewhere in the house and rushed through the open door of the kitchen before he could lose his nerve. Applegate had told him once that most murders occur in the kitchen of the house, with its easy access to knives, but this kitchen was no murder scene. It was clean and tidy, every surface scrubbed and polished, every plate perfectly aligned on the dresser, the tea towel neatly folded in two next to the sink. The knives clean and shiny in the knife block. All except one. Gabriel registered the hole where the vegetable knife should have been and ran back into the hall in time to see Gerard wiping his feet on the doormat.

"Go upstairs!" commanded Gabriel before Gerard could ask what was going on. He must have been able to smell blood too, and he was far more squeamish than Gabriel. "I'll search down here."

Gabriel left Gerard to climb the stairs as he rushed through another door into what he guessed to be the sitting room. Nothing here either. A smart, if sparsely furnished, front room in perfect order. Gabriel turned to make a sharp exit and glanced up momentarily, barely registering the one detail amiss in the room: in the corner of the ceiling just above the door, there was a small, dark stain the size of a penny piece. In any other circumstance, it might have passed as damp, but Gabriel knew exactly what he was looking at and felt his stomach heave. He swallowed the bile rising in his throat and rushed up the stairs, hearing Gerard's unmanly shriek before he had reached the top.

Gabriel took in the details of the horror scene as though he were watching the whole drama unfolding from the out-of-body perspective of a nightmare. Phyllis Baines was lying on her bed, the white sheets saturated in a wide circle of blood. Poor Gerard, for all his horror at the sight of blood, had rushed straight towards her and stood with his folded handkerchief pressed hard against the woman's thin wrist.

Gabriel grabbed one of the cords that tied back the curtains, yanking it free and fumbling desperately to tie it round Phyllis Baines' arm. "We won't save her," rasped Gerard; his mouth and lips were dry with the shock. "Even if we can stop the bleeding, she's lost so much blood. Look at the sheets!"

"It might not be as bad as it looks." Gabriel slipped his hand under Gerard's to take over the act of applying pressure, allowing Gerard to step away. "A little blood goes a long way. You need to call an ambulance. She has a telephone; I saw a receiver on the wall downstairs. If they're quick, they may still save her."

Gerard could not get out of the room fast enough, and Gabriel heard his footsteps hammering down the stairs. He looked at Phyllis Baines' ashen face. He suspected she had fainted with shock quite soon after cutting her wrist, but the effects of haemorrhage would be making themselves felt by now. He tried to calculate how much blood she had already lost, but as she was lying on several layers of bedclothes and a thick horsehair mattress, it was impossible to know how much blood had soaked through. "Miss Baines!" he called, placing his face near hers. "Miss Baines, you must wake up! Wake up now!"

Gabriel thought he saw her eyelids flicker momentarily. He was sure she could hear him, but she had no reason to fight for her life so soon after trying to end it. "Wake up! Please wake up! I won't let the truth die with you!"

Miss Baines did not open her eyes again, but Gabriel heard

the low whisper of an exhausted woman desperately trying to speak. Her lips barely moved, but Gabriel distinctly heard the words, "Leave me alone."

"I'm not going to leave you to die," said Gabriel quickly. "This is the coward's way out, and you are no coward." Gabriel noticed the woman's face taking on that sepulchral look he remembered from other deathbeds. He knew she had started drifting through that terrifying hinterland between life and death, with death so much more attractive than a half life of guilt. "Miss Baines? Phyllis, it doesn't have to end this way. Your life is not yours to take."

A single, pathetic tear slid sideways into Phyllis' hair; she struggled again to speak. "I'm sorry. I shouldn't . . . I'm sorry . . . too late." She spoke the final two words with a sudden surge of energy, as regret turned into anger.

"It's not too late, Phyllis. It's not too late for you, and it's not too late to help Primrose."

Phyllis was squeezing her eyes tight shut, trying to hold on to her self-possession even now, when it could hardly matter. "She tried to tell me . . . I said she was silly . . . silly girl with her stories . . ."

Gabriel shifted his position to ensure that he did not slacken his grip on the tourniquet or the wound. If she was alive now, she might stay alive if the ambulance arrived in time. "What did she tell you, Phyllis? She was frightened of somebody? Someone other than her brother?"

More tears. A steady trickle now, and Gabriel could hear her breathing growing shallow. "I knew where she was . . . I knew . . ."

"Phyllis, please. If you knew where she was buried . . ." But it was no use, and Gabriel knew it. Phyllis was barely coherent, and he could not even be sure she knew what she was saying. Gabriel could hear the sound of male voices downstairs, Gerard talking quickly and a shade too loudly. Then there were two men in the room, bearing a stretcher between them. Someone was telling Gabriel he could let her go now. He could let her go. Gabriel clung desperately to the curtain cord he had tightened around her arm and the blood-soaked handkerchief pressed against the death wound. He could not bring himself to let her slip into eternity like this, even though he knew she had already left this world.

"How did you know?" asked Applegate tersely. He had had the tact to remain silent as he had accompanied Gabriel along the chill, echoing corridor of the cottage hospital, but his patience was already wearing thin. "You knew she was in trouble."

"I didn't know she was a danger to herself," said Gabriel miserably. "I knew she was concealing something, and I barely knew the woman. If I had worked it out, the chances were that someone else had had the same thought. It was something Stevie said that jolted me. But I never thought she'd take her own life."

Applegate was bemused by how distressed Gabriel was. Phyllis Baines had been no relation of his, not even a friend. The sad fact was that she had had no family to speak of and few or no friends to miss her. "If you don't mind my saying so, you're taking this unduly hard. She wasn't even one of yours."

Gabriel smiled wanly, barely noticing the driver opening the back door of the Humber for him. Gabriel got inside and waited for Applegate to get in from the other side. "If you mean she was not Catholic, I'm not sure I understand what that has to do with it. The woman was driven to despair, and she could have been helped. No one should die at his own hand, whispering his regrets."

"They usually do regret it, if it's any consolation," said Applegate, patting Gabriel's shoulder. He was not given to gestures of sympathy, but Gabriel's misery was contagious. "Virtually every time I've ever had to deal with a failed suicide, he will always say he's glad he survived." He waited for Gabriel to respond positively to the information—or at least to acknowledge it—but Gabriel did not flicker. "I don't want to sound indelicate, but did she say anything useful about the murder?"

Gabriel shook his head. "It's not indelicate; you have to ask. She said something about Primrose trying to tell her something, and she had thought her a silly girl telling tales."

Applegate groaned. "So, she spent her final moments telling us what we already knew. This was not a random act of violence by a stranger. Primrose was killed by someone she knew and someone she feared. Like most kids. And like most little children, when Primrose Harding tried to tell an adult she trusted, she was ridiculed." Applegate suddenly noticed that they were being driven in the direction of the constabulary. "No, not this way!" he ordered. "Let's take Father Gabriel home first."

Gabriel sank back in his seat. "Thanks. I think you've more or less got the sum of it, as far as I can tell," said Gabriel quietly. He felt an irrational sense of having personally failed Applegate. He knew Applegate was simply frustrated, but it was not difficult to hear a tone of accusation in what he was saying. *Thank you so much for telling me the blindingly obvious. Thank you for telling me what we both knew. If you hadn't been so busy trying to save her soul, you might have found out something useful.* "I sometimes wonder how many children would be saved from harm if adults only had the decency to listen to them."

"It's possible our victim had a reputation for telling tall tales. It might have been like the boy crying wolf."

"There is no evidence of that. No one has suggested Primrose was a habitual liar." Gabriel looked out the window. A fine drizzle gave the surrounding village the look of an Impressionist painting. He suddenly thought of poor Gerard, who had had to drive alone back to the abbey, shaken to the core by the sight of a woman practically drowning in her own blood. Gabriel really had to stop dragging him into these situations, but he never asked for nasty things to happen.

Applegate cleared his throat, jolting Gabriel out of his malaise. "That's the problem, though, there's not much evidence for anything," remarked Applegate. "After all this time, it's impossible to get a clear picture of the child's character. If she was known to be a liar, how could we know that now? No one ever remembers the debit side of a person's character when he's gone."

That much was true enough. Gabriel was sure Nicoletta had been a little monster on more than a few occasions, flying into toddler tantrums, stubbornly refusing to get into the bath, answering back . . . but for the life of him, he could not remember her like that. She was always an angel in his memories. Nicoletta. Primrose. Gabriel squeezed his fists together until his fingernails pressed hard into the palms of his hands. "Look here, Applegate, whatever

Primrose might or might not have been like, we do know that she was trying to tell the schoolmistress something significant. Whatever it was, the poor child took it to the grave with her. What almost worries me more is why on earth Phyllis Baines should have thought it necessary to conceal Primrose's final resting place."

"She told you that?" demanded Applegate, and out of the corner of his eye, Gabriel could see the inspector glaring at him. He did not dare turn his head.

"Didn't I say that? Miss Baines said she knew where Primrose was."

"Did she, by Jove. And she never thought to tell anyone?"

"Quite. If she really believed Primrose's brother had killed her—dash it all, even if she made that up, there was no reason for her to keep the truth about Primrose's death from the family. It's so cruel! Everyone rushing about trying to find a child, a family hoping and praying that she might be found alive. And all along, Phyllis Baines knew perfectly well that a child was dead; she knew where she was buried, and she said nothing!"

"Did Miss Baines strike you as a cruel person?" asked Applegate curiously. "She seemed to me to be rather cold—well, quite typical of that generation of schoolmistress—but she didn't strike me as malicious in any way."

Gabriel shook his head. He glanced out the car window and saw that he was very nearly home, but unusually, the sight of the abbey unsettled him. There was something about travelling back to this sanctuary with a detective inspector that made him feel as though he were an invading force, inveigling his way into the silence of a house of prayer with his head full of murder and suicide. "I suppose it's hard to know how a person might have behaved towards the children in her care all those years ago. It has been suggested to me that Phyllis Baines singled out Primrose. The children certainly put some ugly rumours out about her."

"Who said that?"

"Archie Wilcox. And Stevie, independently. It didn't ring true, to be honest." Gabriel could not find the right words so just let the thought tumble out. "Yet, to remain in the village all these years, knowing that family members were searching for a missing child and letting them keep searching, letting them hope, when one knew the child was dead . . . it strikes me as an unimaginable act of cruelty."

The car rumbled to a halt, but Gabriel showed no sign of getting out. Applegate turned to him. "Is it your belief that Phyllis Baines knew the identity of Primrose Harding's killer?" asked the inspector warily. "Even if Primrose was never able to tell her teacher who was frightening her?"

Gabriel shook his head, ignoring the sight of Applegate taking his cigarette case out of his pocket. It was never a good sign, and Gabriel felt the need to give Applegate some sort of answer before he could leave the car. "If she knew where Primrose was buried, it does not necessarily follow that she knew who put her there. But she was an intelligent woman. She must have had some suspicions."

"What about her claim that the brother did it?"

"Does that sound plausible to you?" asked Gabriel, looking directly at Applegate, who had begun tamping a cigarette against the silver case with military precision. "Dennis Harding comes home for a week's leave, gets his little sister a dolly he has brought all the way from France for her, murders her, buries her, then pushes off back to the Front?"

"Fair enough."

"If Phyllis Baines had told me she had no idea who had killed Primrose Harding, it would be perfectly reasonable, and I would never have suspected that she was concealing anything. But giving me the name of a conveniently dead man suggests to me that she knew perfectly well who killed Primrose. She may not have allowed Primrose to talk to her—she may not even have witnessed the murder—but in the days and weeks that followed the disappearance, Phyllis Baines would have had plenty of time to consider who might be responsible. And if she stumbled upon the burial ground, I can't help thinking that she must have been looking for clues."

"I don't think she simply stumbled upon that burial place, Father," Applegate responded. "The police were crawling all over the area. If it had been easy for anyone to discover, they would have found it. If Phyllis Baines knew where Primrose was buried, she saw her being buried. That's my guess."

If I can find out why Phyllis concealed that crime, I will know who did it, thought Gabriel as he climbed the stairs in search of Joseph. He was sure Phyllis Baines had not concealed her findings out of malice. Unless there was bad blood he knew nothing about—and he suspected that Florence Harding would have been generous in her condemnation if there had been any trouble there—then Phyllis Baines must have had a compelling reason to keep the information quiet. The only reason Gabriel could think of was that Phyllis cared enough about the killer that she could not bear to see him hang. *But Phyllis Baines had never been intimate with anyone!*

She was not the kind of woman who ever was! The brick wall of thirty years appeared before Gabriel again. He had never known the Phyllis Baines of yesteryear. He had never known any of them.

IO

"Dead?" echoed Joseph, looking up from the letter he had been composing. "Miss Baines?"

"I'm afraid so, Joseph," said Gabriel gently. "I have just returned from the hospital. She took her own life."

Joseph made to stand up, but Gabriel gestured for him to remain seated. Joseph's face had already turned the colour of the plaster wall behind him, and Gabriel worried that he would fall if he rose too quickly. "Suicide? Miss Baines? She'd never do that! She's not the type!"

Gabriel folded his arms, leaning awkwardly against the closed door. These monastic cells were perfectly comfortable, but they were for resting, studying, and praying, not for conversation. "I'm not sure there is a type, Joseph. If we knew who among us would do such a terrible thing, we would try to prevent them. But then, I never really knew the lady, and you did."

Was it Gabriel's imagination, or did Joseph's jaw tighten just a little? "I hardly knew her! She was a grown-up, Father, and she was a schoolmistress! One hardly gets to know one's teacher as a child; they all look the same after a while. Grumpy, bitter, old, ugly." He appeared to register the anger in his own voice and drew in a deep breath. "Sorry, that's not very charitable under the circumstances, but you know what I mean. We probably all looked the same to her. Dirty little ragamuffins she was forced to try to civilise."

"What was she like as a teacher then?" Gabriel persisted. "I take it she taught you?"

Joseph shrugged. "I suppose she was no better and no worse than any other country schoolmistress. She taught us to spell, to do our sums. She made sure our hands were clean, our hair was combed. I don't suppose this helps very much, does it?"

Gabriel smiled, wondering what he himself would have found to say about his own schoolmasters if he had ever been asked. "Would you say she took an interest in you? Any of you, I mean."

Joseph got up abruptly and moved towards the door, causing Gabriel to step aside instinctively. Colour had returned to his face, but his movements still bore the clumsiness of shock. "I need some air," he declared, opening the door on the second attempt. "I'd like to remind myself I'm not in the schoolroom anymore. Loathed the place if I'm honest."

"Was she unkind to you?"

Joseph threw up his arms with unnecessary theatricality before shutting the door with a sharp thud. "She was a schoolmistress! No one liked her, but I don't think anyone hated her either. If she rapped our knuckles, we were cross and sullen for a bit, I suppose. If she gave us gold stars, she went up in our estimation. But no, of course she wasn't interested in us. Why should she have been?"

"What if I were to tell you that I think Miss Baines took her own life because she felt responsible for what happened to Primrose?"

Joseph did not miss a beat, but with his head turned away,

Gabriel could not tell if Joseph had been taken by surprise. "That's ridiculous! What could she possibly have had to do with Primrose's death? Primrose was just a number to her. She was just the child at the second desk from the right, on the first row of her classroom." Joseph's hand drifted back to the door handle, but he hesitated to make a break for it. "Don't you understand, Father?" said Joseph, in a mercifully quieter voice. "Miss Baines could not possibly have had anything to do with Primrose's death precisely because Primrose meant nothing to her. Whoever killed Primrose knew her well, well enough at least either to lure her to that desolate place or to know she would be there."

Gabriel knew he was taking a terrible risk, but he had already gone too far in what he had told Joseph, and he needed to be certain that his suspicions about Joseph were true. "Before she died, Miss Baines said that she knew where Primrose was. Would it surprise you to know that Miss Baines has always known where Primrose was buried?"

Joseph turned slowly to look at Gabriel, his hands shaking unmistakably. "That's impossible," whispered Joseph, squeezing his hands into fists until his knuckles were white and bulging under the skin. "If she had known, she would have told someone. At the very least, she would have tried to stop me digging up that land. She was one of the only villagers I can think of who has expressed no opinion about my work. If she had known that Primrose's skeleton was down there, why would she have allowed me to find it?"

And therein lay the rub. There was simply no reason why a woman who had kept such a terrible secret for years would have stood back and let it be revealed without lifting a finger to stop Joseph. None of this made any sense. Phyllis Baines' suicide made no sense; Joseph's obvious fear made no sense. And Joseph was afraid.

"Well?" asked Joseph.

Gabriel looked at Joseph and realised he was awaiting an answer, but Gabriel could not think of the right thing to say; as always, his mind was too busy scrambling its way out of the rabbit hole it had fallen down to come up with a sensible answer to a perfectly sensible set of questions. "Stevie wanted you to come to tea tomorrow afternoon," he blurted out. "I . . . I went to see him about your car."

Joseph looked at Gabriel in astonishment, throwing open the door as though he half expected to find Stevie Wilcox eavesdropping at the keyhole. "I beg your pardon?"

"I'm so sorry, I forgot all about it in all the confusion. I went to ask him about the damage to your car, and he said he didn't do it." Gabriel ignored Joseph's incredulous snort. "He said he didn't think you were a child killer really; he just didn't want you to build your ugly houses all over the village."

"Now look here—"

"So, he said to come for tea, and maybe you can talk things over."

Joseph clutched his head, but Gabriel was quite used to seeing people do that in response to his comments. He had not been granted the gift of the easy conversationalist. "He wants me to go to his farm and patch up our feud over a nice cup of tea?" Joseph asked.

"That was my impression. If you go, I would take someone with you, just in case."

Joseph turned his back and made his way down the corridor. "I do not need a minder, Father. It's not quite that bad."

"But for your own peace of mind . . ."

Joseph waited for Gabriel to follow. "It's a trap, of course, but I can look after myself. If I don't go, I become a coward. Worse, he'll go around the village saying that he gave me every possible opportunity to sort out this dreadful situation and I snubbed him. So I have to go."

"You know, Brother Gerard—"

"I'll be watching his every move, I assure you. I know the way that type behaves. If you shake their hands, you have to count your fingers afterwards."

"Do you want me to tell them you accept the invitation?" asked Gabriel. He could hear a bell chiming and knew he had to get to chapel. "It will have to be after prayers. I can—"

"Go and be frightfully holy; I shall walk over to Stevie's farm myself," said Joseph, with the first sincere smile Gabriel had seen on his face since this whole business began. "I'll pop a note through his letterbox."

Note . . . Suicide note. So, *that* was what had been troubling Gabriel.

"What are you looking at me like that for?"

"I've made such a stupid mistake!" came Gabriel's anguished cry. "In all the confusion, I didn't check . . ." But the words would not come out in the correct order, and Gabriel fled in the direction of the telephone. He had to tell Applegate his suspicions; if he could speak to Applegate, he might be able to rescue the situation.

Gabriel could already see the other monks processing into the chapel, and he froze, paralysed by an all-too-common quandary. If he could put a call through to Applegate now, he would be late for chapel; but if he waited until afterwards, it might be too late for Applegate to act. Gabriel made an unholy dash in the direction of the telephone, his only sense of relief being that no one else would be using it at such a moment.

Not that there was often a member of the community to be found chatting away on the telephone. The device was there purely for emergencies, and even with Gabriel having taken up residence again at the abbey, there were mercifully few of those. Gabriel slipped into the glorified cupboard in which the telephone receiver was installed and waited for the operator to put him through to the constabulary. It was Police Constable Stevens who answered.

"I need to speak to the inspector!"

"Oh, it's you, Father," came the soft, lilting voice of Stevens. "He's not here. Can I take a message?"

"It's urgent, Stevens. Do you know where he is?" Gabriel did not wait for a response. "I need him to go to the house of Phyllis Baines. He should post a constable there."

"Father, why? It was a suicide. There's no suggestion—"

"Because there should have been a note! We were all so busy trying to save the poor woman, nobody looked for a note!"

Gabriel hung up the phone and pressed his head against the oak-panelled wall, weighing up in his mind the best course of action. He could slip into chapel, knowing he had done his duty, and be only a couple of minutes late. If Applegate were not nearby, however, it could be hours before he received Gabriel's message. Gabriel would have preferred to ask for Gerard to take him to the house in the car, but Gerard was safely ensconced in the chapel by now, no doubt chanting slightly off-key as always.

178

The madness of the situation struck Gabriel, and not for the first time. As he hurried on foot through the fields in the direction of the village, Gabriel was reminded that monks were monks, and policemen were policemen. It was all right for Applegate. He could come and go as he pleased, whenever he pleased. Not that this freedom of movement had helped Scotland Yard catch Jack the Ripper, thought Gabriel, feeling immediately guilty for even thinking such a thing. The very name Jack the Ripper made any honest policeman wince, and the case was said to have done permanent damage to public trust in the police force. It had been an unsavoury reminder that horrific murders went unsolved all the time, and worse, that there were killers walking the streets who would never be identified and brought to justice.

Gabriel groaned much louder than he had intended, quickly looking around to check that no one had heard him. He was approaching the high street now, and there were a few people about, mostly women with young children, but no one had noticed Gabriel's noisy presence. He walked past Joseph's former place of residence, the broken window clumsily boarded up with a piece of chipboard. It might be some time before a glazier could be found to fix the damage.

Murderers on the loose. Giovanna's killer, Nicoletta's killer—or killers; Gabriel did not even know whether there had been more than one man responsible. He thought about his late wife and child all the time, but Gabriel seldom allowed his mind to wander to the unbearable thought that somewhere in this world, on the streets of London, perhaps far away from the country now, the murderer of a woman and a child walked freely, enjoying the life he had denied two innocent people. That was the true horror of Primrose's murder. Even if the police managed to find the killer now, that person had lived contentedly for the best part of thirty years without ever having to account for his crime. Whilst a young child lay dead and a family was devastated, a killer went about his business as though nothing had happened. That was the galling thing about any missing persons case. Not the lack of answers—because someone somewhere had the answers—but the lack of justice.

When Phyllis Baines' house came into view, there was nothing to suggest that anything was amiss. The front door was locked, but it was no difficult business for Gabriel to go down the side passage and into the back garden to force open the back door. Strangely, Gabriel had never had any qualms about breaking and entering; now he felt the added confidence of working under what was almost police authority. Applegate had not specifically told him he could enter Miss Baines' property, but Gabriel doubted he would have him arrested for it. In any case, it looked as though someone else had beaten him to it, as Gabriel had feared.

Under normal circumstances, Gabriel might not have noticed the hint of smoke in the air as he entered the kitchen—at this time of year many households that could afford to would have at least one fire burning—but coming from this lonely home, it made Gabriel's skin crawl. Starting a fire to cover up a crime . . . he knew about that tactic. Gabriel pulled himself together and hurried in the direction of the smell, whispering the prayer to Saint Michael as he raced up the stairs. There was no chance the house could be on fire, the odour was so slight, but someone had lit a fire very recently and it might still be burning, might still threaten to engulf a cottage full of wooden furniture and oak beams.

Gabriel hesitated in the doorway to the dead woman's bedroom, aware of a sense of sacrilege. The blood-soaked bedclothes were not yet dry, and the smell of burnt paper was almost smothered by the metallic stench of blood. He crossed himself mechanically. Gabriel's eyes were drawn to the fireplace which took up much of the opposite wall. The remains of a stack of paper sat disconsolately in the grate, the charred mess still smouldering. Gabriel knew immediately that he would never salvage what he was looking for, but he fell to his knees and swiped at what was left of the paper, burning his fingers in the process.

You imbecile! Gabriel raged, clutching his hands together, but he had a more pressing problem. There was someone in the house. Gabriel could hear the sound of footsteps ascending the stairs, crossing the landing outside, and there was no way he could conceal his presence in the room. His eyes moved towards the window, but even Gabriel was not mad enough to think he could make his escape out of an upstairs window without either being noticed or breaking his neck.

Gabriel hauled himself to his feet, still pressing his singed hands together. Another creaking step, and a male figure walked through the door. It was Inspector Applegate. "Oh thank God it's you!" exclaimed Gabriel, sitting back down on the hearth rug. He let a ripple of relief wash over him. "I thought I was in trouble for a moment."

"You are, technically," Applegate retorted, folding his arms. "You had absolutely no business breaking into a private property. Got a warrant, have you?"

"I haven't broken anything," Gabriel promised, in the manner of a schoolboy trying to convince his teacher that he has not eaten the apple he was caught stealing from the orchard. "You got my message then?"

"I arrived back at the station shortly after your mysterious call to Stevens. He was most keen to find out what was going on. I've left him guarding the front door."

"Could you help me with this, Inspector?" asked Gabriel, pointing to the papers in the grate. "I doubt there's much left to salvage, but it came to me when I was talking to Joseph Beaumont. There should have been a suicide note."

"There's no question about the cause of death, if that's what you're thinking," said Applegate, crouching down near the grate next to Gabriel. "Let's not make the situation any more complicated than it is."

"No, no, I know the poor lady took her own life—God have mercy on her soul—but she would have left a note." He paused as Applegate placed a gloved hand into the grate and retrieved the charred shreds of paper. "And she did leave a note. She never meant to take the secret to the grave with her, but someone else has got here first."

Applegate got up and laid out the salvaged bits of paper on the immaculately tidy walnut desk near the window. Whoever had tried to destroy the suicide note had destroyed a great deal more: even though brown and fire-damaged, with only a few words and fragments of words still visible, Gabriel could clearly see that some of the scraps were the remains of older letters, written on paper of various qualities.

Whilst Applegate returned to the grate to see what else could be salvaged, Gabriel squinted at the papers, but there was little worth reading. He was sure Phyllis had written a suicide note—most people did, and Phyllis Baines had been the sort of woman who would have wanted to put her affairs in order before leaving this world—but Gabriel could find little evidence of it now. He read the words "helped her", which might be a reference to Phyllis' failure to help Primrose, though it could potentially refer to anyone with whom Phyllis had had dealings over the years. The only other intelligible line among the fragments read: "Love as you loved once."

"Look at this!" came a voice from near the grate. Gabriel looked at Applegate, who was blowing the ash off a small square about the size of the palm of his hand. A large fragment compared with the others. "Someone really has gone to town trying to burn the evidence. Does this face look familiar to you?"

Applegate turned the remains of the photograph towards Gabriel for his inspection. Gabriel sucked in a breath between his teeth, trying desperately not to reveal his own sense of shock to the inspector. Applegate was holding a corner of what must have been a much larger photograph containing an entire family or a group of friends and associates, but the only figure still visible was a little boy aged no more than ten in the stiff, lace-trimmed collar so beloved of late Victorian parents. Gabriel had never known the man as a young child, but that sullen little face was quite obviously a young Joseph Beaumont. "I don't understand," Gabriel began. "Why would Miss Baines have a photograph of Joseph Beaumont as a child? I suppose, it might have been a school photograph. Something taken at the beginning of the year, perhaps?"

"I think we'd better talk to your Mr Beaumont," said Applegate testily. "It seems to me he has not been entirely honest with us."

"Whatever he's done, he couldn't possibly have burnt these things," said Gabriel, but Applegate had already slipped the fragment into his pocket and turned to leave the room. "He was with me when I first got the idea that someone would try to destroy the suicide note. How could he possibly have had time to get here and light a fire before I arrived?"

"You walked here, I presume?" asked Applegate over his shoulder as he tramped downstairs. "And Mr Beaumont owns a car, does he not?"

"Well, yes, but the windscreen's been smashed. He could not possibly drive it in that condition."

"Have you seen the smashed windscreen?"

Gabriel faltered, grateful for the moment's respite as Applegate issued Stevens with instructions not to leave the door of the house. He watched Applegate step out into the street, struggling to see through his own confusion as he followed him outside. "I haven't seen it. I suppose it's possible he could have driven here, but it seems a little farfetched. Oughtn't we to try and find out the provenance of that photograph before we jump to any conclusions? It's obviously very old."

"Well, yes," answered Applegate, as though conceding a point to a poor player. "Is Mr Beaumont at the abbey now, as far as you are aware?"

"Yes, he is. No, sorry, he was going to the Wilcox farm with a note."

They reached Applegate's car and got inside. "Wrapped round a brick, is it?" asked Applegate.

"Inspector, that's not fair. Whatever Joseph Beaumont has or has not done, he has had bricks thrown at him, not the other way round."

"We'd better get to the Wilcox farm then," said Applegate, starting the car and pulling away in one deft movement. "If it's all the same to you, Father, I'll drop you back at the abbey first. I think it would be better if you're not involved with this."

"Don't you trust me?"

"Not even as far as I could throw a grand piano," answered Applegate, slamming his foot on the accelerator. The car screeched down the road, narrowly missing a roving cat as they went. "Don't take this the wrong way, Father, but when you decide a man is innocent, you can't see the wood for the trees."

Gabriel sat back in his seat, avoiding the temptation to sulk. He could have added that, as far as he could remember, he had never been wrong in his assumptions of innocence, but he could not think of a way to say it which would not sound prideful. He offered it up instead, trying to think whether there was any way he could warn Joseph that the long arm of the law was reaching out to him. "It might be easier if I accompany you," Gabriel said. "Joseph Beaumont trusts me. He has a bit of a suspicion of the police. Don't take it personally or anything."

"Your kind usually do have a suspicion of the police," Applegate retorted. "The feeling's mutual, if it helps. Don't take it personally or anything."

"Touché!"

"Cheer up, Father. I shan't have you charged with breaking and entering. Let's call it quits."

Gabriel managed a weak smile. This was Applegate's way of hammering home an unwelcome point to Gabriel. He was happy to involve Gabriel in his investigations if it was convenient to him, but it was his investigation, and Gabriel was now surplus to requirements.

Gabriel asked Applegate to drop him off at the edge of the grounds so that he could walk quietly back to the abbey. He wanted to gather his thoughts, but most of all he wanted to arrive at the abbey as unobtrusively as possible. He had to make sense out of the latest findings. He had not expected to find a photograph in the grate, and Joseph's face was the last one he had expected to find peering at him from across the years.

Oh Phyllis, why did you kill yourself? But it was easy enough to lament the silence of the dead. Joseph had a voice; he had always had a voice, and he had chosen to conceal the truth from everyone. Gabriel stopped at his favourite vantage point and turned back to look at the village. The abbey was not on such high ground as to be burdensome to reach on foot, but the incline between the village and the abbey was just enough to afford an unimpeded view of the little settlement. From this distance, the village appeared reassuringly peaceful, all the more so because twilight was falling all around Gabriel. It was what Giovanna had called the golden hour, the in-between time when the stresses of the day begin to slip away and darkness has not yet fallen.

Twilight. It was much later than Gabriel had realised. So much had happened during the day, so much drama that the hours had ebbed away, and Gabriel realised that the distant chiming he could hear was the evening Angelus bell. There was no point in rushing to get to the chapel. From where he was standing, it would take him between ten and fifteen minutes to get there, by which time it would be too late. He wondered whether he had inadvertently misled Applegate as to Joseph's whereabouts. If Joseph had any sense, he would be safely back in the abbey by now. It was still light enough, but even a man very familiar with the lie of the land could become confused, walking across country as darkness fell. And Joseph ought not to be out alone even in daylight.

I I

The monks were filing into the refectory by the time Gabriel reached the abbey. Not for the first time, Gabriel found himself tagging onto the end of the line, hoping nobody had noticed his absence, which they all had. He was walking next to Father Dominic, whose limp forced him to move at a leisurely pace however fraught the situation. "Where's Joseph?" whispered Gabriel out of the side of his mouth. "Our guest. Where is he?"

"He went on a social call earlier. Asked me for a jar of honey."

"He hasn't returned?"

"He's a grown man," Dominic whispered back at him. "I'm sure he can find his own way back."

There was a sharp shushing sound behind them, and Gabriel offered up a prayer that wherever Joseph was, he would not come to grief . . . or cause any. It was hardly a surprise that Joseph had kept important information to himself. Now that Gabriel considered the matter, he had to be honest with himself that he had kept plenty of information away from the police after his own tragedy. Not through guilt or even stubbornness, but because of an irrational fear that his life was no longer his own. Police investigations were notoriously and necessarily intrusive; personal belongings were rifled through, movements and alibis analysed for possible inconsistencies. The intimate nature of the questions he had been asked had appalled Gabriel, and he had felt the desperate need to resist the constant incursions into his privacy, as if this were the only power he retained.

Was it the same for Joseph? Whatever his connection with Phyllis Baines, did he feel some primordial need to be left alone, even by those who might be trying to help him? Gabriel took the bowl of leek and potato soup he was handed, feeling his appetite disappearing at the sight of the unappealing beige liquid. Mechanically, he took his place at the table. The thought crossed his mind that Joseph might not have known about the photograph. Without the rest of the picture to give a context, it could mean anything. It was only the fact that some one had tried to burn the thing that gave it any significance.

The monk sitting opposite Gabriel gave him a light kick under the table, causing him to sit up sharply. All around him there were empty bowls, and Gabriel had hardly touched his food. He was half tempted to plead illness, but Dominic the infirmarian would see through that ruse immediately. Waste was frowned upon in these times of austerity. It was not so long ago that throwing away food had been a custodial offence.

"Are you all right?" mouthed Gerard, looking across the table at Gabriel in concern. The monks were forbidden from speaking during supper, and Gabriel had got his friend into enough hot water with his antics over the years. As hastily as he could without losing his manners, Gabriel ate the soup and bread, putting down his spoon a moment before the monks rose for the words of thanksgiving. He had barely tasted a thing, but at least it was recreation hour now and he could go in search of Joseph. If the photograph were innocent, he would find out soon enough.

"He went out on a social call hours ago," said Dominic when Gabriel cornered him in the infirmary. "He asked if he might have a jar of honey to take as a peace offering. I gather he was off to see a chap who was giving him some trouble over his houses."

"And he's not returned?"

"Not yet, but he said he would be back before the gates were locked for the night."

Gabriel looked up at the infirmary clock. A brisk walk to a neighbouring farm to accept an invitation and deliver a gift would not take a fit man more than half an hour on the outside; even a citified individual like Joseph who would be slowed down by the obstacles of mud, wheel ruts, and tall grass, would not need much longer. "I need to put a call through to the inspector," said Gabriel, backing towards the door. "He was going to go after him. He should have met with Joseph by now."

Dominic looked quizzically at Gabriel. "I'm sure the inspector would have told you if there was a problem. Why don't you go and relax for a while? They're having cocoa in the common room."

Gabriel shook his head reluctantly and stepped out into the draughty corridor. On any other evening, he would have liked nothing more than to sit in the common room with the rest of the community, enjoying a hot drink and some friendly conversation before night prayers. This evening, he could not think of anything more likely to drive him out of his tiny mind than old Brother Aiden talking at him in a steady monotone about the state of the primroses.

He hurried back to the telephone, praying that Applegate would still be in his office. "There you are!" came Applegate's exasperated voice from the other end of the line. "I've been trying to get a message to you for the past hour."

"Is Joseph all right?" demanded Gabriel, not registering the tone of accusation. "He's not returned to the abbey."

"That's because he's enjoying His Majesty's hospitality," answered Applegate.

"Sorry, what?"

"He's nicked, Father. On suspicion of attempted murder."

Gabriel could taste his ration of leek and potato soup as it emerged at the back of his throat. He leant back against the wall, stifling the urge to make any response. He heard Applegate at the end of the line, asking whether he was still there. "I'm here," said Gabriel quietly after what felt like an age. "What are you talking about?"

"I mean that I arrived at the Wilcox farm to find the younger Wilcox writhing in agony. He is now at the hospital with a severe case of poisoning, and Mr Beaumont is in custody."

"But Joseph wouldn't do anything that stupid!" Gabriel protested. "Stevie and Joseph are old enemies. Who on earth would go to a man's house and poison him, knowing he would be implicated immediately?"

"A man who's so angry he can't think straight," answered Applegate dispassionately. "Our Mr Beaumont has had nothing but trouble from the Wilcoxes ever since he arrived—

car vandalised twice, brick through his window. I suppose he couldn't take it anymore."

"But . . . but poisoning isn't the act of a man at the end of his tether; it's—"

"Look, this is all very interesting," Applegate put in, and Gabriel knew, with a sinking heart, that the conversation was over. "But I do have one or two other matters to attend to. If you can find any way to get yourself to the constabulary in the morning, you can talk to the man himself. You might get a bit further with him than I have."

"What about Stevie Wilcox? Will he live?"

"Possibly. I'd get praying if I were you."

With that, Applegate put the phone down and the line went dead.

Gabriel had never expected to pass a peaceful night with the words of Inspector Applegate racketing about in his head, but he did not sleep a wink. It was all happening too quickly, a crime that had lain dormant all these long years, through war and the Depression and the road to another, bloodier war, through the declaration of peace, and the slow return to some form of normality. All those years, as the world crashed and burned, Primrose Harding's remains had lain hidden away in a hastily dug grave; and suddenly, within three days of her discovery, a woman was dead, a man seriously ill, and a third under arrest, with the prospect of losing his own life to the hangman if Stevie Wilcox were to die in hospital.

Gabriel had been certain when he had spoken with Phyllis Baines that he was talking to a woman who had taken her own life. It had seemed so obvious from her behaviour and her final mumbled words that her wound was self-inflicted, but she had bitterly regretted the act in those final moments of consciousness. With what had happened to Stevie, Gabriel was thrown into doubt. Could Joseph really have been so idiotic, so reckless as to poison a man? And not just to poison any man, but a man he was known to despise? Gabriel could not say with confidence that Joseph Beaumont was incapable of murder—Gabriel was beginning to think that anyone might be tempted to commit that mortal sin under the right circumstances—but Joseph was no fool. He might be prone to acting impulsively, but poisoning was not an impulsive method. It was not like punching a man in the face or even pulling a knife. Poisoning took effort and time; it took planning. It took a person very different from the man who had killed Primrose Harding. That was a murder Gabriel was becoming convinced had been committed on the spur of the moment, in the heat of anger or depravity.

Gabriel sat up in bed, his head throbbing with pain. The silence of the monastery felt oppressive with his mind in such turmoil, and it unnerved him that he even felt this way. The broken nights were becoming more commonplace, coupled with that sense of being displaced somehow. He never used to feel these pangs of nostalgia for the bustling London street on which he had once lived, for the lamp lights and the constant background noise. He knew he had no business craving the extraneous noise and light of a world to which he ought no longer to belong.

When Gabriel got up and walked to the window, pushing back the heavy curtains, there was nothing to see as always. Not a single light penetrated the stifling, feral darkness. Somewhere out there, beyond the fields and hills, lay the village. In the cottage hospital, Stevie Wilcox fought for his life, his body stricken by a deadly poison. Not far from the hospital, Joseph Beaumont lay in a police cell—frightened? Confused? Racked with guilt, perhaps?

What have you done, Joseph? What did you do on that far-away April day? Gabriel forced himself to return to bed and closed his eyes, willing sleep to come. If Phyllis Baines had known where Primrose Harding was buried, had Joseph always known too? Might it even be the case that the whole village knew what had happened—at the time at least—and had simply chosen to remain silent? It would not be the first time a whole community had turned its back on the police, preferring to let sleeping dogs lie—to let a *child* lie dead—rather than let uniformed strangers dredge up the secrets of every member of the village. If Primrose Harding's killer had been powerful enough, he might have been deemed worthy of the villagers' protection, however heinous his crime.

As Gabriel felt himself drifting off to sleep, an image passed through his head of a little girl swathed in frills and lace, her big sister's Saint Anthony medallion hanging round her neck . . . Then a different child came to mind: younger, smaller, with a dark Madonna-like face, her hair tied in bunches. A little child sleeping peacefully, unaware of the circle of flames surrounding her . . . Gabriel gave in to the torrent of emotion and cried himself to sleep.

Dawn was invading the room by the time Gabriel was awoken by the sound of a bell chiming. His eyes were crusty from a tearful sleep, and Gabriel tasted acid in his mouth, a warning that he would be tired and unsettled all day. In the chill light of the early morning, those tormented nights always seemed so foolish. It would have been much more sensible to get a decent night's sleep so that he could face the day with energy and sharpened wits rather than allow himself to get caught up in a fruitless cycle of questions he could never have answered from his bed.

Easier said than done, Gabriel acknowledged, murmuring the words of his morning prayers as he dressed. Everything seemed more straightforward in daylight, even in the weak, reluctant light of a day barely begun. He walked out into the corridor and moved mechanically towards the chapel. It would be several hours before the village began to stir; Applegate still had at least an hour of snoring to do before his alarm clock clanged in the new day for him, a thought that gave Gabriel some comfort. He could pray with the community, say his Mass, and possibly even eat some breakfast, all before Applegate was anywhere near the constabulary. *Saint Michael the Archangel, defend us on the day of battle . . .*

It helped Gabriel's sensitive conscience that he was able to find Abbot Ambrose after he had said Mass, to tell him what he was up to. "I see," was Ambrose's anticlimactic response to Gabriel's lengthy summary of the previous day's events. "I had heard that our guest had absconded, but I had not understood the reason. Most unfortunate."

"Which is why I need to see him," Gabriel reiterated. "I don't believe for a second he could have done it; it would be too foolish. Like shooting a man in broad daylight."

Ambrose gave a bemused smile. "I suspect there have been plenty of crimes committed in plain sight before—and there will be more in future, no doubt," he said phlegmatically. "Not all killers are criminal masterminds."

"But Joseph Beaumont?" demanded Gabriel, trying to

put out of his mind the image of Joseph flying at Stevie outside Reggie McClusker's shop. "I'd credit him with a little more sense."

Ambrose smiled. "If you say so, my son. You'd better talk to him and draw your own conclusions. After breakfast."

"Well, actually Father Abbot, I thought I should go straightaway. The early bird—"

"Faints with hunger," finished Ambrose, indicating the open door of the refectory. "Break your fast, then go and talk to this Mr Beaumont. It's not as though the poor chap's going anywhere."

Gabriel knew better than to argue with Abbot Ambrose, especially when he was trying to help, and Gabriel knew his superior was right as usual. Gabriel had no appetite—he was far too caught up by the need to talk to Joseph—but he knew that the exertion of walking to the village would bring on a sudden pang of hunger if he did not eat something while he had the chance. Gabriel nodded impatiently and entered the refectory, where tea and porridge beckoned.

"He'll not be happy to see you," said Applegate, with only the slightest twang of mockery in his voice. "Mr Beaumont has been demanding a solicitor since I nicked him last night. He'll be bitterly disappointed when I open his cell door and you're not a man in a pin-striped suit."

"Hope springs eternal," said Gabriel, standing away from the door whilst Applegate unlocked it. "I might be just the man he wanted to see."

"You look like death warmed up, by the way," said Applegate, the smirk broadening. "Five minutes."

"Why, is he going anywhere?"

When Gabriel came out with comments like that, Applegate could never be sure whether he was being intentionally sarcastic or innocently direct, and the uncertainty wrong-footed Applegate every time. "Just get on with it!" he snapped, heaving open the cell door.

Joseph had raised himself to his feet the moment he heard the key rattling in the lock, and he stood before Gabriel like an exhausted soldier who has been left at his post too long. His hair was unkempt, and he had a light fuzz of stubble across his chin. The sight gave Gabriel some perspective on his own troubled night—Joseph looked as though he had not slept at all. "I wondered if you'd come," said Joseph, but his voice was hoarse, and Gabriel wondered whether he had been given anything to eat or drink yet.

"Are they looking after you, Joseph?" asked Gabriel solicitously. He did not imagine that Applegate would ever be intentionally cruel to a man in custody, but it was a small lockup. The cells were more commonly inhabited by drunkards who had made a nuisance of themselves and needed a few hours to sober up.

Joseph sat down heavily on the bed, the rusty frame making a dull creaking sound under his weight. "They gave me some toast and tea first thing," he said dryly. "I was expecting porridge in the nick. Not that I have much appetite at present."

In the absence of a chair, Gabriel leant against the wall in an unconvincing attempt at nonchalance. "Joseph, what happened yesterday? You only went to the farm to accept an invitation."

"I wish I'd pushed a note through the door now," admitted Joseph, pressing his hands together a split second too late. Gabriel noted the mild tremor. "I asked one of the monks for a jar of honey to take as a peace offering—I was going to pay for it, you understand."

Gabriel stared at the floor, fighting a sudden eruption of nervous laughter. Joseph Beaumont was in about as much trouble as he possibly could be. They both knew that he might be facing a charge of attempted murder—and it could easily become a murder charge if Stevie did not recover. Joseph might be heading for a lengthy prison sentence or the gallows, and he was fretting about the nonpayment for a jar of honey Brother Gerard would have given him without a second thought. "I am sure you have an exemplary credit record," said Gabriel. "Now, what happened when you got to the Wilcox farm?"

Joseph shuffled back until his body touched the wall, and for the first time, Gabriel noticed a newspaper that had been separated into its large individual sheets. The crumpled, torn pages were folded inexpertly at the end of the bed, and Gabriel realised that Joseph must have been cold in the night. In the absence of extra blankets, he had opened up the newspaper he had been given to read and covered himself in the pages. Gabriel made a mental note to discuss the matter with Applegate at a later hour. "There's not much to tell, Father. I knocked on the door; old Mr Wilcox opened it and invited me in. It wasn't quite what I had expected, but it would have been rude to walk away, so I went in."

"And Stevie was there too?"

"No, he was out working on the farm. Mr Wilcox said he'd only just come in himself to get the kettle on. Stevie must have arrived about a quarter of an hour later."

"You ate together?" asked Gabriel. He tried to imagine

those uncomfortable minutes before Stevie's arrival, when the two men would have been forced to make small talk together, neither of them entirely sure how to handle the situation.

"Yes, Father. Well, while we were waiting for Stevie's return, Mr Wilcox made a pot of tea and brought out some scones from a tin. That was what we ate."

"Are you sure that was everything? What about jam or cream? Milk for the tea, that sort of thing."

"You know what would have been on the table, Father," muttered Joseph, betraying his nerves for the first time. "A teapot, a milk jug, a plate of scones, a pot of cream, and my honey. Mr Wilcox said we could have the scones with the honey, since I had so kindly brought it to their table."

"How quickly did Stevie become unwell?" Gabriel persisted, "This is important. What did you see him eat?"

Joseph shook his head. "It all happened very quickly." He paused. "Look, he came bursting into the kitchen in a bit of a temper. I don't think he liked his father starting the tea without him. He was quite rude about it, snatching a scone and stuffing it in his mouth whole, you know, just to annoy his father. But it was old Mr Wilcox he was angry with, not me."

Gabriel stood up straight, looking down at Joseph in a manner that would have been intimidating from Inspector Applegate. Joseph merely shuffled sideways to give himself some space. "Joseph, how did old Mr Wilcox react to Stevie? Was he frightened? Angry?"

"Quite alarmed, as it happened. I think he was embarrassed that he was behaving like such a pig. Families like the Wilcoxes are quite particular about the way they behave at table. It was embarrassing. Mr Wilcox was trying to stop Stevie, telling him that was no way to behave, but Stevie just ignored him. He gulped down the scone, scattering crumbs everywhere, and immediately went and took another. He was guzzling down his second cup of tea when he took ill. Father, what on earth are you smiling about? It was horrible!"

Gabriel wiped the smile off his face immediately, but he could not hide his relief. "Did he snatch that scone off your plate, by any chance?"

Joseph looked up at Gabriel sharply, catching his train of thought. "No, he didn't. It was the scone on top of the pile Mr Wilcox was offering me. Stevie took it before I could."

Gabriel nodded and moved towards the door. He was about to knock, to indicate that he wished to be released from the cell, but he drew his hand away and looked steadily at Joseph. "I know you didn't poison Stevie, Joseph, and I want to help you," he said gravely, "but I can't if you will not help yourself. I know you have not told me the truth about your connection with Primrose Harding's death, and I need you to come clean now." Joseph rose to his feet, but Gabriel put out a hand, warning him to sit down again. This was not the moment for a confrontation. "Did you go to Phyllis Baines' house and burn her suicide note, Joseph? Did you burn this?"

Gabriel held up the fragment of the photograph containing Joseph's childhood figure, watching Joseph's face intently as he did so. Joseph stared at the image, his face deathly white, but he was incapable of answering. "Joseph, Phyllis Baines made some claims before she died, but she lost consciousness before she could tell me everything. I suspect that her suicide note would have led me to Primrose Harding's killer, but someone got to her house first."

"I never went anywhere near that house," said Joseph weakly. "I swear. I have no idea who burnt that photograph."

"Are you sure? Please consider the danger you are in."

"I didn't do it!" Joseph tried to shout, but his mouth was dry with panic, and his words came out as a grating rasp. "I didn't touch her things!"

"Joseph, whatever you know about Primrose Harding's disappearance, you really ought to make a clean breast of it now."

But Joseph had slid to the floor, his head curled in his arms as though he expected Gabriel to strike him. "She knew my father! That's all I can tell you. Miss Baines was engaged to a man who was killed during the Boer War. He fought with my father. It gave her a sort of connection with us. My father . . . he always insisted that we make Miss Baines welcome; she became like a member of our family. That picture was taken in our garden years ago."

"You said you barely knew her, that she was just your teacher."

"I . . . I don't know why I lied. I should have known you'd find out."

Gabriel crouched down next to Joseph, but Joseph turned his back on Gabriel, his head still buried. It was absurd: he was behaving like a little boy. "Joseph, Phyllis Baines is dead. There's no need for you to protect her now. Whatever you know about Primrose—"

"I know nothing; I was barely more than a child myself!" Joseph was virtually shrieking. "You know that! I'm not protecting anyone!"

Gabriel stood up wearily and knocked three times at the door, signalling the end of a conversation that was going nowhere. "Perhaps she was protecting you then, Joseph? The dead tell no tales."

Joseph was incapable of speech. Gabriel turned to face the door as it opened and walked out without a backward glance.

12

Gabriel did not stop walking until he had reached the end of the corridor. "He didn't do it," said Gabriel simply as Applegate caught him by the elbow and propelled him into his interview room. "He wasn't the poisoner; he was the intended victim. Stevie ate the food Mr Wilcox had prepared for Joseph."

"Sit down before you come out with anything else," commanded Applegate, indicating a chair. Applegate sat at his desk, slowly removing the silver cigarette case from his breast pocket. Applegate was going through the unnerving routine Gabriel had seen him him use on suspects before, of performing a mundane task—re-arranging papers on his desk, inking his pen, winding his wristwatch—whilst looking intently at the person sitting opposite him. Gabriel returned the glance as Applegate opened the case and offered it to him. Gabriel shook his head. "I'll make a smoker out of you yet," said Applegate, taking a cigarette out of the case for himself. "Well?"

"Am I permitted to ask what Joseph told you yesterday?" asked Gabriel.

"No," said Applegate tersely. "It wouldn't do you any good anyway. All I got out of him was that he didn't poison anyone. Not that what he says matters particularly. The lab will tell me what the poison was and how it was administered. Not wishing to worry you, of course, but your lovely honey is being analysed as we speak."

Gabriel did not flicker. "I am in charge of the monastic honey, and I can assure you that cyanide is not one of my ingredients."

"It wouldn't be," answered Applegate glibly. "If that scone had been laced with cyanide, Stevie would have dropped dead on his own kitchen floor."

"Inspector, I realise how it may look: Joseph asked for a jar of honey so that he would have a convenient conduit for the poison. But he didn't do it. It was clear from what Joseph said to me that Stevie ate food that was intended for Joseph's consumption, making Joseph the intended victim."

"And the poisoner?"

"Archie Wilcox, obviously. There were only three of them round that table. What with Joseph being the intended victim and Stevie turning into the actual victim—"

"The man's an idiot if he decided to settle the score that way."

"Without wishing to be rude about Mr Wilcox . . ."

"Are you telling me to release Joseph Beaumont without charge because he told you he didn't do it?"

"Oh no, I want you to keep him locked up," answered Gabriel. It was yet another of those moments when it was not clear whether Gabriel was being facetious or blithely direct. Gabriel appeared to register Applegate's uncertainty. "It's important that he remain in that cell, Inspector. He has had a brick thrown through the window of his lodgings and his windscreen, and now this alleged attempt. For his own safety, he's better under your watchful eye."

"In that case, I feel obliged to tell him he is in protective custody. If he doesn't want to be kept here, I've no business locking him up without charge."

Gabriel shuffled uncomfortably in his seat. "This is going to sound awfully underhand, but would you mind not telling him you've dropped the charges? It might be easier in the long run."

Applegate sat forward across the desk, forcing Gabriel to move slightly to avoid the risk of the inspector's cigarette burning his hand. "What are you up to?"

"It's not a lie if you do not volunteer the truth," said Gabriel sweetly, but he could not suppress the urge to cough, and this rather spoiled the gravity of the situation.

"You haven't answered my question."

"I'm not up to anything really," said Gabriel. He should have avoided using the word "really", which always sounded suspect, but it was too late now. "It's just that I do need Joseph to sit where he is and consider what he has done."

Gabriel got up to leave, but Applegate was faster and barred his way. "Don't talk to me in riddles! Do you think Joseph Beaumont killed Primrose Harding?"

"I didn't say that." Gabriel hesitated, unsure as to the next move. Between him and the door there was a vast, glowering mountain blocking his way to freedom. It would be useless to try to push past Applegate and probably even more pointless to mention that he was being held against his will. "Inspector, I never said Joseph killed Primrose, but he is lying to me or at least not telling me what he knows. Phyllis Baines knew where Primrose was buried. If she knew that, she may have known who buried her. It set me thinking about how many people might have been involved in covering up Primrose's death—perhaps not in actually killing her, but in covering it up. Joseph was very young, very impressionable. Easy to bully."

Applegate took several steps back to give Gabriel some space. "It's always a possibility in communities like this," Applegate conceded, "but I can't help thinking that someone would have squealed in the intervening years. Thirty years is a very long time for anyone to keep a secret."

"What if someone did squeal, but he squealed to the wrong person?" asked Gabriel. "I think there's a lot more to this than the death of a child at the hands of a pervert. Joseph knows that too; so did Miss Baines. If Joseph isn't going to play ball, we're going to have to find out who else was in on the secret before we're dealing with another disappearance."

Gabriel made for the door, half expecting Applegate to restrain him, but he made it out of the room and had nearly reached the front entrance when Applegate began calling after him. The constable manning the desk was distracted by an old woman waving the remains of a broken flowerpot at him. As he dashed past, Gabriel heard the squeaking voice protesting, " 'It's the brat next door done it! Second time in a week! And I'll swear 'twas him what stole me bicycle!' "

"Mrs Barnes, it's only a broken flowerpot! A cat might've done it!"

The argument gave Gabriel an unspeakable idea. The constable's bicycle was standing loyally against the outer wall of the building, just waiting to be hopped on and ridden away. The constable in question would be busy all day, and if he were called out, Gabriel reassured himself that he would be accompanying Inspector Applegate somewhere in the car.

Whatever happened, Gabriel was quite sure the constable would not want his bicycle, and Gabriel desperately needed to reach a tormented man before Applegate did.

He took hold of the handlebars, jumped aboard, and cycled away before his better judgement—or Applegate—could stop him from stealing a policeman's bicycle in broad daylight under the nose of a senior member of His Majesty's police force. He had done madder things before. Gabriel headed directly out of the village, quickly losing himself on the narrow roads that led round the back of the abbey grounds. Not much farther and he would reach the gated entrances to a cluster of farms that began with the Wilcox property.

Gabriel felt safe on a road such as this. Very few people came this way unless they had business at the farms; anyone heading for the abbey on foot would cut across the fields. He was protected by the dense, tall banks on either side of the path that were thick with Queen Anne's lace, nettles, and dock leaves at this time of year. Gabriel was already wondering how he was going to explain his moment of madness to Applegate later, but he allowed himself to be distracted by the intoxicating odour of vegetation all around him, the peaty, primitive, fertile aromas of uncultivated land a world away from the manicured lawns and angular buildings of the cities the Victorians had planned so meticulously. Overhead, a flock of sparrows were in full flight, ready to find safe places to build their nests and raise their young, now that the winter frosts were over and they were back from their southern migrations.

How could a village as beautiful as this have become a child's grave? When Primrose Harding had been killed, the most brutal and bloody war was being fought just across the water in Flanders. Men were being shot, gassed, blown to pieces by the tens of thousands . . . but this was no battlefield. A tiny village had not even held the dangers of the cities, whose armaments factories always threatened to explode without warning; nor had it suffered the pressures of the coastal towns, which had become targets of German U-boats and Zeppelins. Primrose Harding should have been safe here. But every child ought to be safe, and Gabriel knew better than most that the adult world failed to protect children all the time.

There was no sign of old Mr Wilcox when Gabriel came to the gate. Instead, a farmhand stomped over, indicating the house before walking away in sullen silence. Gabriel had not expected a warm welcome, but in the absence of Stevie, the farm felt more desolate than ever. He tried not to think what would happen if Stevie failed to recover, or if he were too debilitated by the poisoning attack to be of much help on the farm again.

Gabriel could see Archie Wilcox through the kitchen window, sitting at the table drinking from an enamel mug. He looked listless and tired, but Gabriel calculated that the man must be nearly eighty, ill-equipped to deal with the guilt of his son's sudden danger. Gabriel was not sure whether Applegate thought it plausible that Archie had accidentally poisoned his own son, but it could be only a matter of time before events caught up with the old farmer. Gabriel braced himself for a hostile response and knocked at the door.

Archie was unnaturally startled by the noise and scrambled to his feet, looking anxiously out the window to see who was disturbing him. Gabriel knew that he must be expecting a policeman to turn up, probably not to arrest him but to be the bearer of bad news, and he relaxed immediately at the sight of Gabriel's black-clad figure. Whatever Gabriel was, in Archie Wilcox's eyes he was harmless. "I'm so sorry, Mr Wilcox," Gabriel began, then realised how ominous he sounded. "I'm sorry to hear Stevie is in hospital. I just thought I'd pop round to see how you're bearing up."

Archie gave a weak smile. "Last thing I heard, they said he would recover but he could be laid up for weeks. It's a nasty business, that's for sure. Have they arrested Joseph yet?"

Gabriel sidestepped the question. "If you wanted to go to the hospital to see Stevie, I could always—"

"I'm not going to no hospital," said Archie forcefully. "If I had my way, he'd be home by now. Doctors these days can't keep their noses out, always wanting to interfere. Soon as they done pumping out his stomach, they should've let him home."

Gabriel understood the hostility. He doubted Archie Wilcox had ever been visited by a doctor in his entire life and had certainly never been a patient in a hospital. He was from a generation of men too proud and too confident of their own physical strength ever to seek medical help—too poor to afford doctors and medicines, if truth be told, but money was one of many forbidden topics of conversation in these parts. "Would you like me to take anything to Stevie?"

Archie shook his head. "He'll be home soon enough. If the doctors won't let him out, he'll up and leave." Archie pointed at a framed photograph standing in pride of place on the mantelpiece. It depicted an attractive young woman, radiant in her best clothes, with spring flowers woven into her hair—Archie's wife on her wedding day. "That dear lassie were stronger than she looked. Brought all her babes into the world with just her ma for company. When her time came, she curled up under a tree and slipped away. Never made no trouble for nobody."

Gabriel smiled, taking time to admire the photograph so that he did not have to say anything. Gabriel had no doubt at all that Archie's late wife had made no trouble, but he wondered how many of her babies might have survived infancy if she had had access to a skilled midwife. Gabriel wondered, too, whether she might have enjoyed a good old age if the warning signs of the illness that had struck her down had been noted and treated early enough—stroke, heart attack, it was probably not even recorded. Gabriel was sure that Archie had loved his wife, but it was a tough, dispassionate love, rather like the love the old man felt for his son.

"How old was she when she died?" asked Gabriel, looking intently at the necklace around the young bride's neck. As was the custom in this part of the world, the young woman was very simply adorned. Her ears had probably never been pierced, and she wore no bracelets or rings, just that one simple necklace Gabriel recognised immediately.

"She were just thirty-seven years old when she slipped away," said Archie. "But they don't make old bones in her family, poor girl." Archie touched the frame of the photograph as though it were an icon, a gesture Gabriel suspected Archie carried out every time he walked past. Whatever sort of a union it had been, it had been a close one. Archie could easily have married again but had preferred widowhood to taking up with another woman. "They'll be putting Joseph on trial before long, I'll warrant."

Gabriel floundered for a moment, his thoughts still on Archie's doomed bride. "I suppose . . ." He was desperate to avoid a deliberate lie. "These things take time."

"Don't see why it should. In my grandfather's day, they would have hanged him from the nearest tree, and no one would have thought twice about it."

Gabriel shuddered. He doubted that that sort of rough justice had happened nearly so often as the older members of the village liked to imagine, but a place like this had already proven to be dangerous for a man like Joseph—the unpopular outsider stirring up the village with his plans, a convenient scapegoat for a sleeping murder, and now a suspected poisoner. He might not have to face a baying crowd with torches and pitchforks, but someone was out to get him, and even the abbey was not safe enough for him now.

In the end, Archie gave Gabriel a thermos of soup to take to Stevie, as he could not be sure the poor lad was being fed properly. As Gabriel took his leave and cycled back towards the village, he thought that the only person who was going to go anywhere near this soup was a laboratory technician. Whether or not Applegate believed Gabriel's assertion that Joseph had been the intended victim, it was unlikely that any food from outside the hospital would be allowed anywhere near Stevie.

"You do realise I could have you arrested for that?" blustered Applegate when Gabriel arrived back at the constabulary with the soup and the constable's bicycle. "Theft of police property is a very serious matter; in case you really didn't know that."

"I didn't steal it; I borrowed it," protested Gabriel, putting the thermos on the desk like a libation. "I brought it back, and it's in perfect condition."

"I'd like to see you try that line when you're up before the beak."

Gabriel had never been arraigned before the magistrate before, and the sudden, horrible picture presented itself to him. He was standing in the courtroom with Abbot Ambrose, Inspector Applegate, and a gallery full of reporters, confessing to the unlawful borrowing of a bobby's bicycle. He sidestepped the subject as usual. "That soup is for Stevie from his father," said Gabriel, pointing at the thermos. "Almost as soon as I'd agreed to take it to the hospital, I realised he would never be allowed food from outside until it's been determined who poisoned him."

"Leave it with me," said Applegate gruffly, snatching up the thermos and carrying it away with him, no doubt to ensure that no one took a sneaky sip and inadvertently topped himself. "I'm prepared to admit that your idea about Joseph being the man Archie meant to poison sounds credible. I'm going to bring Archie Wilcox in for questioning."

Gabriel waited until Applegate was safely out of sight before making his way to Joseph's cell. He knocked softly before pushing back the metal flap covering the grate. "Joseph, it's me," whispered Gabriel, peering through into the room. He could make out the figure of Joseph getting up and moving towards him. "Joseph, I don't have very long, but I have to ask you this once again." Gabriel swallowed, praying that this whole sorry journey might be coming to an end. "Will you please tell me what you know about Primrose Harding's death? If you're afraid of the consequences, you needn't be. You were a juvenile at the time; you are not going to hang."

There was a cripplingly long silence. Gabriel could hear the long, laboured breathing of a man in a state of uncontrolled distress. "For pity's sake, Father!" came a voice that was almost a whimper. "Why would I start digging up that grave if I had put her there?"

"Joseph, you can be straight with me, or you can be straight with Inspector Applegate. You can be straight with one of His Majesty's judges. Time is running out!"

"Just leave me alone!"

"Joseph, there may not be another opportunity for you to tell me what you know. You must—" Gabriel was stopped short by the sound of footsteps directly behind, and he turned round to see Inspector Applegate glaring at him.

"I hope you weren't trying to steal my suspect too?" asked Applegate, reaching past Gabriel to throw down the flap across the grate. The clatter of metal against metal echoed all around them; it must have been maddening inside the enclosed space of the cell. "Haven't you somewhere better to go? On foot."

Gabriel certainly did have somewhere to go, though he would have done anything to avoid entering that soulless old house again. Joseph could have spared him the need to trouble Florence Harding and her mother. They had been given only days to accept the certainty of Primrose's death, and experience told Gabriel that they needed to be left in peace. At the risk of having the door slammed in his face, Gabriel left the constabulary and walked to the Harding family home.

To Gabriel's intense relief, Florence was in the garden when Gabriel reached the front gate. There were several large lavender bushes lining the garden path, and Florence stood over them with a pair of pruning shears the basket at her feet already full of the blooms. With any luck it might be possible to talk to her outside without having to venture into the house at all.

It was cold and overcast, but there was no sign of rain, and Florence was protected from the elements by a long woollen coat with a velvet collar and cuffs. She looked up as soon as the gate squeaked open. "Please forgive the intrusion," said Gabriel hurriedly as Florence straightened up and looked quizzically at him. "I happened to be passing and wondered how you were bearing up."

Florence gave a smile that might have been accompanied by a roll of the eyes if such rudeness had not been beneath her dignity. "Father, I may count on one hand the number of visitors we have received in the past year. My sister's body is found, and suddenly our home has become Piccadilly Circus! You are the first visitor who has at least taken the trouble to apologise for the intrusion."

Gabriel closed the unfriendly gate, with its taut latch poised to take his fingers off. "I'm sure many people are concerned for you, Miss Harding," he said, taking two small steps into the garden. "It was a terrible discovery."

Florence sighed audibly and returned to her pruning. "Why should anyone in this village be concerned for us?" she asked, the tendrils of bitterness already creeping into her voice. "No one cared when Primmie first went missing; no one has cared during the long years that have passed, other than to whisper and gossip. The village forgot about her, but we have had to live with her loss every single day." The pruning shears snapped shut savagely, condemning another purple-adorned stem to the basket.

Gabriel understood the cause of Florence's resentment. When a person died—or in this case, disappeared—there was always a short period of frenetic activity, when everyone in the vicinity seemed to be trying to help in some way. Letters of sympathy would be sent; cakes and biscuits and bunches of flowers would appear on the doorstep; there would be a steady stream of neighbours popping in for tea and conversation. Then, suddenly, it would come to an abrupt stop. Everyone else would get back to their humdrum lives as though nothing were amiss, when the loved ones mourning the loss were condemned to live out the nightmare of grief for weeks, months, and perhaps years after the event. Gabriel doubted that a day passed without Florence and her mother being taken back to that terrible moment during the Great War when Primrose had failed to return home.

"Miss Harding, I hate to ask you this, but—"

"Florence, please," Florence retorted, staring fixedly at the lavender flowers. Gabriel suspected that there were tears in her eyes that were causing her considerable embarrassment; only by focusing on an incidental detail could she be sure of keeping control of herself. "I really don't know what you could possibly need to ask me now. I will survive, and my mother will survive. At least now that Primrose has received a Christian burial, we might be able to find some peace. I'm not sure there's any more to be said on the matter."

"Florence, before Miss Baines died, she voiced a suspicion that your brother may have killed Primrose—accidentally perhaps." Gabriel found himself taking a backward step towards the gate. There was no easy way to tell a woman her brother was suspected of being a murderer, but he definitely had not said it correctly.

"I can't think why she would have made such an accusation," said Florence, and her shock looked convincing to Gabriel. "How could she have known who killed her? It's preposterous!"

"Did your brother know that you were walking out with Stevie?"

Florence's face hardened into a glare. "I was never walking out with Stevie Wilcox. We were scarcely more than children at the time!"

"Then how would you describe your friendship with Stevie?" asked Gabriel. But he could not bring himself to string her along and came to the point. "Florence, that necklace Primrose was wearing when she died was a gift to you from Stevie."

Florence's glare did not flicker. "What if it was? Young men give girls gifts from time to time. It's not a crime, is it?"

"Certainly not a crime, but this was no ordinary gift. Stevie cared for you so deeply that he gave you his dead mother's wedding jewellery."

Florence turned away, not quite quickly enough to prevent Gabriel from seeing the first hint of uncertainty creeping across Florence's face. "I didn't know that! It looked like a cheap little thing to me."

"Are you sure about that?" asked Gabriel, moving towards her, but Florence spun round in a rustle of skirts, causing him to move away again. Her eyes glistened with tears she was now trying desperately to hold back.

"Of course I'm sure, Father!" She was all but pleading. "I would never have accepted it if I'd known its significance! I could never have attached myself to such a man; it was a ludicrous notion!"

"Did it seem ludicrous at the time?" Gabriel noticed Florence looking awkwardly past him towards the road, but there was no one in sight. Gabriel doubted that casual passersby ever came near the house if it could be avoided. In a village, there were always dwellings like that from which people instinctively shied away, either because the house was in disrepair or because the occupants had earned a reputation for being unfriendly. In the case of the Hardings, they had deliberately cultivated a reputation that made other people steer clear of them, but it might still be risky to have a personal conversation in the open air. Against his better instincts, Gabriel said, "Would it be better to go indoors, Florence?"

Gabriel's suggestion caused Florence to revert to type, as though those few moments of evident distress had never happened. "Father, there's nothing to talk about. If Stevie imagined we were courting, then I'm sorry for him. I barely saw the poor boy as a friend, let alone a sweetheart. I suppose I rather enjoyed the *frisson* of a dalliance with a man so far beneath me. But it was only a dalliance. I quickly grew bored, then what with Primrose's disappearance and my brother's death, there was no time for games anymore. I had to pull myself together and look after my mother."

"Florence, I must ask you this. Did you let Stevie know your true feelings? Did you ever tell him you did not care for him, or did you simply—"

"This is going to sound frightfully rude, Father," Florence cut in, picking up her basket in one elaborate movement, "but I really think you might mind your own business. My actions may have been foolish and selfish, but I am quite sure I was not the only young girl to toy with a man's affections. I regret hurting Stevie, if that's what you want me to say, but I fail to see what any of this has to do with my sister's disappearance."

Gabriel opened his mouth to speak, but Florence was making her way purposefully down the garden path to her home, and he knew better than to try to follow. He waited while Florence let herself into the house and closed the door heavily behind her, harbouring a vain hope that she might change her mind and decide to talk to him. It was only as Gabriel was turning to leave that he noticed two faces staring at him from the drawing room window of the house. Old Mrs Harding and her nurse sat in the bay window, watching him intently. Gabriel wondered with a shudder how long they had been watching and what difference it could possibly make to anything. It was unlikely that either of them had overheard any part of the conversation, but at the very least, they knew that Florence had been talking to him and that there had been a disagreement.

She would be all right, Gabriel told himself as he walked in the direction of the constabulary. He ought to update Applegate, find out how he had got on with Archie Wilcox, and perhaps take some food to Joseph to cheer him up. It would not be too much of a detour to go to Reggie's shop and see if he had any biscuits or fruit Gabriel could take with him—perish the thought that he might be able to purchase a bar of chocolate! Gabriel was hoping that Joseph's unfortunate predicament might not last much longer. And not just for his sake.

The conversation with Florence had reminded Gabriel of the vulnerability of the two women. That sad old face peering through the window in mild accusation. It was the face of a woman who had been condemned to grow old while the younger generation had been denied that right. Like so many women of her generation, she had lived out much of her life in mourning, not just for the son killed in dubious duty's cause but also for a daughter who should have lived. For Florence, it had been even worse. She could probably not even remember now what it felt like to live without the shadow of grief all around her—dead father, dead brother, permanently missing sister. During those few moments when Florence had allowed her harsh, steely mask to slip, Gabriel had been made aware of the fragile young woman she had once been, and of the person she might so easily have become if her life had not been engulfed by grief and bitterness when she had barely reached adulthood.

The village shop should have been quite quiet at that time of the day, but when Gabriel entered he noticed that Jimmy the paperboy was sitting on a crate behind the counter, eating a piece of seed cake whilst Reggie plied him with questions. Neither of them looked up when the bell over the door tinkled, and Gabriel was virtually at the counter before Reggie turned to greet him. "Oughtn't you to be at school, Jimmy?" enquired Gabriel, secretly encouraged by the sight of the child eating. If there were spare treats for Jimmy, Reggie would have something to sell him.

"I bunked off school," said Jimmy, giving Gabriel a

charming view of the half-chewed seed cake in his mouth. "It were an emergency!"

"I hope it was worth the punishment you'll get when you slink back to school," commented Gabriel, but his curiosity was getting the better of him as usual. "What's the emergency?"

"He's been telling me all about it," said Reggie, and he at least had the decency to look a little shamefaced. "It looks as though they've found the miscreant who's been threatening our Joseph Beaumont."

Gabriel looked at the conspiratorial pair in astonishment. "But I thought he was in—" He swallowed the rest of the sentence just in time. For all he knew, Applegate might have paid Stevie a visit in the hospital to answer a few questions, even if he was not yet well enough to be placed under arrest. But Gabriel realised almost immediately that Reggie was not talking about Stevie. Safely ensconced in his classroom, Jimmy could not possibly have known whether Stevie had confessed.

"Not he, she," came Jimmy's muffled reply, his mouth still full of food. "*She* done it."

"Jimmy, would you please swallow before you say anything else?" demanded Gabriel. He was secretly squeamish about bad manners and could not bear to see the inner workings of Jimmy's mouth again. "Who is she?"

Jimmy swallowed loud enough for the entire village to hear and looked triumphantly at Gabriel. "You'll never guess who threw them bricks. Susie Austin!"

If Jimmy had hurled a bucket of ice-cold water at Gabriel's head, he could not have been more astonished. "Little Susie Austin? Don't be silly!" Gabriel looked to Reggie for reassurance, but Reggie nodded in confirmation. "But she's only a child!"

"She's a naughty little minx," Reggie retorted. "Always said she were trouble. Headstrong like her mother."

"Mr Austin were cutting up his old newspapers for . . . for, well you know . . . " said Jimmy.

Gabriel laughed to himself at the boy's pained expression as he avoided saying "toilet paper".

"He found holes where she'd cut out the letters," Jimmy added, delighted to be able to share his information again. "Then he remembered she'd cut her hand the other day and had said she done it falling in brambles." Jimmy sprang to his feet and stood, hands on hips, legs apart, mimicking the posture of a forbidding older man. " 'No child of mine will be a liar!' 'No child of mine will be a vandal!' "

"Jimmy, how do you know all this?" demanded Gabriel, directing his gaze at the half-empty shelves behind Reggie's head. He could not risk bursting out laughing, but Jimmy's impression of Susie Austin's dragon of a father was perfect.

"I heard, didn't I?" Jimmy explained, sitting back down on the crate; he looked up expectantly for more food. None was forthcoming. "I were delivering his paper when I heard the row."

Gabriel suspected that Jimmy had heard only a fraction of the information he had related, then used his fertile imagination to fill in the details, but Gabriel would have found such a tale irresistible at that age. "I still don't understand why you felt the need to play truant."

Jimmy blushed, sensing that he was sliding onto thin ice. "Well, you see, I were so busy listening, I didn't notice how late it were getting. Next thing, I see Mr Austin marching

Susie out the door, saying he's going to have her locked up for this."

"So you followed them to the police station?"

Jimmy shook his head. "I tried, but Mr Austin noticed I were following and told me to clear off. I didn't dare go to school so late, so I come here. I'll slip in at break time and say I took sick."

Gabriel shook his head. "You haven't covered yourself in glory this morning, have you, son?" Jimmy looked away. "You jolly well ought to think about what you've done. Eavesdropping on a conversation that was none of your business, then skipping school, and now you're going to lie to get out of a sticky situation. Not your finest hour, is it?"

"I could feed him a spoonful of salt if you like," suggested Reggie cheerfully, "then it won't be a lie when he says he took sick." Reggie turned to Jimmy. "You should get yourself to school, sonny. Whatever happens, it won't be half as bad as what our Susie's facing. I wouldn't fancy being in her shoes."

A thought struck Gabriel. "Jimmy, was Mr Austin really taking Susie to the police? It wasn't just a threat?"

Jimmy shook his head firmly. "Oh no, I'm sure that's where they were heading. It's the sort of thing he would do."

"Thanks." Gabriel made a bolt for the door and hurried down the road.

13

The first sound to greet Gabriel as he dashed into the constabulary was a high-pitched wailing that would not have disgraced the torture chambers of the Tower of London. Gabriel followed the racket to the door of the room Applegate always used when he was in residence, letting himself in without stopping to ponder the etiquette of barging in on such an intense interrogation.

Susie Austin stood before Applegate, bawling her pretty little head off, whilst her father stood behind her, exuding the menace of a Komsomol officer handing over a dissident to the KGB. Susie was so completely commanding the attention of the room that it took a moment for anyone to notice Gabriel's entrance, and when Applegate looked up, he barely registered the presence of an intruder. "Everyone was saying he was a child killer!" shrieked Susie, tears of rage pouring down her face. "Everyone was talking, and nobody was doing anything about it!"

That was the curious thing, thought Gabriel, watching silently as Susie Austin defended herself against the charges brought before her. Whatever fear she must have felt when her father had confronted her that morning, the only emotion she was expressing now was boiling anger. She was typical of the sort of precocious child who listens to the conversations of the adults around her, only to discover that no one is interested in anything she has to say. She was a child who thought deeply about everything and had been given no assistance in making sense of the muddled, confusing, and sometimes terrifying world around her. Susie must have taken seriously every bitter word, every accusation, every piece of malicious village gossip, and had acted on the knowledge in the only way she knew—direct action.

"You'll rot in jail!" shouted Susie's father, silencing her almost immediately. She was angry, not suicidal—Susie knew better than to engage in a shouting match with an adult, especially him. "Do you understand? You'll go to prison! Vandalism is a crime!"

Applegate was just raising a hand for silence when Mr Austin's grim pronouncements were drowned out by an infernal banging of fists on metal. Joseph had heard every word of the row from his cell and was hammering on the door, demanding to be released. "What's that?" gasped Susie, turning towards the door in genuine fear. "What's that noise?"

"Wait here," said Applegate before marching out of the room. The commotion stopped, and they heard the clatter of keys and doors, Applegate telling Joseph firmly to be quiet and a murmured response too quiet to hear from the room.

Then Applegate and a visibly distressed Joseph were entering the room; it was Gabriel's turn to gasp with shock. He thought he had seen Joseph at his lowest ebb already, exhausted, anxious, but nothing could have prepared him for the state Joseph was in as he advanced into the room. His eyes were red and swollen; his face had taken on the blotchy tincture of a man struggling with powerful emotions. Worse, he was shaking violently and making no attempt at controlling the movement.

"Stop shouting at her!" exclaimed Joseph, glaring at Mr Austin over Susie's head. "You're not going to send a child to prison on my account."

Applegate stepped in before Mr Austin could reply. "There is no need to trouble yourself, Mr Beaumont," he said, the picture of diplomacy. "No one's going to prison for this. However, the child must understand that she has done something very serious, and there may be consequences I cannot prevent. If you press charges—"

Joseph let out a strangled cry of frustration. "Why the devil would I press charges against a child? Whatever she's done, it's hardly her fault. With half the village spitting poison, it's no wonder she's taken the law into her own hands! She thinks I'm a murderer, for heaven's sake!"

Mr Austin cleared his throat to get everyone's attention, only to find himself unable to speak. There was no way he could have known that the victim of his daughter's shenanigans was being held on the premises, and Joseph's intervention was taking the conversation in entirely the wrong direction. "Look here, sir," Mr Austin began, his voice several decibels lower than before. "It's awfully decent of you to let Susie off, but I must insist upon paying for the damage she has caused. She's my daughter and my responsibility; it's only reasonable."

Yes, you'll pay for Susie's actions, thought Gabriel in growing irritation, *then you'll make her pay*. The same thought had not escaped Joseph, as he shook his head vociferously. "You do not owe me a penny," he said firmly. "I will cover my landlady's costs immediately. The car will be easy enough to repair."

"Sir, I must protest . . ." The rest of the sentence was drowned out by the whine of Susie bursting into renewed floods of tears—and this time she was not angry. "Pull yourself together, girl! Crying won't help you!"

"It didn't help another girl either," said Joseph, so quietly that only Gabriel heard, but Joseph was dropping to one knee before Susie, forcing her to look him in the eye. "My dear, do you think I killed that little girl all those years ago?"

"I . . . I don't . . . yes," she forced out, but she had started hiccupping with the effort to control herself, and Gabriel doubted anyone would get a word of sense out of her now. Susie should not have been in a police interview room; she should never have been dragged before a detective inspector, an experience so terrifying for a child that she might have nightmares for months. "I don't . . . don't know!"

"Inspector, I really think—" Gabriel began, but Joseph signalled for him to stop.

"Susie, isn't it?" asked Joseph. Susie nodded miserably, wiping her nose on her sleeve. The gesture caused her disgusted father to look sharply away, but Susie did not notice. "Susie, you are not so far from the truth. In some ways, I did kill her, because the grown-ups didn't listen to me when I needed them." Joseph stood up and turned to Mr Austin, his demeanour a little more composed now. "Sir, please give me your assurance that this child will not suffer in any way for what she's done. This visit to the police station will have been quite lesson enough."

Mr Austin looked at Joseph with such profound astonishment, it would have been comical if there had not been a
weeping child in the room and Joseph had not just dropped
a bombshell large enough to tear the building down. "I . . .
well, if you are satisfied . . ." Mr Austin trailed off, and
Joseph made no attempt at answering. Gabriel did not dare
look at Applegate, busying himself instead with trying to
cheer up Susie, who returned his friendly smile with a look
of Dickensian misery. Susie's father might have been prevailed upon to leave her alone, but Gabriel suspected that
Susie would spend the rest of her life trying to forget the
events of this day.

"You are free to go," said Applegate, taking back control of the situation. He looked sternly in Susie's direction.
"You've got off very lightly indeed, young lady. I hope I
shan't see you here again."

Susie shook her head hastily before following her father
out of the room. Gabriel closed the door before turning to
look at Joseph. "Are you ready to tell me the truth now,
Joseph?"

"I want him out of the room," said Joseph quietly. "Please."

Applegate grimaced at Joseph's back, but he was too much
of a professional to argue. If Joseph had a confession to
make, Applegate was only going to be a hindrance. He nodded to Gabriel and left, closing the door soundlessly after
him. "Why don't you sit down, Joseph?" suggested Gabriel,
but Joseph was already seating himself on Applegate's desk,
the errant schoolboy till the end.

"How did you know?" asked Joseph, looking wearily at
Gabriel as the priest pulled up a chair. "You knew right
from the start, didn't you?"

"I knew that you had something very serious on your conscience, yes," Gabriel explained. "When a man returns home determined to leave his mark on a community he abandoned years before, one may surmise that he is trying to atone for something. It was the location you chose for your houses that first made me wonder, despite your claims that you were trying to avoid spoiling the natural beauty of the place. That plot is not just ugly. To build your houses, you would have had to tear down those remaining outbuildings and deal with the dangerous and expensive problem of filling in the old mineshafts. With death duties forcing landowners to sell up left, right, and centre, you could have had your pick of the best plots and still kept your new houses out of sight of the village. You bought that land because you knew perfectly well what was hidden there."

Joseph had begun nursing his temples as though the memories of long ago were tearing at the inside of his skull. "I knew she was there all right. I wanted everyone to know."

"Why now?"

"I'd heard that her mother was getting very frail," he said hastily, but he shrank back from Gabriel's glance, closing his eyes rather than make eye contact with him. "I hate trying to lie to you."

"You don't have to," Gabriel reassured him. "The heart condition that kept you out of the war is coming to claim you, sooner than you would like."

"Have you been prying into my medical records as well?"

Gabriel shook his head. "Come now, Joseph, you know I could never do that. And it does not take a doctor to notice how out of breath you get after a relatively short walk. You are not fat; you are clearly not lazy. You must therefore be unwell."

"I had rheumatic fever as an infant. It damaged my heart," said Joseph tonelessly. "I've always known I was living on borrowed time; the prognosis is very poor. And when the end comes, it will be quick. My heart will stop wherever I am, and I will die." The statement was curt and to the point, but Gabriel knew that Joseph must have gone through months of mental torment coming to terms with the situation. There was something terrifying about a lethal heart condition for precisely the reasons Joseph had enunciated. There was unlikely to be a slow decline for him, an opportunity to put his worldly affairs in order and reflect on his own mortality. One minute he would be there, pottering about the garden or walking down the street; the next moment he would be gone from this life.

"I'm sorry, Joseph."

"I don't need pity," he answered, without a trace of anger or bitterness. It was a statement of fact. Joseph was used to bearing his troubles alone and had no need of kind words or the sympathy of friends who had no idea how to treat him. "I wasn't lying when I said that Mrs Harding was getting very frail. I thought she had a right to know the truth."

"She has always had that right."

"I *know*!" Joseph all but shouted. "It wasn't the way I wanted it!"

Gabriel waited calmly for Joseph to continue, speaking only when he was sure Joseph had nothing further to say. "You wanted to show the Harding family—what remains of it—where Primrose was buried; you wanted to give them the chance to mourn her death after years of wondering what had become of her. That was admirable, Joseph, but you could have spared Primrose's loved ones many years of suffering."

"Father, you have no idea what you're asking!" exclaimed Joseph, and he really was angry now. As so often happened, fear had turned into anger, and Gabriel found himself shifting position to ensure that he had a clear run to the door if he needed it. He did not truly imagine Joseph would do him any harm, but he had been attacked before. "Father, I was absolutely certain Archie would kill me! If he could do that to a little girl, he could do it to me. Would you have confessed the truth if you knew you'd pay with your life?"

"What thought did you give to the living death to which you subjected a grieving mother?" demanded Gabriel, feeling his own anger rising now. "If you had gone to the police as soon as they began searching for Primrose, they might have protected you. You could have told the police at any time that you saw Archie Wilcox burying Primrose's body."

"No one goes to the police for protection, you know that!"

"Your silence scarcely helped you, did it? You took a terrible risk meeting Archie—"

"I wanted to talk to him! I wanted to persuade him to come clean!"

"You must have known the risk that he'd—" Gabriel broke off, jumping to his feet so violently that Joseph recoiled.

"What?" blustered Joseph. "What are you looking at me like that for?"

"Wait here!"

Gabriel dashed out of the room, almost colliding with an eavesdropping Applegate, who only just had time to step away from the door to avoid being flattened. "You really do look like Dracula when you swoop at me like that!" complained Applegate, desperately clinging to his dignity. "Can't you just walk nice and calmly like a normal person?"

"Archie Wilcox!" Gabriel blurted out. "You haven't taken him in for questioning!"

Applegate rolled his eyes. "Is that what you're in a flap about? I haven't had the chance, what with the Austin man marching in and all."

"But . . . but . . . you can't have a poisoner on the loose!" blustered Gabriel. "He might have done anything by now!"

Applegate gave Gabriel an indulgent smile which served only to infuriate him, not that Applegate appeared to notice. "There's no need to fret, old man. Stevie's safe in hospital, and Joseph's with me. Old Mr Wilcox can't make another attempt on Joseph's life even if he wants to. Even he's not that hare-brained."

"It's not Joseph you need to be worrying about now," said Gabriel breathlessly. "We need to get to the Harding house. We need to go now!"

Applegate blinked in surprise. "Why the Hardings? If you think Archie's a danger to anyone, shouldn't we go to the Wilcox farm?"

Gabriel gave Applegate a disrespectful shove in the direction of the outside world, thankful that the inspector took the hint and started to walk towards the door. "We could, but I don't think Archie will be there. I'll explain everything, but there isn't time now."

Applegate grunted in resignation and led Gabriel outside to the car.

Gabriel had never been a passenger in a car moving quite this fast, and he told himself there was nothing exhilarating about zooming around hairpin bends with the sleeping Wiltshire fields vanishing in a blur on either side of them. Gabriel had not hurtled this fast on anything, not even a train, and if Applegate had not been such an excellent driver, Gabriel would have been clinging to his seat for dear life. "Am I allowed a teeny-weeny hint as to what this is about?" asked Applegate, swerving violently to avoid a pothole big enough to break a car's axle. "I must be going deaf or something, or Joseph is a mumbler, but I could hardly hear a word."

"Serves you right!" exclaimed Gabriel over the growing roar of the engine. "As I always suspected, Joseph witnessed Primrose Harding's body being buried. Susie Austin's misdemeanour left me certain."

Applegate took his eyes off the road momentarily but was soon forced to refocus his attention on avoiding a crash. "Joseph was a brick thrower as a child, was he?"

"No, it just got me thinking. Children are invisible. No one takes them seriously. Now, we all know that children are sometimes threatened into keeping secrets—"

"You don't need to tell me that!"

"Quite. Well . . ." Gabriel was momentarily distracted by an unfortunate thought: Applegate driving out of the village like a Valkyrie was going to alert the entire gossiping population to the fact that something was amiss. "The fact is, even a very frightened child might still try to share the secret with somebody. In Joseph's case, he might have told the priest in the confessional—" Applegate's exasperated snort broke into Gabriel's thoughts, but only for a moment. He had known the inspector would react like that. "But who else? Probably not parents—they're too close to home, and probably not Reggie McClusker. Good man, but far too talkative. Even a child would know he'd never keep the secret. But a teacher perhaps?"

Applegate sounded the horn as he turned a blind corner. Gabriel was aware of a vast blur of black-and-white shapes covering the road ahead, as far as the eye could see. He covered his eyes, whispering an *Ave Maria* as Applegate slammed his foot down and brought the car lurching to a halt. A farmer had chosen that moment to transfer his herd of cows across to greener pastures, and the hoof was always mightier than the wheel in these parts. They were stuck.

"How urgent is the situation?" demanded Applegate, glaring at the cows as they lumbered past the car. The animals gazed back, unimpressed. "It's only about a five-minute walk from here if we take it briskly."

Gabriel was already getting out of the car. Applegate led him through the entrance to a lane so overgrown it would have been easy for an untrained eye to miss. "I never had to worry about cows in London," mused Gabriel, desperate to think about anything other than what might be waiting for them at the Harding family home.

"We never had to worry about German doodlebugs in Wiltshire. Those flying bombs were the work of the devil!" Applegate retorted.

The chalky path was littered with horse manure, and there were stinging nettles running along either side, four or five rows thick, defying anyone to cut through into the neighbouring fields. Gabriel tried to get his bearings, but he had never walked this way before and hoped Applegate had not got himself disoriented as well.

"If Miss Baines knew the truth from Joseph, why didn't she tell anyone?" asked Applegate. "Or are you telling me she was killed before she could?"

"No," puffed Gabriel. The slight incline of the path and the need for haste had left Gabriel out of breath. "Sometimes a suicide is just that. I think Miss Baines took her own life because recent events brought back memories she could not live with any longer. I have a theory about why she kept quiet, but I will never be able to prove it. What I'm sure of is that she left a note revealing everything, and the killer got there first. Burnt everything incriminating—not just the note but anything that linked Miss Baines with the child who knew the truth from the start."

"I fail to see how a man could get into Miss Baines' house without anyone noticing," protested Applegate as they hurried round a bend in the path. "She lived on a nosy street; she was an old spinster."

"Inspector, I never said the killer was a man. No one would have noticed a woman entering. The neighbours were used to seeing a woman walking in and out. If such a visitor were wearing a hat and coat, it would be easy to assume it was always the same woman." Gabriel could feel a stitch stabbing him in the side and was about to tell Applegate to go ahead, when the house came into view. "Too late," he said dully, but Applegate had also noticed the front door hanging open and ran hell for leather in the direction of the house, disappearing inside without a backward glance.

Gabriel slowed down, knowing that there was little left

for him to do. He could hear raised voices—Applegate's off-key baritone, the shrill, waspish voice of the nurse . . . and, as Gabriel drew closer, the desperate, wavering sobs of a feeble old woman.

It was the sound of the old woman crying that pierced Gabriel to the heart as he stepped inside, but he was immediately assailed by the stench of blood in his nostrils. *Too late . . . too late . . . too late.* He saw himself, a much younger man, running down a London street, with the acrid fumes of a house fire catching at the back of his throat. Gabriel felt again the agonising crunch of his ribs contracting and expanding as he raced down the smooth, hot pavement, calling his wife's name. Except that he could not call very loudly, and his words vanished amidst the noise and panic of that hideous night. A fire engine stood next to the burning house. He heard the bursts of water exploding against the flames at high pressure. From the nearby houses, Gabriel noticed his neighbours being shepherded outside and away from the scene: women in dressing gowns and curlers; anxious men in their slippers, overcoats slung awkwardly over their shoulders; fretful little children in their nightclothes being led or carried away.

Not Gabriel's wife, not Gabriel's little girl. The roar of the flames tearing the house from the inside out was so deafening, he barely heard the crash of glass shattering from the windows. He made one final dash forward, but powerful hands grabbed his arms, holding him back. He fought with every scrap of strength he possessed, screaming their names at the top of his voice. "Giovanna! Nicoletta! Giovanna . . . per favore, Giovanna . . ." He knew nothing could walk alive out of that raging inferno. He knew they were already dead, but he called for them as though they might still hear his voice and come running out, frightened, fighting for breath, but alive. Even if they were injured, there would be hope. Gabriel could nurse them back to health; they might recover and resume their happy lives together . . .

A piercing scream, like that of a fox caught in the rusted teeth of a trap, sent Gabriel shuddering back into the present, to a house where violence had erupted and he had been powerless to come to the rescue. He was standing in the faded grandeur of the hallway. Around the staircase in a grotesque tableau were three members of the household and one unwelcome guest. Old Mrs Harding sat huddled up on the stairs like a frightened child, sobbing hysterically into her arms. It looked as though she had attempted to hurry downstairs at the first sound of trouble, only to be overwhelmed by the disaster unravelling below.

Standing directly behind Mrs Harding, the nurse was struggling to console her patient, but she was too shocked to pay the old woman much attention. She was gazing fixedly at Florence Harding, who stood as imperious as ever, her clothing and face mottled by a spray of fresh blood. Her hands were drenched like something out of a cheap Hollywood horror movie, but she held no weapon. At her feet, his body still twitching as the last threads of life left him, lay Archie Wilcox. The wooden handle of a kitchen knife protruded from his chest.

Gabriel had not seen blood pumping so relentlessly out of a wound since the first war, and he trembled with the effort of keeping his composure. The blade had missed Archie's heart but had severed a major artery, and his body was lying in a pool of blood. Both Applegate and Gabriel knew that

Archie was beyond help, but Gabriel found himself dropping to his knees next to the body whilst Applegate shepherded Florence into another room.

"Do something, Nurse!" shouted Gabriel, infuriated by the thought that a woman in uniform had stood there watching a man die without lifting a finger to help him. "At least tell me what to do!" *So much blood . . . so much blood everywhere.* Archie's beige shirt was drenched. Gabriel reached for the knife to yank it out, but a cool, thin hand reached out from behind him and held his arm. He heard the nurse speak in her clipped accent, "Don't do that. Don't touch the knife unless you know what you're doing." The nurse stepped past Gabriel, pressing her fingers against Archie's jugular. She paused for a moment, feeling for a pulse, then looked round at Gabriel and shook her head.

Gabriel felt himself trembling again, this time with something that felt unnervingly like anger. The nurse was behaving as though nothing had happened, almost as though she had expected an unarmed man to be stabbed to death in front of her. He rose to his feet and turned to look directly at her, but it was only when he was standing quite close to the nurse that he realised her cold professional detachment was no such thing. The nurse's eyes bore that glazed, weary look of intense shock he had only ever seen before on the faces of bewildered young men as they blundered through no-man's-land. Like old Mrs Harding, the nurse had clearly had no inkling that anything downstairs was amiss until a commotion—a cry perhaps—had brought them to the top of the stairs.

Mrs Harding was quieting down, her sobs replaced by a low, continuous moan of despair. Gabriel looked from one haunted face to the next, wondering what to do. Applegate was busy with Florence—arresting her, Gabriel presumed—and the nurse was in no fit state to care for anyone else. "Nurse, we need to get Mrs Harding comfortable," he said, unsure whether the nurse could hear him. She was not even looking in his direction, staring fixedly at Archie Wilcox's dead body. Gabriel tried again, speaking as though to a sleepwalker. "Nurse, let me help you get Mrs Harding into the drawing room."

The nurse nodded mechanically, walking over to Mrs Harding in the manner of a puppet being pulled and jostled in the right direction. Quite gently, though with no attempt at reassurance, the nurse held out her hands to assist Mrs Harding, and she and Gabriel walked her slowly to a comfortable chair in the drawing room.

"I'm sorry, Father," said the nurse hazily. "There was never any possibility of saving a man's life with a knife wound like that. Florence knew what she was doing. As soon as I saw what she had done, I knew it was hopeless."

"If he had time to scream . . . ," Gabriel began but trailed off at the sight of the nurse's penetrating gaze. "He didn't scream, did he? There was no time."

"Florence screamed. It's a terrible thing to end a life, especially like that. So close up and so bloodily. Even if she thought he deserved it. He just cried."

"Cried?" Gabriel demanded. This was not a detail he had expected to hear. "Archie was crying? But if he had no time to scream when he was stabbed, surely he couldn't—"

"He was sobbing when he broke into the house. I distinctly heard it," the nurse affirmed. "Then Florence screamed, and it was all over."

Gabriel shook his head, but there was no time to question the nurse any further. He could see Mrs Harding's bloodshot eyes moving from the nurse to him and back, as though completely unaware of where she was and who these people were who had invaded her home. The nurse would recover from the shock of this afternoon, but Gabriel doubted old Mrs Harding could survive this. "I think you had better attend to your patient," said Gabriel, giving a little bow before heading for the door. "I should find out what's happened to Florence."

"Father?"

The question was wheedling and breathless. Gabriel turned back and saw Mrs Harding looking pleadingly at him, fresh tears coursing down her face. "Father, please don't let the inspector take my daughter away," she said, shrugging away the nurse's attempts to pacify her. "I've no one else left, nothing to live for. She . . . I'm sure she was only trying to defend herself. The man was a brute! You do not know the half of it!"

Gabriel looked steadily at Mrs Harding, marvelling that a woman who looked so confused and shocked could be so lucid. He wondered again how much longer she would survive if she were forced to grieve the death of her only surviving child. "I will do everything I can to help Florence over the death of Archie Wilcox," said Gabriel slowly, "but I fear you must prepare yourself for the worst."

14

Once Florence had recovered from the initial shock, she was as outwardly composed as Gabriel might have expected. She stood impassively as Applegate read out her rights and formally arrested her; she spoke only to request that she be permitted a few moments with her mother before leaving. "I wonder if you might dispense with the handcuffs," Florence added. "I'm not going anywhere and should rather not suffer the indignity of being shackled like an animal."

Gabriel stifled the resentful thought that a woman of a lower social class than Florence Harding would have been shackled whether she fancied the idea or not, but Applegate was happy for a lady to have a quiet cup of tea whilst he arranged transport to the constabulary.

It was just as well Applegate was such a snob. Gabriel knew that Florence would be a great deal more open with him, seated in her own domain, rather than surrounded by the bare grey walls and harsh lights of Applegate's interview room. "You should speak with a lawyer," said Gabriel, pouring Earl Grey tea from a porcelain teapot into two gold-rimmed cups decorated with pink roses. "But I daresay you have already considered that."

"I shall telephone the family solicitor directly," said Florence, taking the cup without a word of thanks. "I shall plead self-defence, since the brute forced his way in here and threatened me."

Gabriel nodded. "I noted the damage to the door as I walked in," he said. "That will certainly count in your favour. And since your assailant is dead, Archie Wilcox cannot tell the court why he threatened you."

Florence gave Gabriel a condescending smirk. "I could hardly expect you to understand such things, Father," she said pertly, "but when a man threatens a woman, the motive is usually fairly obvious."

"Possibly," said Gabriel, taking a sip of the weak, bland tea which was useful only as a means of breaking up an awkward conversation. "We both know that Archie burst in here because he was at the end of his tether. His clumsy attempt at silencing Joseph ended in his very nearly poisoning his own son. He'd encouraged Stevie to stir up the village against Joseph, hoping to stop Primrose's burial place from being discovered. He'd had enough of covering up your crime for you."

"I don't know what you are talking about," said Florence without a flicker of comprehension. "When a man breaks into a house, he is a thief or something rather worse. I knew what he was going to do to me. I had a right to defend myself."

Gabriel regarded Florence's cool countenance with a sense of growing despair. This woman had stabbed a man to death in a frenzied attack, and her hand did not so much as tremble as she held her cup daintily between her fingers. Within minutes of feeling the knife slicing into human flesh, Florence had dismissed the raw, visceral horror she had experienced. She sat now without human feeling or the slightest shred of remorse for her actions. All that mattered was planning her defence, and she expected Gabriel to be her unquestioning audience.

"Florence, common criminals who break into other people's houses do not tend to weep as they go about their work. The nurse clearly heard Archie sobbing before you stabbed him and began to scream yourself."

"She was mistaken," said Florence unhurriedly. "How could she remember a detail like that in all the panic?"

"Hardly a detail, and she did not have long to remember," answered Gabriel. He was going to find the chink in this woman's armour. He was going to see her repent of her actions. "Florence, you need not worry about the jury taking your side. The man was trespassing, and I am sure any good legal counsel will build a strong case that you acted out of necessity. As to the death of Primrose, you will probably be spared the noose for that as well."

The shock tactic worked. Florence dropped the teacup onto the saucer so abruptly that it toppled onto its side, breaking and sending tiny shards of china skittering across the mahogany surface. A moment later, she had risen to her feet, glaring at Gabriel with such hatred, he instinctively stood up to avoid the woman towering over him. "You dare mention my sister to me?" she spat. "You sully her good name just speaking it!"

"She was a good girl, wasn't she, Florence?" said Gabriel, taking a step towards her. Florence's hands were curled into bony-white fists, and he did not risk getting any closer. If she had had easy access to a knife when Archie had appeared before her, she might have access to others, and Gabriel knew better than to tempt her. Florence had spent her life playing at being self-controlled, but Gabriel had some understanding of the torment that lay beneath the surface. "She was a good girl, but she must have driven you mad, always following you about, constantly demanding your attention. The lonely little sister with no one to turn to but you. No friends, a distant mother, a volatile brother. And you wanted a life of your own."

Florence raised her arms, pressing her fists to her temples with such force that her whole upper body shook. "I am not a murderess! She was never meant to die!"

Gabriel reached out a hand to Florence, but she turned around, flattening herself against the wall. Before Gabriel could speak, Florence let out a terrible cry. Her hand went to her mouth, but it did nothing to stifle the hideous animal scream as years of mental agony were finally released. Gabriel braced himself against the sound; but he could feel his flesh crawling with the intensity of it. He might have been watching an attempted exorcism, with the subject writhing in agony but stubbornly resisting deliverance.

Over the sound of Florence's laboured breathing, Gabriel heard the door open and turned to see Applegate looking in, understandably concerned. Gabriel signalled for him to leave as quietly as possible, and Applegate took the hint, slipping out immediately. Gabriel suspected—and rather hoped— that the inspector would remain stationed outside the door until the conversation was over.

"Florence, why did you lure her to that old mine?" asked Gabriel, when he was sure Florence was capable of hearing him. "It was the old mine where you trapped her, wasn't it? Those fractures on her skeleton were self-inflicted, caused by a hysterical child hurling herself against a locked and bolted door."

But Florence began to wail again, and this time, Gabriel noticed her tearing her fingernails down the oak panels lining the wall. This was a memory that had tortured her for years, but the telling of the tale was no less painful than bloodletting. "I was teaching her a lesson, that was all!" she sobbed. "I was fed up with her following me about. She was jealous of Stevie; she kept threatening to tell Mother about us. I even had to give her that love token just to silence her."

"So you lured her into that old mine and locked her in, just to frighten her."

"Yes."

Yes. A young woman—barely more than a girl herself—had coaxed her own little sister into a dark and frightening place. Florence had no doubt brought her there with promises of sweets or toys, though it scarcely mattered how she had enticed little Primrose into that dungeon. Gabriel could almost see the interior of the mine through the eyes of a petrified child. The oppressive darkness, the sliver of light creeping in from under the locked door. The cold, damp walls and the twisted remains of old machinery threatening to spring to life and tear her to pieces. The echo of her cries in a dizzying drop into the bowels of the earth . . .

"Can you tell me what went wrong?"

But Florence was struggling for breath, sobs racking her body as grief poured out of her after years of denial. Wordlessly, Gabriel took Florence by the arm and led her to a chair. He waited in silence as she wept, intervening only to press a clean handkerchief into her hand. Gabriel knew better than to hurry her or attempt to question her until the grief had burned itself out. He had experienced it himself before—that desperation to maintain control, the weaving of a tissue of lies around oneself as a protection from the savagery of the pain. The pretence never lasted, and Gabriel counted himself fortunate that his own sorrow had erupted before self-deception could become habitual. He had also been blessed to have been alone when the dam had burst, and nobody had witnessed him curled up in the foetal position on the floor of his room, weeping until exhaustion overcame him.

Florence continued to cry. At one point, Gabriel was aware of Applegate putting his head round the door again, this time with an air of impatience. Gabriel shook his head, indicating Florence's bowed head. Applegate rolled his eyes before leaving, too sensible to interfere but clearly unimpressed by Gabriel's handling of the situation.

"It's all right, Florence, I know what went wrong," said Gabriel, as Florence grew quieter. Her cries had given way to gasps and hiccups, but she was still in no condition to speak. She nodded her head jerkily, as though answering a question, but looked steadfastly at the handkerchief crumpled into a ball in her hands. "I think it would be fair to say that what you did to Primrose was a cruel trick, but you never intended it to end in tragedy. Not to begin with, at least."

Gabriel's eye was drawn to the family photograph showing Primrose holding her favourite toy, a rag dolly wearing a jacket held shut by a single button. "I realised that Primrose must have died in the old mine when I was told that a thorough search had discovered an old metal button. I was warned that it was too generic to be used to identify the killer, but it did create the false impression that the killer was a man, since the button was of the type commonly found on a man's jacket years ago. In fact, the button had become detached from Primrose's toy, which she took with her everywhere. She must have picked and tugged at it as she stood in the darkness, desperately waiting for help to come." Gabriel looked from the photograph to Florence's red, swollen face. "Or it may have come off when the toy was snatched up along with Primrose's body, by the person who attempted to conceal the evidence."

"He said he'd buried her with her toy because he didn't want to think of her being lonely," whimpered Florence, making concerted efforts to breathe more slowly. "No one seemed very interested in that button at the time."

"They were looking for a body." Florence covered her face at the word "body" as Gabriel had known she would. The grim finality of it was still impossible to bear. "Florence, why did you walk away after you had locked Primrose in that mine? What possessed you to leave her?"

"I meant only to be gone a few minutes," said Florence, "just long enough to give the little minx a scare." She dropped her hands into her lap and looked listlessly ahead of her as though falling back into the nightmare of her youth. "I don't know what got into me, but I was so angry with her that I just kept walking. I wasn't thinking. I never even stopped to check the time. I just walked and walked."

"Once she was out of earshot, it must have been easier to

put her out of your mind," suggested Gabriel, but the point was greeted by a glare from Florence. She was not going to admit her negligence readily.

"I swear, Father, I wasn't gone more than an hour!" she blustered. "Probably less time than that!"

"There was enough time for Joseph to hear her and run off to tell Miss Baines about the strange sounds he had heard," said Gabriel. "There was enough time for Miss Baines to convince Joseph that he was mistaken, depriving Primrose of her final chance of survival. Did you see anyone when you returned to Primrose?"

Florence shook her head. "I saw nothing. I went to find Stevie and told him what I'd done. He was the one who saw sense and told me it had been a despicable trick to play on a child. He and his father insisted upon coming with me to let her out. I'm not sure they trusted me."

"So, it was Archie who found her?"

Florence's face had clouded over again. "You were wrong about one thing, Father. She didn't batter her head against the locked door."

"Florence, be careful." Gabriel could hear Florence's breathing becoming rapid and shallow. "Breathe!"

"It looked . . . it looked as though she'd pitched forward into the shaft," panted Florence, forcing out every word with considerable effort. "She didn't fall far . . . they'd, well they'd blocked it years before with wood and soil, but over time, the wood must have rotted away, leaving a gap of a few feet. It was just a few feet! She slammed her head . . ." Florence was breathing too quickly and swayed forward, pale and listless, her eyes glazing over.

"Florence!" shouted Gabriel, grabbing her by the arms to prevent her from falling. "You have to calm yourself."

Applegate was in the room, lifting Florence's limp body onto the floor. "See if you can find some brandy," instructed Applegate, fumbling with the buttons on Florence's pie-crust collar. "The shock's setting in."

Gabriel hesitated in the doorway, regarding the grey, prematurely aged woman lying in a swoon on the floor. The role had become so much a part of her identity that, even in the depths of her despair, Florence Harding was still playing the part of a Victorian matron. Gabriel suspected that—if the judge were harsh enough—she would die like a Victorian heroine too, with a rope around her neck and some fine words of repentance on her lips. It might be the one honest moment in Florence Harding's sad life. It was cold comfort, but she truly was sorry for causing the death of her sister.

"Are you sure you wouldn't prefer to drive?" asked Gabriel, watching anxiously as Joseph struggled to keep in step beside him. "You may be a free man, but you're going to need time to recover."

Joseph shook his head emphatically. "I've been cooped up in that cell for quite long enough. I need some air. I need to feel the grass beneath my feet."

They were walking to the hospital to see Stevie. Gabriel hoped that Joseph would stay on at the abbey a little while longer, making the most of the opportunity to spend some time in quiet reflection whilst he decided what to do next. With the death of Archie, and Florence's arrest, Joseph was no longer in any danger and was at liberty to get on with his life. The trouble was that life is seldom so straightforward, the threads refusing to tie up as neatly as anyone would like. Joseph had much to ponder before he went back to building his houses. If he ever did return to that task.

"Joseph, you don't have to see Stevie yet, if it's too painful—"

"His pain is a good deal worse than mine," Joseph cut in, "and if I don't make my peace with him today, I doubt I will ever pluck up the courage to do so. I owe him that much."

Gabriel could not help noticing how slowly he was having to walk to allow Joseph to keep up with him. Joseph's movements were already becoming more laborious than when Gabriel had first encountered him a few days ago, but the distress caused by recent events had inevitably made its mark. "Joseph, I understand, at least I think I understand, why you did not tell the police that you had witnessed Archie burying Primrose's body. But why could you not have told me? What did you have to lose after so long?"

Joseph stopped, ostensibly to catch his breath. "When I told Miss Baines what I'd seen, she told me I'd been mistaken. Even when the village was out trying to find Primrose, she didn't report what I had told her. If she didn't believe me, nobody would. When I returned to the village, I meant to meet her, but events overtook us and suddenly she was dead." He started walking again, his brows furrowed in thought. "I suppose, when I heard that all Miss Baines' papers had been burnt, I thought . . . I imagined perhaps that she was trying to protect me." He shook his head impatiently. "Ridiculous, I know. I'm not so important. I just couldn't get it out of my head that she'd been prepared to die rather than talk."

Gabriel rested a hand on Joseph's drooping shoulder. "If it helps, I don't believe Phyllis Baines took her own life to protect anyone. I think that the discovery of the grave and then the funeral threw her into despair."

"But I was the one who made sure that body was discovered!" exclaimed Joseph, shrugging Gabriel off. "If I'd let well alone, she might be alive today!"

"You know you could never have taken that secret to the grave. You yourself said that you owed it to Primrose Harding's mother to reveal the truth before it was too late."

"But at the cost of another life?" demanded Joseph. "Morally, I killed Miss Baines. If I hadn't confided in her, if I'd let sleeping dogs lie . . ."

"Phyllis Baines killed Phyllis Baines, Joseph," said Gabriel gravely. "Suicide is never the answer; it never had to end that way. And she didn't burn her papers; she meant to reveal what she knew. It was Florence who burnt those papers."

Joseph made a sharp intake of breath. "Florence? But why?"

"This would never stand up in court," said Gabriel, "but my belief is that she saw Phyllis talking to me after the funeral and realised she knew something. The full story may or may not come out at the trial, but Florence had good reason to ensure that Phyllis Baines' confession was never made public. She was good at getting others to do her dirty work for her, but I could not see Stevie or Archie entering an elderly spinster's home unnoticed or acting so carefully.

They would have burnt the entire house down rather than go to the trouble of seeking out incriminating material and burning it neatly in the fireplace."

"There might not have been a confession," Joseph ventured. "She'd kept the secret for so many years."

"Most people who take their own lives leave a note. Phyllis Baines is the sort of person who would have left a note. She was not the type to leave this world without putting her affairs in order."

Gabriel and Joseph walked on in silence. They were nearing the hospital now, and Joseph was moving ever more slowly, either through fatigue or through reluctance to face Stevie. "Even if Miss Baines did not end her life on my account, I will never stop being haunted by what happened to Primrose," said Joseph, lowering his voice as they reached the inobtrusive entrance to the cottage hospital. "I will always wish I had followed my own instincts, even though I was only a child."

Gabriel was about to answer when he noticed the matron moving in their direction; he groaned inwardly. Gabriel had had a few run-ins with the implacable woman before and knew she would throw every possible obstacle in their way. He liked to think that her hostility had nothing to do with her Ulster Protestant background, but he was not entirely naive.

"If you've come to see Mr Wilcox, I must ask you to leave," said the matron curtly, addressing her comments to Joseph as though it were entirely beneath her dignity to converse with a papist priest.

"It's very important that we see him," said Gabriel, ignoring the sight of the woman's icy profile. "He will want to see us."

"The inspector has only just finished with him," the matron responded. "He is in no state to entertain anyone else."

"Please, Matron," Joseph said, "We're childhood friends. He shouldn't be alone at such a time."

The woman gave Gabriel a glacial glance. "I was not aware that Mr Wilcox was one of yours. I hardly see why you should go anywhere near his bedside."

Gabriel gave a little bow of acknowledgement. "I quite understand, Matron, and I do not intend to interfere. If Mr Wilcox would rather I remain outside, I will do so."

The matron narrowed her eyes, looking from one man to the other before making a great ceremony of checking the watch pinned to her uniform. "It is nearly the end of the visiting hour. You have ten minutes, no more."

With that, she turned on her heel and led them wordlessly down the corridor, to the private room where Stevie was recovering away from the prying eyes of other patients. The matron pushed open the door, signalling for the two men to wait in the corridor. Gabriel heard her artificially cheerful voice informing Stevie that he had visitors but that she would send them away if he preferred. As inevitably happened in these situations, she gave Stevie every possible signal that she would like his permission to tell his visitors to clear off. Gabriel waited for the words of dismissal, but instead, a weak but insistent voice said, "No, I want to see them, Matron."

"As I said, ten minutes," said the matron as she brushed

past them in the direction of the door. "He's still very weak, and he's had a horrible shock."

Gabriel nodded, but the woman had already swept away down the corridor, apparently determined to avoid any further conversation with him. Gabriel glanced at Joseph before walking into Stevie's room with Joseph close behind him. Stevie was propped up in bed. His skin was pale, almost translucent, with the effects of arsenic poisoning, and his eyes were red-rimmed and bleary. Stevie took a deep breath before saying, "I'm not sure who I was expecting, but it weren't you two. What do you want?"

"Well, to begin with, we would both like to offer our sympathies," said Gabriel mildly, looking steadily at Stevie. "I am so sorry for your loss."

Stevie gave a rasping laugh. "Really? Joe here is so very sorry for the death of the old goat who tried to poison him? That's what happened, weren't it? Silly beggar couldn't even bump off the right man."

"I know why he did it," said Joseph cautiously, "but the truth's come out now. I've confessed that I saw your father bury the body."

A single tear ran down Stevie's face, which he brushed away with a slap of his hand across his face. "If Florence is going to hang for this, we should all hang. We were all in it up to our necks." Stevie looked accusingly at Joseph. "You didn't just see my old man burying Primmie, did you, mate? I got there too late to save her, but you could have got her out of there in time."

Joseph winced, the muscles in his face tightening. It was Gabriel who spoke next. "Joseph, that is true, isn't it? Your guilt runs deeper than merely failing to reveal a burial place. You heard her calling for help."

Joseph closed his eyes as though he could shut out the image that was flooding his mind, of a locked door and the sound of a moaning, whining cry, the *tap-tap-tap* of little fists against unyielding metal. The sounds of childhood nightmares. "How did you know?" he whispered.

"It was something Miss Baines said as she was dying. 'I knew where she was.' At the time, I thought she meant the place where Primrose had been buried, but somehow it felt as though she were confessing to something far more heinous than the failure to reveal a burial place. And would a woman really commit suicide for that?"

Joseph shook his head, his eyes still firmly shut. The word "no" barely registered between them. "Phyllis Baines spoke as though she could have saved the child's life," Gabriel continued. "She therefore knew where Primrose was before the child died. Since it was unlikely that a respectable woman would have been out wandering in such a place at that hour of the morning, I could only assume that a child had alerted her. It was only a short stretch of the imagination to assume that it was you."

"I ran to find Miss Baines," said Joseph softly, not looking at either man. "She was always in the schoolroom early on a Saturday morning. It was when she did all her work. Marking our copy books, tidying the schoolroom."

"Why Miss Baines?"

"Because the schoolroom was the closest place. Because I knew she would be up and about." Joseph gave a low, guttural laugh. "Because I trusted the old stick, I suppose.

But she told me not to be silly. Said I was making a lot of fuss about some wild animal or some such."

"She refused to come with you."

"She was adamant. The more I pestered her, the more determined she was that I was being a silly boy, trying to send her on a wild goose chase. She told me I was to go home immediately, or she'd tell my father I'd been playing near the old mine." Joseph looked across at Gabriel, with the embarrassment of a grown man admitting to having been a nervy child. "I was forbidden from playing there; my father said it was dangerous. She knew I would never admit to my parents that I had been there. When I told her about Archie later on, I thought she'd have to believe me then. But she didn't."

There it was. An act of infantile spite on the part of an exasperated older sister had taken a young life and left others wounded: Florence, Stevie, Archie, Phyllis, Joseph. They had all paid the price for their collusion, condemned to live a half life haunted by guilt and the omnipresent fear of discovery. They had all been punished many times over, long before the law had descended upon them to exact overdue justice. "Like I said, Father," said Stevie, breaking into Gabriel's thoughts, "if Florence is going to hang, I should go with her. We were so loyal to her. She were good at getting people to do what she wanted. I've never rightly known how."

"Florence will not hang for Primrose's death," said Gabriel. "She was a juvenile at the time. At most, she was guilty of manslaughter. She may well hang for your father's murder, Stevie."

For the first time, Stevie seemed to come to life. His eyes

258

grew hot with anger as though he had only just heard—or registered—what had happened. "The little she-devil should hang for that," he snarled, and Gabriel noticed out of the corner of his eye that Joseph was stepping slowly towards the door. He was still afraid of Stevie's rage, even in a hospital room with his old adversary lying helpless in bed. "We covered up her filthy secret all these years. It destroyed us, Father! Every day since, I've woken up with the memory of that kiddie's broken body. She were like a little doll, even more when she were dead. Her skin were all cold and white like she were made of china. Me dad couldn't leave her there. He said the poor little lass ought to be buried proper. I said he shouldn't touch her. If he left her, everyone would say she just come to grief wandering off. But Florence said they'd know she done something to her. Her ma would say Primrose were afraid of the dark. She would never have gone in somewhere so dark and gloomy by herself. They'd know, they'd know . . ."

The door was thrown open and the matron walked in, taking in the sight of her distressed patient before glaring at Gabriel in cold reproach. "I think my patient has had quite enough excitement for one day," she declared, indicating that Gabriel and Joseph should step outside. "He needs to rest."

Joseph left without a word, incapable of arguing with anyone in his current state. Gabriel ignored the matron's demands and turned to Stevie. "We'll leave you now, Stevie; you need time to recover. Things are going to be very hard for you in the weeks and months to come, but I'm only at the abbey. You don't have to face this alone."

"Just leave," snapped the matron, stepping between Gabriel and Stevie to make conversation as difficult as possible. "You had no business distressing him like this. If anything happens to him, I will have you held responsible."

"Leave him alone, Matron," said Stevie, reaching out a hand to Gabriel to signal that he wished him to come closer. Gabriel took his life in his hands and moved around woman's substantial bulk, kneeling at Stevie's bedside. "I know what Florence said about my father," said Stevie, the anger stirring in him again. "The inspector told me she said it were self-defence, but she'll tell any lie she likes to save her own neck. I'll not have my father's name sullied by no one. He would never have hurt a hair on her head. He loved her like she were the daughter he never had. He couldn't live with himself anymore. He were going to tell the police what happened, and she tried to stop him. She were that heartless. After everything we'd done to protect her."

Gabriel felt the matron's hand on his shoulder, and he rose to his feet. Stevie was still looking knowingly at him, and Gabriel understood the message precisely. Stevie would not see his dead father framed as a common criminal who had broken into a house and tried to assault a woman. Whatever else he had done, Archie Wilcox had been neither a thug nor a thief, and Stevie would proclaim it to the courts, even if it meant that Florence's one defence would crumble. Gabriel raised his hand in blessing and left.

15

It seemed a long time since Gabriel had witnessed Marie Paige's trial and rejoiced at the sight of that brave woman standing on the steps of the court, ready to embrace the life that had so nearly been taken from her. Abbot Ambrose had denied Gabriel permission to attend Florence Harding's trial, and Gabriel had reluctantly accepted that it was for the best. In the end, Florence had faced several charges: manslaughter, prevention of the lawful and decent burial of a dead body, perversion of the course of justice, and the murder of Archie Wilcox. Abbot Ambrose had reasoned that the loss of Gabriel's own daughter might weigh too heavily on his mind if he were forced to listen to the horrible details of another child's final moments.

Stevie had had no charges brought against him for his part in concealing the child's death. It was not an offence to fail to report a crime, and there was no evidence that he had assisted his father in the burial of Primrose's body. He could have faced charges on account of the false statements he had made to the police during the original investigation, but the Crown Prosecution Service showed no interest in pursuing the matter. It may have helped his case that Stevie was so forthcoming with evidence against Florence Harding at her trial.

Stevie's description of his last encounter with his father

made a powerful impression on the jury. He described how Archie had come to Stevie's hospital bed to beg his forgiveness, claiming that he could not live with the secret of Primrose's death any longer and would have to go to the police. Florence's defence counsel had done their best to cast doubt on the credibility of Stevie's evidence but to no avail. It came as no surprise when Florence was found guilty on all counts, and there was no escaping the grim reality that Stevie's evidence had been a deciding factor in the judge handing down the harshest possible sentence.

Having kept Gabriel away from the trial, Abbot Ambrose permitted him to visit Florence in the county jail, as long as he made the journey with Brother Gerard. No one could be disconsolate for long in Gerard's company, but even he was subdued as they walked together down the dimly lit, grey corridor to Florence's lonely cell. The warden who led the way had told Gabriel that Florence was refusing to see any visitors, including her mother, but that she had agreed to seek the spiritual solace of a priest. "Perhaps you can help her," said the warden over her shoulder. She was a plump-faced, cheerful young woman who looked entirely incongruous in such a dismal labyrinth, almost as though Central Casting had blundered and sent the minor heroine of a Charlie Chaplin picture to audition for Lady Macbeth. "She's not said a word since they brought her over from the court. She won't eat either, but she's only got a week."

Gabriel shuddered. Florence's execution was to take place on the following Wednesday, at eight o'clock in the morning, as was customary in the provinces. It gave her just eight days left on this earth. The warden stopped outside a door and took out a bunch of keys, smiling apologetically at Gerard. "Just the one visitor at a time, I'm afraid. Why don't you stay out here with me?"

Gerard shrugged, looking at Gabriel for guidance. "Will you be all right?" asked Gerard.

"Don't worry, I doubt this will take very long," answered Gabriel, feeling a pang of envy for Gerard. Gabriel suspected that, as soon as he had entered the condemned cell, Gerard would go off to the warden's room for a restorative cup of tea and a light-hearted natter, as though a woman were not about to be put to death in the prime of her life.

Gabriel put such thoughts behind him as the door opened and he stepped inside, pushing the heavy door shut behind him before Florence could change her mind and order him out. The woman in question was standing ramrod straight in the middle of the cell, her back to him as she stared up at the narrow, barred window just above her eye line. "Have you come to hear my confession, Father?" came the cold, clipped voice, with only a hint of a sneer. "A little late to be turning me into a saint, isn't it?"

"I would never say that," said Gabriel to Florence's turned back. "I can hear your confession if you wish."

Florence gave a long sigh, pressing her head against the wall before answering. "I have been doing penance for little Primmie's life for years. I never believed I deserved happiness, and I have enjoyed none. I am almost relieved that it will soon be over."

Gabriel wished Florence would turn around and look at him, but she was creating a barrier akin to the grille in a confessional; it might be easier for her to speak honestly if she could not see his face. "I gather the judge advised your defence counsel to appeal to the home secretary for clemency. You refused.''

"I let my sister die. One must pay one's debts.''

"Florence, you are to hang for Archie's murder, not Primrose's death.''

Florence turned on Gabriel so abruptly that he flinched, not so much from the rage that had appeared out of nowhere but from the sight of her face. Gabriel had not seen Florence since the day of her arrest, and he would barely have recognised her if he had not known the sound of her voice. Her face was so thin, he could see every bone, every hard line. Her eyes looked sunken and far too large, making her look like the sort of figure one might see haunting a Pathé newsreel about displaced persons. Either Florence had deliberately starved herself, driven by some destructive desire to suffer for her past crimes, or the anguish of the trial and the knowledge of her impending demise had reduced her to the wreck she had become.

"That thing? That loathsome man?'' she spat, reaching out to snatch Gabriel by the arm. He made no effort to prevent her, swallowing a cry as her clawlike fingers fastened themselves around his arm, squeezing until the pain was almost unbearable. "I never asked that ridiculous oaf to interfere! I never asked either of them to come running after me that day! They chose to make my sister's death their business, and they have paid for that!''

Gabriel opened his mouth to speak, but the words would not come. As calmly as he could, Gabriel took hold of Florence's wrist, endeavouring to pull her hand away. She realised what she had done and let go as abruptly as she had attacked him, backing away into the corner. "Florence, they acted out of loyalty to you, and they have certainly paid a heavy price for that loyalty. Archie—"

"I could have looked after things myself! I never asked them to interfere!" shouted Florence. "Men are such fools. They take it upon themselves to rescue women who never ask for help, then think themselves martyrs when they suffer. I'm only amazed I restrained myself from killing him sooner."

Gabriel blenched. He had suspected that Florence's frenzied attack on Archie had been motivated more by anger at the man's hold on her life than fear of discovery, but her hatred for the man she had stabbed chilled Gabriel to his fingertips. "Archie's life was not yours to take."

"His life? What life was that?" demanded Florence, that spectral face of hers creasing into a horrible sneer. "We've none of us had much of a life, and his was the most worthless. No one will miss that little man, not even Stevie for very long."

"Whatever you think of Archie's life, he had a right to live it." Gabriel watched as Florence clenched and unclenched her fists, desperately trying to regain her composure. "Florence, have you no remorse at all for killing a man because he begged you to make a clean breast of things?"

Florence sat daintily on the edge of the bed, her fists still clenching and unclenching in her lap. "I have not," she said emphatically, looking past Gabriel as though he were not in the room. "I know I will hang for Archie Wilcox, but it will be little Primmie I remember when they put the rope around my neck. She deserved better than a lonely death and an unmarked grave. She might have been someone."

That was the nub of the problem, as far as Florence Harding was concerned. It was not so much that Primrose had been an innocent little girl betrayed by the sister she adored. It was that—according to the view of the world Florence had imbibed as a child—Primrose's life had been valuable, whereas the life of a poor farmer who had long outlived his usefulness was dispensable.

"Florence, would you like me to accompany you?" asked Gabriel, moving towards the door. He rapped sharply on the discoloured metal. "You can ask for a chaplain to be present if it would help you." Gabriel felt queasy just thinking of standing in the same room as a woman being dropped to her death through a trapdoor, but it would give him one last opportunity to offer her the sacraments.

Florence shook her head wearily. The anger had burnt itself out. "I don't think so, Father. There was no one to comfort Primrose as she died."

"Then let me hear your confession now, before I have to leave."

Florence looked up at him, and Gabriel noticed her expression hardening again. "I'm not sorry, Father. I know I should be, but I would hesitate to kill a sheep longer than I hesitated to kill Archie Wilcox."

Gabriel could barely put one foot in front of the other as he processed into the chapel for Vigils. Sleep had refused to come to him yet again, and he had spent the stilly watches of the night before the Blessed Sacrament, praying for a miracle. Weariness had struck him just as the rest of the community were getting up to start the day, and he walked punch-drunk towards his place, hoping against all hope that he would not drop off to sleep.

He had heard nothing further from Florence Harding, and she was to hang in just over twenty-four hours. *Perhaps she has had a change of heart,* thought Gabriel, too preoccupied to hear the distant chime of the doorbell over the sound of the bell calling him to prayer. *There are plenty of priests who might have heard her confession.* He tried to focus his mind on prayer as he intoned the opening response with the other monks, "O God, come to our aid."

The weight of a hand came down on Gabriel's shoulder, followed by the sound of Dominic whispering, "Come outside, Gabriel."

It helped that Gabriel was in too much of a trance to react, and he followed Dominic out of the chapel as quiet as a mouse, registering no surprise when he found himself in the corridor, face-to-face with a police constable. "Fetch your knapsack; I'll fetch the oils," said Dominic gently, noting Gabriel's sleepy bewilderment. "The constable here is going to drive you to the county jail."

Gabriel's dreamlike state persisted as he returned to his room to pack for an overnight stay. The days since his encounter with Florence had sent him into a spiral of dread that had left him numb, not unlike those ghastly days following the deaths of Giovanna and Nicoletta. He packed the essentials, resisting the urge to take his purple keepsake bag with him. It was a fault, but even in the weary fog into which he had fallen, Gabriel struggled to leave it behind. He should have no attachment to any material thing, but he felt the need to hold those two souls close to him at moments like this.

A soft knock at the door brought Gabriel back to earth. Dominic was standing in the doorway, holding the case containing the oils in one hand, and a small paper bag in the other. "Try to eat something on the journey," said Dominic solicitously. "You're looking a bit peaky, if you don't mind me saying."

Gabriel smiled, taking the case and the bag. Dominic the infirmarian was the sort of inoffensive, softly spoken man who was at liberty to say whatever he needed to say. It was so impossible to imagine him uttering an unkind word to anyone; he could tell the truth and—in general—expect to be heard. "I can't say I've much appetite at present." He looked into the paper bag, which contained a round of bread, an oat biscuit, and an apple. "I'm sorry, I shouldn't keep the constable waiting."

"He's waiting for you outside the chapel. You'll need to take the Blessed Sacrament with you," Dominic reminded him.

Gabriel nodded, feeling the first glimmer of relief piercing through his gloom. Florence Harding had called for a priest. She might make a good death of it yet, consoled by the rites of Holy Church.

"You should prepare yourself, Gabriel," said Dominic cautiously, as they walked together towards the chapel. "She may ask that you accompany her into the death chamber."

Gabriel suppressed a shudder, nodding with as much nonchalance as he could muster. "I offered to," he said weakly, trying desperately not to imagine watching a woman being tied up, hooded, and dropped through a trapdoor with a rope around her neck. It was an image that had haunted Gabriel since his last encounter with Florence, but he had said he would accompany Florence on that last journey if she wished, and he would not fail her now.

Ten minutes later, with the pyx hanging around his neck, Gabriel climbed into the car that was to take him all the way to Bristol and the county jail. The work of a detective was easy, Gabriel mused, clasping the pyx in one hand as they left the village behind. Gabriel had lived many lives—schoolboy, soldier, husband, father, priest. And the work of a priest was more perilous, but perhaps more blessed than anything else he had ever known.